# In His Eyes

by

Barbara Lohr

Purple Egret Press
Savannah, Georgia 31411



Cover Art: The Killion Group
Editing: The Editing Hall


ISBN -10: 1-945523-03-4
ISBN-13: 978-1-945523-03-8

# Chapter 1

Diana Prescott had a bad history of being with the wrong man. And here she was again, walking into a dance with a guy crazy about another woman. Desperate to make friends in Gull Harbor, she'd agreed to come to the Firemen's Ball with Cole Campbell, who had it bad for Kate Kennedy. Right now Cole and Kate were having a communication problem. Why had Diana offered to help with the solution? Sarah and Chili, her new book group buddies, had been so persuasive. "*Pobrecita*, Kate needs to realize how much she loves Cole, no?" Chili had pleaded. "They see each other at the dance and boom! They will know."

Right. The lovebirds would realize they needed each other and Diana's life would still be a mess. Outside, the muggy July air clung like Velcro. Luckily, the Whittaker Woods Country Club had pumped up the air conditioning. These volunteer firemen could generate a lot of heat. Diana's eyes swept the ballroom of strangers. She could be at home watching *The Notebook* one more time. But tonight she was a woman with a mission.

"My buddies are over there." Cole pointed to a table.

"Lead the way." Tugging up the halter top of her sea-blue gown, she followed Cole into the crowd. This felt like senior prom in Newtown, where she'd grown up.

Soft ringlets tickled her bare shoulders, and she'd spent time on her eye makeup. This was as perfect as she got. Cheers went up when they reached Cole's group and introductions began. Seemed like nice couples but every guy was taken.

Cole left to get their drinks. The bolo tie and western boots were a nice touch. Diana smiled to see Kate Kennedy's eyes sweep Cole like a soft serve cone at the Swirly Top. His return glance could have made a puddle out of any woman. Feeling like collateral damage, Diana straightened her shoulders. She'd agreed to this, and she was getting them together tonight, no matter what.

A while back, Diana had gone out with Cole for drinks but hadn't felt that spark. Maybe it was too soon. At the time, she was still recovering from the biggest mistake of her life. And Cole? On top of being a single father, he had a busy construction business. They hadn't clicked so no hard feelings. No fault, no foul.

Things were different now and she glanced around. Her eyes skidded to a halt at the guy seated with Kate. Drop. Dead. Gorgeous. Dialing back to the conversation with Chili and Sarah, Diana struggled to fill in the blanks. Wasn't Kate's date in charge of some nursing home? This sexy, beach boy blond caring for seniors? She could almost hear Grandma Kit and Aunt Ethel cackling with delight. Kate and the hottie got up to dance. Diana's eyes followed. Just something about him looked familiar.

Cole returned with icy margaritas. "Good job, Cole."

She'd hardly had her first sip when he shot up from the table. "Dance?"

"Why not." The disc jockey was playing "Lady in Red" as he led her onto the crowded dance floor. In the right situation, this song could be a major turn-on. But she wasn't wearing red tonight. Kate was and the dress looked great on her. Diana ran a hand over her own gown that had felt so right...until now.

Arms in a stiff arc, Cole was treating her like his sister. She almost burst out laughing. "You like this song?" His eyes drifted.

"Sometimes. Obviously you do."

His lips twisted into a guilty smile. "Sorry, Diana."

"Not a problem. You and I decided long ago we weren't each other's happily-ever-after." His body relaxed and so did hers. They had an understanding.

While the song flowed over the crowd like a liquid aphrodisiac, couples drew closer. Palms probably started sweating. But not Diana's. When Cole stepped on her toes, she groaned. "Watch where you're going, buddy."

"God, I am so sorry."

She'd never seen him so flustered. This was getting aggravating. After all, Diana wasn't exactly chump change.

When Cole swung her around, Diana faced Kate and the ridiculously attractive man, who looked like Diana felt. Irritated. Puzzled too. And yes, sort of familiar. A fabulous dancer, he twirled Kate out and back but she stumbled. Her eyes flew back to Cole like a homing pigeon. Catching the eyes of Chili and Sarah, Diana threw daggers. Chili held out both hands, as if to say, *what can we do?* Instead of circling the floor, Cole and Diana danced in place way too long.

She pinched his shoulder. "Enough of that, big boy. Dance or get off the floor."

Cole cocked his head to one side. "Sorry, what was that?"

"I said, move it or lose it."

"Sorry, I was just…" Cole had the good grace to blush.

"Drooling over Kate," she supplied. "Take out a hankie and wipe your chin."

He brushed his face with one hand.

"Kidding, Cole. I was kidding." Really, he was useless tonight. What she'd give to have some guy this crazy about her.

"We worked on her flower stand all summer," he stammered. "You ever stop there?"

"Never had much of a green thumb myself." Who was he kidding? Kate and Cole did way more than plan a roadside stand.

"She's brought a lot to Gull Harbor," he said with the reverence usually reserved for Nordstrom.

The song ended. Cole led her back to their table. "How about another drink?" he asked, tugging at his bolo tie.

"Sure. Why not?" He left for the bar. Two tables over, Kate said something to Sarah and Chili, and the three of them made tracks to the ladies room. When the Rolling Stones wailed about not having any satisfaction, Diana knew just how that felt. Drumming her fingers on the tablecloth, she snuck a peek at her phone. Leaving now would look strange. Time to tie this up.

"Here you go." Cole set two frosty margaritas on the table. Diana took one hearty gulp and grabbed her beaded bag. "I'll be right back."

"Okay, and Diana…?"

With a sigh, she turned.

"You really do look beautiful tonight." He offered the compliment like an apology.

"Thank you." After all, she'd agreed to this.

Customers she recognized from her store Hippy Chick complimented her on the dress as she swept past. Waving, she made a detour to talk to the disc jockey then continued on her way. When she pushed open the door of the ladies room, the discussion was well underway. "What's this? Planning the next book club meeting?" She planted her silver sandals squarely on the tiled floor.

The three of them looked guilty as sin. "You two need to talk." Pointing, Chili circled the air between Kate and Diana. "Diana, you explain please, yes?"

So, they were handing her the ball? Kate looked totally confused. Obviously, she hadn't expected to see Cole here, especially with a date. Diana didn't blame her one bit. Here was her chance to be one of the group. She was closing the deal. "See you later, Chili and Sarah." She waved them away.

The door whooshed shut behind them, leaving Diana alone with Kate.

"Nice dress." Taking out a small brush, Diana worked on her limp curls. "Where did you get that, Chicago?"

"Second Hand Rose. The consignment shop up the road."

"No way. Really?" She'd have to check it out.

"Amazing, right?" Kate applied lip gloss as red as her dress. "But what about you? Your gown is drop-dead gorgeous. Kind of a sexy mermaid look."

"It's a sample. The vendor let me keep it. So did Sarah and Chili clue you in about why I'm here with Cole?"

Kate kept jabbing at her lips like they were a dart board. "Sort of."

"Just so you know, I have no designs on him. When Sarah and Chili came up with this scheme, I wanted to help." *I wanted to be part of the group.* Taking out a small hand mirror, she checked the back of her hair.

"I don't get it." Kate gave up on the gloss.

"You and Cole need to settle this. At least, that's what Sarah and Chili think. A ladies' choice is coming up. Ask Cole to dance, and I'll entertain your date." How Diana hated relationship drama. She'd had enough to last a lifetime.

Frowning, Kate snapped her tiny purse shut. "But Cole's with you!"

"Sarah and Chili arranged it. The temperature in the ballroom goes up ten degrees every time you and Cole look at each other. I'm definitely in the line of fire and so is whoever you're with...?" She waited.

"Will. Poor guy. You think he's noticed?" Kate frowned.

"Would you notice a forest fire?" *Will. I like the name.* "Cole's done nothing but talk about your flower stand tonight." Not exactly true but close. "You need to work this out. I'll keep your date busy."

"Oh lord. Really?" Kate scrubbed a hand over her forehead. "Be kind to Will, okay?"

Now that hurt. "Come on, Kate. Do I look like Cruella

Deville?"

"I didn't mean that. It's just that Will's such a nice guy. A good person." Kate could be describing paper towels, not the hottie she was ignoring tonight.

Time to drill down on the details. Diana liked clarity, especially after what she'd been through. "I mean, did you...does Will have...any ties to you?" *Any mistaken fumblings I should know about?*

"No, no. I was surprised when he asked me." Kate plumped her long chestnut curls. "He was so nice to Mom after her stroke. A real sweetheart. We met at the Gull Harbor Care Center. He's the administrator."

Okay, Kate had vetted her date. Diana didn't have any plans beyond one dance. Time to get on with it. When the two of them returned to the ballroom, the sound level had kicked up a notch and a buffet line was forming.

"Hungry?" Cole asked, eyes flitting to Kate's receding back.

"Famished." Her own focus drifted to the tall blond, who was pulling out Kate's chair. Did she dare? Uncertainty fluttered in her stomach.

Cole and Diana joined the buffet line, where he heaped his plate with enough food for a construction crew. Thick slices of ham studded with cloves nestled beside cheese-crusted potatoes. Diana spooned some green beans and a thin strip of ham onto her plate. Back at the table, the guys talked about beach preservation techniques. This summer had been especially bad for sand erosion. Listening with half an ear, she nibbled on her beans.

While Cole left for the restroom, Diana made tracks back to the band. "That ladies' choice coming anytime soon?" She batted her long lashes, and the man checked the list on the paper in front of him.

"You bet. It's my job to please the ladies." Was he winking at her?

"Right." She turned on her heel.

Cole returned with a plate filled with cookies—chocolate chip, Mexican hot chocolate, and snicker doodles. Her grandma used to make those, and she snapped one up. "Thanks, Cole."

The sound system squealed when the disc jockey grabbed the mic. "We have a special request for a ladies' choice. Ladies, choose your man." Diana hunkered down behind her snicker doodle.

"I Only have Eyes for You" started playing. The cookie melted in her mouth and she stopped chewing. Diana remembered Grandma Kit peeling potatoes at the kitchen sink while this song played in the background. Grandpa Stanley would come in from his shop out back, wash his hands, and then kiss Grandma on the neck. She wanted that someday.

"Cole, I'm going to ask Kate's date to dance. If she doesn't head over here, take matters into your own hands. That okay with you?"

The poor man looked surprised but relieved. "Sure. Whatever."

Was she about to make a fool of herself? Diana got up. Wouldn't be the first time. Her heel caught in the hem of her dress and she stumbled. *Slow down.* Grabbing the nearest chair, she got her bearings while women led men to the dance floor. The song poured over them in a wave of longing. By the time she got to

Kate's table, her confidence was faltering. She didn't even know the man. But she hadn't gone through this uncomfortable evening for nothing. With Sarah and Chili beaming at her, she tapped Kate's shoulder. "Mind if I steal your date for a minute?"

The blond looked surprised but not unhappy.

"Oh. Well, s-sure. Will, this is Diana Prescott, a friend from my book group." Kate's attention was already drifting toward Cole. "Diana, this is Will Applegate. Is this okay with you?"

He was already getting to his feet. "Sure. Fine. Glad to meet you, Diana."

For a second, Diana felt desperate and foolish. Then Will threw her the smile of a co-conspirator. Had he been ignored all night too? "I'd like to hear more about the book group."

Sure. Right. Chili elbowed Sarah. They didn't even try to hide their giggles. Nacho, Chili's husband, rolled his eyes. Diana heard him mumble, "*Madre de Dios.*"

Dodging tables and chairs, she felt boldly conspicuous. Why had she done this?

Will took her in his arms. "You're shaking."

"Am I?" When his left hand closed over hers, the trembling stopped.

"Better?" He looked down at her with wise eyes.

Her shoulders loosened. "Much." This might be fun.

"Good, let's dance." He swept her into the music then twirled her, passing her under his arm with elegant moves. But still he kept her at a polite distance, like they were in an eighth grade dancing class. No grabby hands wandering from her waist. No sweaty cheek sliding onto hers. Just movement and rhythm. The man knew how to dance. Her stomach tightened with admiration, chased by a tumbler of lust.

Diana lost the beat. He raised a brow. She got back into it and he smiled. If this was a test, she wasn't about to fail it.

After a few turns, he slowed down. Heat burned through her body when his hand tightened on her waist. "So why me?"

She blinked. "What do you mean?"

"Why did you ask *me* to dance and not your date?" His left arm remained rigid, keeping his distance. She liked that. Needed that separation right now.

"Cole and I were fixed up." How embarrassing to admit this.

"Really? A beautiful woman like you could have anyone."

His matter of fact tone made her smile. "You think so, huh?"

"I know so, not that I'm complaining. I'm kind of new here, trying to learn the ropes." He whipped her around and broke into a brisk two-step.

"So you're not mad?" Diana gasped when she could breathe again. "After all, you did invite Kate, and she said yes."

He trained those all-knowing eyes on her. "Look, I may be a country boy, but I didn't just fall off the turnip truck. I hardly knew Kate when I invited her. The dance sounded like fun, and I felt like coming. I don't meet many women... I mean, not under the age of sixty." A rueful smile tugged at his lips.

She chuckled. "So, you're the administrator of the nursing home in town?"

"Nursing home?" His forehead wrinkled. "I like to think of us as a home away from home. You know, a safe place. Do I sound preachy?"

"Nope, not at all." Those words might sound scripted from another guy, a page from a promotional brochure. But not from Will. "My grandfather spent his final days in a care center following a bad fall. They were really nice to him. That meant a lot."

Now, what pulled that truth from her? Diana rarely shared that memory.

"I'm sorry, Diana." Had Will pulled her closer?

"Yeah." His nearness soothed the sting. "Well, it happens. What made you choose that field?"

"I've always liked old people." They did a few more swirls and twirls.

"Me too," she said. "I was raised by my grandparents. Then my grandfather passed away after that accident. We really miss him." How she wished she could roll back time and visit her grandfather more at that nursing home. She'd been trying to keep up with her classes. No one expected him to take that sudden turn.

As if he could read her mind, Will's hold on her hand tightened. "My grandfather died in Vietnam way before I was born, so I never knew him. My grandmother lived with us. It was like having two moms."

How was he able to keep up this pace and talk? Diana was starting to pant.

"Two moms? You were lucky." She would have settled for one. Will had probably grown up in the ideal, loving family. That would figure. Twirling her out, he did the two-step and pulled her back in.

She followed. Amazing.

"California swing, right?"

His eyes widened. "You know?"

"Yes, as a matter of fact."

"Game on."

What followed was exercise enough to glue Diana's dress to her body like a leotard. When they passed under an overhead fans, she squeezed his firm bicep and stopped. "Stay. Just for a minute."

"Right." He inhaled. "So, do you have any siblings?"

"I'm an only child." The air from the fan felt glorious, and Diana shook back her damp hair.

"Too bad." Will cupped her right hand on his chest, as if for comfort. They swayed in place. She felt the steady thud of his heart under his damp shirt.

But just when her resolve was weakening, he spun her out and whipped her back again. Breathless, she landed against his firm, muscled chest. "What was that?"

"I like to surprise people."

"I'll keep that in mind." She laughed at his pleased smile. This guy could be a lot of fun. But she couldn't let her guard down. Not after what had happened last time. "Back to the interrogation. Any brothers or sisters?"

His full lips flattened the smile. Maybe she'd hit a nerve. "An older sister. Just the four of us, well, and my grandmother but she's gone now."

"I'm sorry. At least you have four in your family." This was becoming uncomfortable. Over Will's shoulder, Diana caught a glimpse of Kate and Cole. "Our dates are finally talking."

Smiling, he spun her around for a better view. "Good. Kate's not much of a dancer. "You..." He glanced down at her silver sandals. "You're really light on your feet, and you can follow me."

"Glad I'm getting points. This hasn't been easy tonight."

The blue eyes warmed. "Doesn't sound like you've been having enjoying yourself."

"I am now. Life can't always be fun. Hey, why are you staring at me?"

"It's just that... Well, you're so beautiful."

Disappointment pushed the breath from her body. She used to enjoy lines like that.

He stopped dancing. "Was I wrong to say that?"

"Nope, absolutely not." She gave him a nudge, and they slipped into a slower rhythm. "It's just that I've heard a lot of lines. That sounded like you meant it."

He jerked back. "Of course I meant it. You're gorgeous."

"And you're handsome. So what?" Cripes, they were practically shouting at each other. She glanced around at a few staring faces and then buried her face in his shoulder. "Are we causing a scene?"

A chuckle rumbled through his chest. "Do we care? We just established that we are two fine-looking people."

Really, he was a trip. She drew herself up. "I don't usually act like this. Don't take me seriously."

"What if I want to take you seriously?" Will pulled her closer. Tighter.

"Guess we'll just have to see about that."

She couldn't. She wouldn't. *But maybe.*

When had this evening gotten out of control? Will rested his cheek against Diana's forehead. "I feel like I've seen you before," he murmured. "Know you somehow."

She tipped her head back. "Me too. Clancy's maybe? What day do you shop for groceries?"

The chuckle returned. "My groceries consist of coffee and peanut butter. I eat most of my meals at the facility. My work is pretty time consuming, so I didn't see you while you were squeezing the tomatoes."

"I wouldn't do that." She feigned horror.

"Good to know."

His eyes were lapping at her like July waves along the shore. "Know what?" Where were they?

"That you don't squeeze tomatoes. Smell the melons or..."

"Oh, now *that*. Yes, yes, I do smell melons." What was she saying?

The chortle became a belly laugh. "You are so much fun, Diana."

He sounded wistful, like this was rare. "What, you usually don't have fun?"

Will's wry smile was growing on her. "Maybe I never make time for it." He raised his brows.

Was that an invitation? After all, she'd asked him to dance. Was he asking her for more? Was she ready for more?

She sighed.

He jerked. "Ouch! You just stepped on my foot."

"Sorry, sorry. It's just that, well. Forget it."

"Not a problem. Didn't hurt. Much." She could feel his grin on her forehead.

What a bizarre night this was turning out to be. Gull Harbor didn't offer a lot of dating material. That had been just fine for Diana. Tonight? Dancing with Will had given her body a wake-up call. Sleep wouldn't come easy tonight. They danced past an open door, and a gust of warm night air blew over her just as the air conditioning shot on overhead. Her body and her mind blew hot and cold.

"You always tell the truth, right?"

"Scouts honor." He held up a hand. They both looked at it and burst out laughing.

The resigned shake of his head made Will look adorable. "Sorry. Sometimes I can be a real dork."

"Not a bad quality. Can a man ever be too good?"

The smile faded. "So...you're dating Cole?"

"Come on. Does it look like it?"

She could see the wheels turning in Will's mind. He glanced over at Cole and Kate in front of the french doors. They should get a room. "Point taken. So, tell me about the book group."

"I kind of fell into it. About a year and a half ago, I opened a shop in Gull Harbor. Carolyn Knight, a book group member, stopped in one day. We got to talking and she invited me to join." Sure, the other women had welcomed her, but they didn't really know her yet. No one did and she liked it that way. "I'm still getting to know the group. I don't have many..."

"What?" He bent closer.

"Nothing." She'd almost admitted she didn't have many friends. How pathetic was that?

His head tipped to one side. "You're so mysterious, Diana."

"The pot calling the kettle black." The song had ended. They were still dancing.

Will looked around. Only a few couples remained on the dance floor. "Kind of conspicuous, right?"

"Right." She snatched her arms from around his neck.

"Thanks for the dance, Diana," Will said softly. "Glad I was your lady's choice." When he stepped back, cool air swooshed between them.

"You're welcome." Somehow, her life had shifted in the past five minutes. Could she trust that feeling?

"Guess we should get back to—" Will nodded to his table where Cole was pulling out Kate's chair.

"Sure. Right. Thanks for the dance." She brushed her dress, discreetly shaking out any shameless wrinkles.

"I'm glad you asked me."

Gazes tangling, they stood there.

"Maybe we'll see each other around."

"Right. Maybe." Diana sure hoped so. She'd opened up her treasure trove of memories for him. Well, some of them anyway. She followed Will back to her table.

"Bye, Will," Diana whispered before he walked away.

"See you."

"Uh huh." Her heart raced while her head told her to slow

down.

Hands in his pockets, Will ambled away. Then he turned back to smile, nearly stumbling over his own feet. They both laughed. She gave a little wave.

"Will seems like a nice guy," Cole said, sliding into the seat next to her.

"Yeah, he is." Sitting back, Diana pressed a hand against her fluttering stomach.

Will wasn't the type of man who'd ever interested her. Kind of homespun, squeaky clean, and funny. Cheeks burning, she chugged the rest of her drink. "Ready to leave?"

Cole leapt up with a surprised smile. "Guess so."

~.~

Taking Kate home, Will kept his eyes on the road but his mind was back at the Firemen's Ball, with a beautiful woman who knew how to dance. Diana's sense of humor wasn't bad either. At first, he'd dismissed Diana Prescott as one those gorgeous blondes that spent a lot of time in front of the mirror. But her sassy humor shook him up and so did that glimpse of vulnerability. She was complicated, sexy, and fun.

Kate stared out the window with a tiny smile on her lips. If not for Diana tonight, he'd be pissed. "So, Diana's a friend of yours?"

"We're in the same book group, but I can't say I know her. She's not from Gull Harbor. We didn't go to high school together."

"Got it." So, Diana was an outsider too. He couldn't help

feeling a stronger connection with the woman whose hair felt so soft against his cheek. But he was getting way ahead of himself. One dance did not make a relationship. Her spontaneity was eroding his usual caution.

Not much traffic on Red Arrow Highway tonight. The drive would be short, and he had to make use of every minute. Why hadn't he just asked Diana for her number? But they had both come with other people. Exchanging contact information on the edge of the dance floor would not be cool. Damn, he was no good at this. He could ask a sick resident where she felt pain and in five seconds have it located for the doctor's visit. But with women under sixty? Totally different story.

"She has a shop, Will." Kate broke into his thoughts. "It's called Hippy Chick. She might carry some gifts for a mother or sister?"

"Sure. Right. If I ever need one." Opening his window, he let the cool air stream over him. "Beautiful night, isn't it?"

Kate's laughter pealed like St. Mary's church bells. "If you say so."

When they turned down the Kennedy driveway, he took it easy. The graveled road needed work, just like the house. Sitting under huge pine and birch trees, the cottage could use a fresh coat of paint and some new window boxes. But Cole was a contractor. He could handle it. Will pulled up in the back parking lot. Kate nearly tripped getting out. She didn't strike him as a big drinker, so that had nothing to do with her loopy gait. They walked to the back door. A night wind whistled through the trees and waves lapped the shore somewhere below. He breathed in the night air. Hippy

Chick, was it? The path seemed clear.

At the door, she turned. "Thanks for inviting me, Will." Obviously, she was preoccupied and at this point, he didn't care. The evening had turned out well for both of them.

"You're welcome." Backing away, he jiggled the car keys in his hand. "Give my best to your mother."

"I will." She worked the key, stepped inside and then turned. "See ya...and good luck."

"Right. Thanks."

An owl hooted deep in the woods, low and mysterious as he walked to his car. All the way back to his condo, he hummed "I Only Have Eyes for You." And Kate was not the woman on his mind.

# Chapter 2

Not a man who rushed into things, Will waited until mid-week to make his move. Diana exuded sophistication that made him painfully aware he came from Beanblossom, Indiana. Still, he hadn't imagined the interest in her eyes, the soft pressure of her body while they danced. Or had he? He'd find out soon enough. When he pulled up to the store called Hippy Chick, he sat in the car and let the air run.

August pressed down with a heated hand. Despite the air vents blowing full blast, Will started to sweat. The windows of the tidy, freestanding shop shouted Sale in big red letters. Suddenly the door opened and Diana stepped outside. Will checked his watch. Eleven o'clock. He valued punctuality. Then she turned back and tried to wrestle a display rack through the front door. The clunky metal looked heavy. Turning off the car, he jumped out. "Need some help?"

She glanced up in surprise, her long, beaded earrings swinging. "Always glad for a hand." Pushing a wisp of blonde hair from her eyes, she gave him a shy smile. The heat kicked up a notch.

The clothing on the rack looked like stuff Diana would wear. The colorful, fluttery, and soft fabric swayed as he moved the rack around. "This where you want it?"

"Perfect." Shading her eyes with one hand, she smiled up at him. "Thanks, Will. What brings you here?"

"I'm looking for someone, er, thing." He hoped to hell she didn't ask what.

"Good enough. Glad you thought of my shop. Come on in."

She glided toward the glass door, and he rushed to open it. Perfume that smelled like his mother's peonies enticed him when she swept past. Inside, the shop was dim and cool. He drew a deep breath and looked around. Yep, he was clearly out of his league.

"You're looking for women's clothing?"

"Right. A gift." His new loafers squeaked when he shifted.

"Okay. Give me just a minute." She hurried toward the back and lights flipped on.

Glancing at the stuff hanging here, he tried to pull together a game plan. In the back was a glass counter with sparkly jewelry. Off to the side, shoeboxes were stacked under a rack of dresses. The entire place was crammed with clothes that might not be right for his mother. That left Delinda. His sister might dress like this. He doubted it but he hadn't seen her in years.

"Well?" Diana blinked up at him. With a rush, he remembered her soft cheek on his chin. His mouth felt dry and sandy. Words wouldn't come, and he casually reached for a rack. Bad move. With a clatter, a box of pins went flying like a disturbed porcupine. "Good God."

"Oh, Will! Let me see." Diana reached for his hand.

Feeling like a total fool, he opened his palm. Her cool fingers sent heat coursing through him. The accident was almost worth it.

When she plucked a pin from his palm, a bubble of blood rose. "I'll get a tissue. Stay right there."

Yep, totally worth it. Diana in motion was a sight to treasure. But his hand wasn't. As he pulled out pins, drops of blood rose. He might bleed all over her merchandise.

Muttering to herself, she came back with a box of tissues and began blotting. Her hair swept over his hand and he pulled in a deep breath, almost disappointed when the bleeding stopped. Diana gathered the tissues and tossed them in the trash. Coming back, she ran her hands over those slim hips. "I can take care of these pins later. Now what was it you wanted?"

Right now? He couldn't be honest, or he'd get kicked out.

"You came in looking for a gift, right?" Her delicious chuckle rippled like a bubbling fountain. "What did you have in mind?"

Will slid his eyes to the nearest rack. "A shirt would be good."

"You mean a blouse? Now we'. Okay, what size?"

He had no idea. "What size are you? I mean, if I could ask."

Her cheeks flushed. "Me? Oh, a small."

"Well, then larger. Yes, I think large."

"Okay. How fancy? Are you thinking glittery or embroidered? Maybe a print?"

The questions spun in his head. "Anything."

Her lips twitched.

"Anything casual, I meant. Casual would probably be nice."

Turning to the circular metal rack, she began pushing hangers around. "Any particular color? Solid or pattern?"

"This looks pretty." He fingered something blue draped from a display.

"That's a scarf, Will. Does your sister wear them?"

His mouth opened and closed. He had no idea. Delinda and her little girl had been MIA for years. She'd caused a lot of hurt for their parents. Made him furious. "Maybe something else."

Thank God, Diana was on a roll. What followed was a dizzying array of clothing, colorfully described. He enjoyed her sweet, uncertain smile and delicate hands. Her pale pink fingernails were edged with white tips. While she ran through a list of possibilities, his head felt like a sieve being filled with her words.

"Will, Will. Are you paying attention?"

"Sorry." He ran a hand over his brow, and it came away damp.

Diana was waving a white blouse in front of him. Flowers decorated the neckline and sleeves in pink and green. "Do you think she'd like this?"

"It's pretty, right? Women would like this?" Why had he worn his khaki jacket in the store? He felt like he'd stepped into the sauna at the racquet club. This stuff was way over his head. His mother had worn a lot of jeans for tending cows and chickens. When Grandma Trudie was alive, she stirred his oatmeal wearing a tidy housedress every morning. He couldn't recall any patterns or designs, none of the stuff Diana was running through like chords on a piano.

Turning to another rack, she pulled out a black number with sleeves. "Maybe your sister's more sophisticated?"

"Not at all." The words came so fast that Diana smiled and put the dress aside.

"Probably something flowered." Where had he pulled that from?

"Follow me." Leading him to a corner, she pulled out a top with yellow and brown flowers.

"Do you think the brown is perky enough?" Clothes were closing in on him. He pretended to consider the shirt as if he cared. His sister could be a walking rainbow for all he knew and so could her daughter. Maybe he should just buy the pink and green one. But then he'd have to leave.

"Tie dyes are back," she said with excitement, as if announcing the president was coming to visit. "They come in a rainbow of colors." Diana loved her work, and he loved watching her. When her long blue skirt swished around her feet, hot pink nails peaked out. His stomach felt squishy, and he wondered if he'd eaten anything for breakfast. He also wondered where those pretty feet could lead.

"Isn't this fabulous? Just came in." With her bewitching long fingers, Diana held up a top that started as pale pink and ended up dark blue at the bottom. It looked pretty. She stroked one hand over the front. "And it's so soft."

With a jolt, he imagined his own hand caressing the material over her soft curves. "I'll take it," he gasped.

Will was dripping wet and breathing hard. Somehow, this shopping trip felt like great sex. Not that he'd had any in a long time.

"You really like this tie-dye thing, huh? Maybe you're wilder than I thought." She wiggled her brows.

Perspiration trailed down his backbone. He'd have to stop at his condo for a shower before going into work.

"Well, what do you think?"

"Yes, yes to all of it." Looking down into Diana's eyes felt like skydiving. "Your eyes are so, so...b-blue." He was stuttering like an idiot.

Nudging him with an elbow, she laughed. "So are yours, goofus."

"Goofus? Is that what you think?"

Her eyes darkened to velvet. "No. No, Will. I sure don't." Her tongue darted out to lick her lips, and she dropped her gaze.

His insides imploded. He wanted her arms around his neck, the way they'd been at the dance.

"Who is this for?" The bright overhead light glinted off the long, golden hair he longed to curl around his hand.

"My sister."

"That's so sweet." Perspiration beaded her upper lip. Maybe it was warm in here. Maybe it wasn't just his body running riot. "What's her name?"

"Delinda. She's my older sister."

"That's a pretty name you don't often hear. What size again?" Diana smiled. He fought the urge to take out his hankie and slowly blot her sweetly curved lips. Instead, he shifted his attention to the blouse. "Large might work," he breathed. "As big as the sky."

Will had no idea what he was saying.

Checking the labels, Diana gave a squeal of delight. "Oh goody. We won't have to order it. Anything else?"

He felt like he might combust. "Yes, as a matter of fact."

Diana stood waiting, mouth open and lips moist. "What would that be?"

"Would you have dinner with me?" Great. So cool...like a blow torch.

A blush tinged her cheeks. Taking the blouse, she slipped behind the counter. "Oh, well. I'm kind of busy right now. Summer season and all." Eyes down, she knotted her fingers in the fabric.

What? Had he imagined the chemistry at the dance? "But summer's ending."

"Yes, yes it is." With a sigh, she twisted the blouse from its hanger. The graceful movement of her hands had him imagining all kinds of things. Inappropriate. Mind-blowing. Shaking his head helped dislodge the mental picture. But his body didn't get the message.

He rooted himself in the worn carpet. "Just something casual. A bite to eat. Wouldn't take much time." The words battered at her defenses. No way was he giving up this easy.

Golden lashes fluttering, she gazed up. The distrust in her eyes shook him. "What is it, Diana?"

With a pretty shake of her shoulders, she looked away. "Oh, nothing. Guess I'm just being silly. Sure, a casual dinner would be nice. When?"

*Tonight.* But instinct made him say, "Saturday?" She wanted distance. He'd give it to her even though the weekend felt like a year away.

Spreading the blouse out flat, Diana folded it with precise movements. Her hands took his imagination on a roller coaster ride.

"Do you have a favorite place to eat?"

Diana tipped her head to one side. "Well, I like Brewster's."

"Sounds good. Six o'clock? Will your shop be closed by then?"

"I have someone to help me on weekends. Rachel. Hippy Chick stays open until seven Fridays and Saturdays. You know. Tourists."

"We can make it later." He wasn't letting this slip away.

"No, six is fine." She motioned for him to run his credit card through the machine. "Rachel will be glad to have the hours."

The door opened and a bell jangled. "Oh look, Diana's got some new merchandise." The newcomers waved and Diana waved back.

"Check out the sale rack," she called out. "I just took some new markdowns. Be careful of the pins on the floor."

He recognized Sharon Dalby, whose father was rehabbing at the care center. Sharon and her friend bustled toward him like chickens pecking for corn.

"Saturday it is then," he said.

Knowing glances were exchanged by the two newcomers. Definitely time to get out of here. "Pardon me, ladies." Skirting them, he marched toward the door. "See you, Diana."

"Oh, Will."

With one hand on the plate glass door, he turned. "Yes?"

A lime green bag dangled from her hand. "Don't you want this?" Diana's lips twitched.

"Yes. Yes, of course." With a tight grin, he went back for the bag but not before he'd heard the giggles. The entire town would know about this before he reached the care center. A burst of perspiration bathed his body.

"And don't you want my number?"

Sharon and her friend leaned forward to catch every word.

"But I have your card." He jerked his head in the direction of the display.

Confusion clouded her face. "That's the store. Sometimes it's very busy."

Feeling like a complete clod, Will set the bag on the floor and retrieved his pocket planner. Under the watchful eyes of three women, he jotted down her number. Yep, might as well take out an ad in *The Beacher*, the local weekly.

The ridiculous bag swinging from his hand, he left. Outside, bright light glanced off the stones in the parking lot as the sun marched toward noon. He felt blinded and incinerated at the same time.

But his mood lifted as he backed out of the parking place and took a left onto Whittaker. One block later, he was back on Red Arrow and headed to his condo for a shower. As he lathered up, he remembered the warm honey of her hair, the blue blaze of her eyes. The bright pink toenails and the feminine way she folded the blouse. He began to hum "I Only Have Eyes for You" or what he could remember of that song.

Thirty minutes later, he parked in the administrator spot outside the care center. The bag sat accusingly on the front seat. What the hell was he going to do with it? "Oh, all right." Slinging the bag from one finger, he approached the front door, where one of his residents sat sentinel every day. "Morning, Harold."

"Good morning, Mr. Applegate. Any food in that bag?" The notorious forager always wore a hat with earflaps, even in August.

"Sorry. Not today."

Inside, cool air greeted him along with the smell of cookies baking. Will wanted Gull Harbor Care Center to feel like home. His grandmother had always had fresh-baked cookies in her cookie jar.

Kelsey looked up from the reception desk, eyes zipping to the bag. "Good morning, Mr. Applegate. Looks like you've been shopping at Hippy Chick. I just love that shop."

Shoving the bag her way, he felt relieved. "You do? Good, maybe you'll like this. Isn't it your birthday or something?" He had no plans to see his sister anytime soon.

Flushing, Kelsey cradled the bag in both hands. "Thank you, Mr. Applegate." Was she fluttering her eyes? He turned toward his office. The only eyes in his mind were blue and often guarded by long lashes.

Why had Diana thrown up a shield and how could he penetrate it?

Penetration. Will tripped on the tile floor and nearly went down.

## Chapter 3

Eye makeup was a necessary evil. Diana sponged off the expensive Stormy Sky eye shadow and started over. Heat swelled in the small bathroom, which didn't help. She tried to keep her electric bill down so she had the air conditioning set at seventy-six. The small pedestal sink had no room, and her products kept rolling off the closed toilet seat.

Brush in hand, she stopped.  Would Will even care about her makeup? He had an appealing homespun look. Maybe he'd be one of those guys who didn't go for a lot of eye shadow. Not Bryce. He'd told her she had Cleopatra eyes.

But she was finished and done with him.

Stomach clenched, she tapped her brush against the sink. Was she ready to start over, especially with Will Applegate? Mr. Perfect...which she wasn't. She could be setting herself up for disappointment, especially if she told all. Her head told her to run for the hills. But her heart? Maybe it was time to take some chances.

Snatching her eye palette, she started over. Cream powder first over the eyelid, a swath of white at the top and then Warm Taupe feathering from the outer crease. Blinking for the effect, she scrutinized herself in the mirror. Right. Moderation. This looked more natural. More Will. Then she carefully lined her eyes with the tiniest brush she owned before applying a base coat of mascara.

"Remember, Diana," her mother had told her. "Beautiful girls have an easier life. And you're prettier than the rest of the girls. Make the most of it, kiddo." Diana had been what, six at the time? Grandma Kit didn't believe in that "rubbish." That's exactly what she called it.

The "easier life" part? Diana snorted.

When she was seven, her mother bought a one-way ticket to a Chicago rock concert and just kept going. They were living with her grandparents at the time. Her grandfather spent a lot of money to find Star, their only child. Didn't matter. By then, she was eighteen and not coming back. Diana blinked fast so her eyeliner didn't run. Stupid to cry after all these years. Her absentee mother lived in Ibiza with her third husband, Paulo. Or so she said on the postcards that arrived on Diana's birthday, or close to it anyway. Sometimes she sent a refrigerator magnet instead. Ibiza was just one in a string of quaint villages and skyscraper cities.

A quick sniff and Diana blotted the corners of her eyes and finished the job. Next came a dash of cream rouge on the upper apple of each cheek. Her lips looked fuller when she outlined them just outside her natural line before filling them in. Last was the Summer Peach gloss dabbed in the center of her lower lip. A quick wide grin allowed her to check her teeth. Almost perfect. Packing up her supplies, she hurried to get dressed.

She was adjusting the soft blue top that hugged her shoulders when the doorbell rang. Excitement rippled through her. That one dance with Will had awakened all kinds of crazy feelings. Those sunset blue eyes with smoky green rims? Slipping into her white miniskirt, she wished she weren't such a romantic. The bell rang again, and she padded to the door in her bare feet. Where had she left her sandals?

Will's silhouette showed through the lace curtains. She smiled to see him run a hand through his hair. Maybe he was nervous too. When she opened the door, he held a bouquet of red roses and the perfume curled around her. "Oh, Will. How beautiful."

His blue sport coat and bright red tie had her wondering if they'd gotten their signals crossed. Gull Harbor was summer casual all year long. Still, his cluelessness tugged at her heart. So did the flowers. "Come on in."

When Will stepped inside, the ceiling seemed to drop. She closed the door against the persistent heat. "You're sure looking beautiful. Peach, not pink?" His eyes fell to her feet.

She wiggled her toes. "Peach."

"Am I overdressed? I figured the restaurant will be air conditioned." He ran a hand down the tie, eyes lifting from her white miniskirt to the pale blue top. "You look, well, beautiful. Did I say that already?"

"Trust me, a girl never minds hearing it twice. So do you. I mean, not beautiful but, well, you know." Her tongue felt knotted.

"Yes, guess I do." Laughter danced in his eyes, and she wondered if Will Applegate ever had a bad day. It wasn't difficult to picture his smile charming the older women at the care center.

When she took the flowers from him, the tissue felt damp.

"How sweet. You didn't have to do this." When was the last time any man had brought her flowers?

Two years. The memory cut deep. But she wasn't going to let a past mistake spoil tonight. "I'll just put these in some water." Diana led the way past the island into the cramped kitchen space.

"Nice place." While she poured water into a bowl, he looked around.

"Small but I like the open concept. Isn't that what they call it? This counter kind of divides the kitchen from the living room." To stop her nervous babbling, she buried her nose in the sweet blooms. Diana drank in the lush scent before slipping them into the cool water. That should hold them until later. She wanted to take her time arranging the stems. Whirling around, she found Will's eyes pouring over her bare shoulders. "They're beautiful, Will. Thank you."

"Yes, yes they are." Then he jerked upright and flushed scarlet, like he'd been thinking about more than the roses. A laugh tickled her throat, but she swallowed it. Will might be the type who embarrassed easily.

"Did you have any trouble finding the house?"

"Nope. My car's got GPS."

She glanced at the clock. "And right on time."

"I try to be." Another nervous tug at the tie.

"Let me just grab my purse." She dashed into the bedroom and did a quick check under the bed for her shoes. Thank goodness they were there, and she slipped into the silver sandals. Checking her hair in the mirror, she tried to smooth her curls, hopelessly frizzy in the humidity.

When she returned, Will was studying one of the Monet prints on her living room wall. Glancing around, she saw her tiny living space with new eyes. Magazines she never read were stacked on the coffee table, the TV remote buried under them. Retrieving an empty coffee mug, she hustled back to the sink. This open concept thing was fine except when you had guests.

"Don't straighten up on account of me, Diana."

"I bet you're neat as a pin."

"Not really." He looked deflated and endearing. "*Neat as a pin.* Sounds so exciting."

"I didn't mean it in a bad way." She nudged her scuffed tennis shoes under a side table.

"Sometimes it's nice to just let things go. I think you'll be surprised when...if you see my place."

*When. If. Really?* Happy talk. She stiffened with disappointment. Oh, she'd heard plenty of those casual comments men threw out about the future. As if there were one for the two of them. Still, Will didn't seem to be that type and she reined in her unfair assumption. "Watch what men do, not what they say," her last therapist had told her.

Maybe Will really was different. He didn't seem to be one of those guys with slick manners and well rehearsed lines. The stubborn cowlick in the dirty blond hair and his way of laughing at himself made him seem different.

The light dancing in his eyes sure looked like mischief. When he flexed his shoulders and went back to looking at the prints on her walls, his clean male scent rolled over her. The thoughts that unfurled in her head could get her into trouble. Time to lock up, and she scurried to slide the side door bolt but it always stuck.

"Here. Let me." Will's hand closed over hers, so warm. The bolt slid into place. He glanced down as if he didn't know how she'd ended up in his arms.

Ducking, she skipped under his arm. "Thanks, Will."

Hand still on the lock, he looked dazed. "You're so beau...welcome. You're welcome, Diana." Stepping away from the door, he gave his head a little shake.

They were quite a pair. Hands trembling, she felt like a sophomore on her first date, heading out for pizza with Tim Johnson.

"So you like the Impressionists?" They were back to Monet.

"Sounds like you know them?" Not every man recognized artists from the end of the 19th century. "The pastel colors are so peaceful."

He ran a hand over his chin. "Maybe I should get one for my office."

"What do you have in your office now?" Looping her fringed shawl over one arm, Diana snatched her keys from the counter and shoved them in her bag.

Will hitched up a shoulder. "Mostly deer hunting and fishing stuff. You know, outdoorsy."

"You're into that?" Stepping out onto the porch, she pictured stuffed heads hanging on his office wall and shivered.

"Kind of." Will followed her out the door. "Aren't you going to leave the light on? Might be dark when we come home...back, I mean."

"Good idea. The sun's setting earlier now." She flipped a switch inside the porch door.

"My mother always says a welcoming home keeps the front light on."

How simple and wholesome. "She was probably right."

Crickets sang in the tiger lilies blooming in the front. They'd had a few days of rain and an earthy smell hung rich in the air. Everything had gone through a growth spurt, including the grass. "Sometimes I wish I'd rented a house without this big yard."

Will closed the door and then twisted the knob to make sure it was locked. "Isn't your landlord responsible for upkeep?"

"That wasn't our arrangement. I took on lawn duty in exchange for part of my rent."

"Good for you."

"Yes, when I have time to do it. Did you know how hard it is to cut grass that's three inches high?"

His chuckle floated on the soft night air. A sensible white sedan sat at the curb. "Want to walk over? We're only about three blocks from the restaurant."

"Great idea." Sliding out of his jacket, he tossed it in the back seat of his car and then clicked the lock. They took off together.

"Watch yourself," she told him. "The city keeps saying they'll fix this. The roots push up and crack the sidewalk. They even talk about taking down the trees." Throwing back her head, she glanced up into the leafy greenness up above and Will followed her gaze.

"I'd vote for the tree every time," he said.

"You *are* an outdoor guy."

"I've done a lot of fishing and hunting, in season."

The evening air caressed her body. "What a beautiful night. Want to eat outside? Brewster's patio is great in the summer."

"I'm up for anything," he said, very matter of fact. When they reached the corner, he took her arm. The asphalt street gave off summer heat, invasive on her bare legs. With his hand cupping her elbow, dangerous thoughts chased through her head. She tripped on the curb but his grip tightened.

"You okay, Diana?" he asked softly.

"Fine. Just not watching my step."

"Happy to help with that." And easy as that, he took her hand.

First date? But she laced her fingers with his. For a few seconds they just walked until the silence made her nervous. "I hate to see summer slip away. September comes so fast." And then sales would drop.

"I suppose summer is your busiest time."

"Absolutely. The winters can be long for the shops. Some of them close up during January and February."

"Head to Florida?"

"Right. But I can't afford that. I'm experimenting. Ordering stock for the cross-country skiers."

But she didn't want to be a buzzkill with her work worries. Her gaze slid up. Will Applegate was definitely easy on the eyes. Every time they came to an upended sidewalk block, his grip tightened. The protective gesture sent heat spiraling through her. "How about you? Any seasonal shift in what you do?"

"Not really. Of course, Christmas is a little different. Over the holidays, adult children often realize their folks can't handle being at home alone anymore."

"And that's where you come in."

"Exactly. I've got a good team. Trust me, we never spend January in Florida." The words were said with good humor.

When they reached Brewster's, cars lined the street. The Italian café was always crowded. Tiny lights were strung over the outside seating area. With any luck, they'd get a table out there. The smell of garlic, warm bread and tomato sauce drifted through the front doors.

Dropping her hand, Will stepped up to the receptionist. "Table for two, please?"

The young girl consulted her screen. "The wait is about one hour and fifteen minutes."

"You're kidding." His voice held dismay.

"Next time, you can call when you're on the way," the girl told him. "There's still a wait but at least you're on the list."

Diana's stomach shrank. She'd forgotten about their phone policy.

"What do you think?" Will half-turned, as if considering other options.

"Let's just wait at the bar. There's no hurry, right?"

He looked uncertain, as if he didn't want to disappoint her. "You're sure that's all right? We could try our luck on Red Arrow."

But tonight she wanted the romance of the darkened patio.

"No, really. Let's have a drink." Diana led the way to the side bar. She loved this place in the summer, even though it held some memories. They took the last two bar stools.

"You must think I don't get out much. Sorry, I didn't know about the wait." His lips twisted.

"Not a problem. I'm happy they're crowded. Brings me business."

Settling in, they ordered margaritas. In the background, Dean Martin crooned Italian love songs. The evening felt strangely perfect, like a fabulous dress she forgot she owned. She was on a date, the first in a long time. Sales had been good that day. Best of all, Will was being sweet as could be. When the drinks came, she raised her glass. "To a good day."

"I'm for that." He clinked her glass with his. "What's a good day for you?"

Salt rimmed her margarita glass and Diana licked her lips. His eyes followed. "I-I hit my target today, which was last year's sales. Don't you have goals at work?"

Nodding, he took a gulp. The tendons in his neck worked. Will's neck was broad, strong. Cripes, she practically felt his icy drink drip down her spine as he swallowed. Maybe she was sweating.

"Sure," he said, while she gave herself a mental head slap. "The company that owns Gull Harbor Care Center has daily census goals."

His words sounded muffled. *Stop thinking about his neck and concentrate.* She pulled her attention back while he continued, "My personal goal is the health of my residents."

Words like that usually belonged in TV commercials. But on Will's lips, they sounded sincere.

It was so hard to gather her thoughts. She needed rock music, not Italian love songs. "Where is the care center? I don't remember ever passing it."

"Just off Red Arrow Highway. Greenwood Road."

She searched her mind, licking her lips again. "Don't think I know where that is."

His eyes clung to her lips. "Don't feel bad. No one knows where it is until they need it. Then we're there for you."

Will's glance wandered from her lips to her eyes. She was glad she'd spent so much time on her makeup.

"You look so mysterious. What are you thinking?" With a mischievous smile, he leaned closer.

God, he smelled good. "For what it's worth, you'd be the guy I'd want taking care of my family." She was tempted to sweep back the lock of hair that fell into his eyes. Instead, she clenched one fist tight in her lap and reached for her drink. She had to take it slow. In lots of ways.

But her body was humming a different message.

# Chapter 4

"What a compliment, Diana. You'd entrust your family to me?" Will's eyes flowed over her bare shoulders like a warm July wave. Goose bumps rose on her skin. "I'd be waiting in the hall for your visits."

"Visits." She almost dropped her glass. He had just filled in the blanks. "Will, do I look familiar? Did you work at a rehab home in Indianapolis?"

He blinked. "Yes, Westwood. That's where I started out. Why?"

"My grandfather rehabbed there." At first, she thought he was another visiting relative. But that tall, good-looking guy was there all the time, walking the halls. "After my grandfather broke his hip, he was taken to Westwood Care Center on the north side of Indianapolis."

Will seemed to be thinking back. "Right, okay. You did look a little familiar at the dance. Guess I thought that was just wishful thinking. Westwood was my first job. I was assistant administrator."

"My grandmother adored you. She called you that cute young man in the suit."

"Really?" Loosening his tie, Will unbuttoned the top button of his shirt. Was the evening getting warmer or was it them? "You remember all that?"

"I do now." She was toast.

He shook his head. "Life is funny, right?"

"Funny? Sometimes." If she could only go back to that time when Grandpa Stan was sick. She'd do it differently, that's for sure.

"And your grandfather? Hope we treated him well. He's doing okay?"

She dropped her eyes. "He never made it, Will. But it didn't have anything to do with your staff or the place. He hated the whole thing. Hated that he'd fallen in the first place. The rehab? Grandpa just gave up." Her voice had turned hoarse. Dean Martin and his music faded into the background. Yep, she'd do anything to go back and spend more time with her grandfather. She'd been too busy worrying about calculus and American Literature back then. Working part-time and going to night school.

Will squeezed her hand. "I'm so sorry, Diana."

"That's okay. Your staff did what they could. He had a stroke and that was that. My great-aunt Ethel moved in with my mother, and they're still in Newtown."

"Newtown. Think I've heard of it."

She leaned back in disbelief. "Come on. Newtown is almost too small to be on the map."

He chuckled. "Look, I'm from Beanblossom, Indiana, if that puts things into perspective."

She swallowed a giggle that turned into a hiccup.

"What a name to hang around a kid's neck all his life, right?"

"Do they sell t-shirts? I want one!"

His eyebrows disappeared into that crazy cowlick. "Okay, now you're putting me on."

By that time, she was laughing. "I'm not one to point fingers. The only people who ever drive through Newtown are probably on their way to Ball State University, which is in Muncie."

"Did you go to Ball State?"

"No. A community college in Indy."

"Are your parents still in Newtown too? Do they live near your grandmother?"

She should have known. Will was the kind of guy who'd want details. "My mother lives on the island of Ibiza with her third husband."

"Sounds glamorous."

"I've never been there. Those magnets you may have noticed on my refrigerator? That's all I know about the island."

His smile faded. "That's too bad."

Will no doubt came from the perfect family. She pictured Sunday dinners with his family gathered around a table.

"Maybe." Diana hated questions like this. "We're not close."

"How about your dad?"

Wasn't their table ready yet?

What would he think? She forged on anyway. "I don't have a father. Star—that's actually my mother's name—was pretty wild in high school. None of her partners wanted to narrow down the field with her."

The silence stretched. Will didn't look away, and he didn't jump into the usual "I'm so sorry." If anything, he looked angry. "You deserve better."

"I can handle it." She tossed her head back. Time to change the subject. "How did you end up running a care center?"

"Like I said, I just liked old people. They need people who care looking out for them." His brows pinched together. "I hope to succeed at my job."

She sat back. Most guys defined success with money, big houses and everything that went with it.

"Okay, you're quiet. What are you thinking?"

"Nothing." Why go into this? Instead, she lifted her glass. "Here's to people from small towns with cool names."

They sipped. Will checked his phone but still no text about their table. "What do your parents do in Beanblossom?" Diana wanted to hear more about his family.

"My dad was the mayor for a while. He has a small hardware store. But it's really a place where guys come to sit and talk about their crops, stuff like that."

Right. Of course. Her drink turned tart. The Applegate family sounded like good upright folks. Apple pie and strong principles. Honesty. She shivered.

"Anything wrong?" When he leaned closer, she saw the green ring around the iris of each blue eye. Felt his warm breath on her face.

"Oh, no. Just thinking." She ran her finger down the stem of her glass. "Do you ever miss your home town?"

"Sure, but my folks give me all the news. I go back when I can." The way he talked, she knew he had great memories.

"Is it pretty in that part of Indiana?"

Will grinned. "Yeah, it's awesome. In a couple of months, the leaves will be changing color. But Michigan was pretty last fall, so that made the move easier."

"Did you hate to leave Indiana?"

"Not really. I never pictured myself staying in Beanblossom." He scooped some peanuts from a bowl on the bar. "Don't you miss your home town? Newtown, right?"

"More than the town, I miss my grandmother and Aunt Ethel. But I go back to visit."

"So, you went to school in Indianapolis. What brought you up here?"

She'd learned to choose her words carefully. "For a while I lived in Chicago. A small inheritance from my grandfather made that possible. I ended up in Gull Harbor by accident. The recession, you know." That seemed like the best excuse.

"At least you weren't in real estate, although I imagine the shops took a hit."

"Retail's not an easy career. I jumped into it without enough training and made some mistakes. But I like what I do."

Will had grabbed a menu from the pile stacked in a corner of the bar. "Maybe we should check this out so we're ready when our table comes up."

"They have great pizza."

He flipped over a page. "What do you like on yours?"

"Everything. Spinach, mushrooms, onion, peppers, lots of black olives." The list made her drool.

His eyes had widened. "You really do come here often."

"Take out. One pizza lasts me a couple of days. How about you? I suppose you want sausage or pepperoni."

"What you described sounds fine to me. Order whatever you want."

"You're sure easy to please." She couldn't recall when she'd been this comfortable with a man.

Nipping his lower lip between his teeth, Will nodded. "Usually, yes."

Picking up the menu, she fanned herself. "Lordy, it's hot in here, or is it me?"

His eyes settled on her. "You. It's definitely you."

She stopped breathing until it hurt. When Will went back to studying the menu, she exhaled. "They should be calling us soon, don't you think?" She craned her neck toward the front desk. The crowd had thinned. Wouldn't be long now. She could almost taste the pizza.

Will's phone rang. Finally. She was starving. Hopping off the stool, Diana grabbed her drink and glanced toward the patio. Everything was going so well.

But Will was frowning. "When did the staff last see her?"

Diana set her drink back on the bar.

"Call the Emergency Team. I'll be there in ten minutes."

"What's wrong?" Diana snatched her shawl and purse. Digging out his wallet, Will threw some bills on the bar. "I'm sorry, but I have to get to work. Fast. An emergency."

Following him out into the gathering dusk, she tried to keep up.

Will's legs ate up the sidewalk with long strides. "What is it? What's wrong?"

"One of our Alzheimer's patients is missing. Damn, wish I'd brought my car."

Running wasn't easy in her sandals, but Will broke into a jog and she kept up. "How could you know? Does this happen often?"

"No." Giving her a side-glance, Will said, "You don't have to run along with me, Diana. I'll call you after this is over." They were both starting to pant.

"Absolutely not." He looked so worried. "How will you find her?"

"We map out a grid and search the fields. Most patients are found within a mile. Unless Luanne grabbed a ride from someone. My nursing director has alerted the police." By the second block, Will was starting to sweat. He looked warm and worried. But she had to watch the blasted sidewalk or take a nasty spill.

This off-the-shoulder top was just not cutting it. Glad that Will was preoccupied, she folded her arms under her breasts to keep everything in place. "The Gull Harbor police force is small. Who helps you search?" Darkness had crept over the street. They were running in and out of pools of light thrown from street lamps.

"We have a First Alert Team. Every staff member available. Folks from the community like the volunteer firemen."

"Can anyone pitch in?" Her side was killing her. Thank God she hadn't eaten yet. Her yellow frame house came into sight, the light glowing over the front door. The last stretch felt like forever. "I'm coming with you."

"No, you're not." He looked down at her shoes.

Will had a point. She couldn't search the fields in this getup. "You go," she told him, pushing her front door open. "I'll be there. And I won't get in your way. "

"I'm not going to argue with you." Hard to believe this was the same man who had stood calmly studying her Monet print only an hour ago. Will told her where to turn off Red Arrow and then he was gone, tires squealing as he took a corner.

In less than a minute, she shed her white skirt for jeans and ditched the sexy top for a navy hoodie. Then she jammed her feet into socks and tennis shoes. The whole time, she thought about how frightened the poor woman must be. What if this were Grandma Kit? After locking up the house, she jumped into her bright yellow VW and headed for Red Arrow.

Will might think she was crazy and maybe she was. She just had to help. Sometimes you get a chance to catch up in life. And this was one of those moments.

Greenwood Road wasn't hard to find. Up ahead of her cars were turning, headlights arcing in the dark. When she pulled into the parking lot, red lights flashed from police cars and guys in uniforms were studying GPS maps. She parked, got out and hurried inside. A girl at the reception desk told her where to find Will and the crisis team. Her tennis shoes squeaked on the shiny tile as she raced to the conference room, standing room only when she arrived. Sleeves rolled up, Will stood pointing to a chart pinned to a board. "Team A will begin at this sector and move south to the quarter mile point. Then we'll flip and head north. Team B will start across the road. Stay ten feet away from each other and keep a steady but thorough pace. Be sure to look in every depression or gully. Check under fallen trees and shake bushes all the way to the creek."

At the mention of the creek, the group fell silent. She didn't have to be a clinical person to know how dangerous any body of water could be for a confused older woman, especially at night.

"Let's move." Will snapped them back to attention. "Count off." They counted off and Diana ended up on Team A, which he led.

Grabbing flashlights from the table, they went out into the fields. What was she doing here, stamping through high weeds in the dark? But she wanted so desperately to help. This could be her Grandma Kit or Aunt Ethel lost out here. Lightning split the sky and thunder rumbled overhead. The group picked up the pace. She could practically feel the terror of the older woman. Was there a daughter somewhere who would be called? She pressed forward in the long line of searchers calling one name, "Luanne! Luanne!"

The name echoed through the fields. They stopped to listen every so often, but no response came on the still night air. They pushed on. Thank goodness she'd changed clothes. Bushes slapped her legs, and once, a branch whipped back across her cheek. She pressed a hand against the sting. Had it left a scratch? She'd deal with it later. From across the road came the calls from the B team. The quarter mile stretch felt eternal, and Diana could only imagine how it would feel to Luanne.

Of course, she might be out on the highway, even more

terrifying. The police were stopping along Red Arrow, asking questions at gas stations and restaurants before leaving a flyer. Was Luanne tiny like Grandma Kit? Would a motorist see her along the road in the pitch darkness of Michigan? Her empty stomach heaved while Diana's imagination went wild. She hadn't thought to bring bug spray, and the mosquitoes buzzed about her face. She scratched her neck, face and wrists as they walked. Will stayed in the lead, his white shirt a beacon. Then it came time to turn, and the line repositioned to scour the next quarter mile.

When they came to the creek, they picked their way slowly along the shore. Diana's breath tightened in her throat when she swung her flashlight over the gurgling water. The only thing they found was a family of raccoons, who scurried away into the night. Then the rain came. Not a sprinkle—the skies opened and soon Diana's clothes and hair were plastered to her body. The tennis shoes felt like wedges of concrete.

She tried to stay near Will, who was on his phone with the other team across the highway. "Anything?" she asked when he hung up, but he just shook his head. In the darkness she couldn't read his expression, but his tense body sent signals. Streaked with dirt, his shirt clung to him. The tie had disappeared, and his slacks were torn in at least two places.

Relentless, he led the charge. How did he stay so calm? His pristine image faded under the wet rain and mud but he kept on. There was nothing not to like about Will tonight.

Finally, a shout went up from the far end of the search area. "Over here!" Everyone turned. They swept through the high, damp grass, and Diana prayed they'd found Luanne, and that she'd be all right.

She followed Will toward the excited voices. The search party pulled back when he arrived. Surrounded and safe, Luanne looked scared to death. Will approached her. "Hey Luanne, it's me. Will. You're all right now."

"I want to go home," Luanne wailed, plucking at her wet shirt. "I want my mam."

Just a tiny thing, she cowered from all the attention. Her white hair was matted, and she shivered in a light summer top. Shielding her face when the light hit her, she turned toward Will, no doubt responding to the kindness in his voice. "I'm looking for my mam. She'll be mad that I'm not home."

Keeping a little distance between them, Will held out a hand. "We'll go to your mam's right now, Luanne. Can you take my hand?" When her knuckled hand reached out, the group exhaled.

One of the EMTs appeared with a stretcher, but Will warded them off with a shake of his head. But he did accept an umbrella. Together they all walked back to the building. Diana could hear him talking to Luanne in soothing tones. What an amazing man.

How embarrassing that she was ogling him like this, but Will looked riveting in that wet shirt. Was anything more attractive than compassion? Time to turn down the hot-o-meter. A confused elderly woman was safe, and that was the main concern tonight. Luanne looked up at Will as if he were a savior, and he was probably was for her. In Diana's eyes, he was a hero.

Relief made her knees wobbly as Diana followed the group

back. She couldn't recall another time when she'd experienced this life-and-death urgency. And she'd been a part of it. Once inside the facility, Luanne blinked in the bright lights of the reception area. Will whisked her down a hallway with comforting words. "Let's just get you settled, Luanne. You're home now."

Jan, the head nurse, thanked the crews. "Hot coffee in the break room," she told them. "Good work tonight, everyone."

The crisis had passed and now Diana felt she didn't belong, a familiar and unwelcome feeling. While the EMTs and the First Alert team clapped each other on the shoulders and headed down the hall for coffee, Diana slipped out into the dank night air. The rain had stopped. Clouds moved stealthily across the sky, allowing just a glimpse of a moon. Exhausted and lost in thought, she took her time on her way back to town.

Tonight she'd seen Will in a completely different light. How could she measure up to that? Indecision gnawed at her empty stomach when she reached the house and hurried into the bathroom to check the damage. One glimpse in the mirror and she froze. Red bumps swelled all over her face, along with an angry streak from that branch. Her eye makeup had streaked, giving her serious raccoon eyes. The hairdo? Forget it. Her shiny blonde curls had been reduced to a dirty brown mess.

And Will had seen her like this?

# Chapter 5

Climbing the steps to Diana's cottage the following afternoon, Will heard a lot of slamming around. Warm pizza box in hand, he listened. She was belting out "Be My Baby," and he smiled. Hadn't heard that in a while. Was she dancing too? With a hot rush, he remembered how she'd felt in his arms at the Firemen's Ball.

He shut that down fast and rang the bell. The singing stopped.

A few seconds later, she peeked out from behind the curtain. Maybe he should've phoned first, but he'd been in a rush. She'd been so amazing the night before. He never would have pictured Diana Prescott slogging through the fields, looking for Luanne Gummer. It really touched him to see her eyes fill when they finally found his missing resident. A pizza was the least he could do. Besides that, he wanted to see Diana. Their date had been cut short.

The door cracked open. "Will?" Diana was wrestling a blue bandana from her head.

"Hey, beautiful. Want a short visit from a tall friend?"

A Rosie the Riveter t-shirt clung to her figure, and she was yanking her curls over her face. "Hey, are those bites from last night?"

Her hands flew to her cheeks. "Do they look that bad?"

Will wanted to bite out his tongue. "You can hardly see them. Have I come at a bad time?"

The helpless look in her eyes told him yes. He shifted uncomfortably in his dockers. Her eyes fell to the box, and she opened the door. "First you bring me roses and now pizza?"

Coming inside, Will made sure he didn't step on her bare feet. "I figured I owed you dinner after last night. How about lunch instead?"

"You really are too cute. I'm just straightening up." Following her to the kitchen island, he was pleased to see his roses in a vase.

"Where should I put this?" He lifted the pizza box.

She pointed to the open side door. "How about the picnic table?"

"Fine with me. Beautiful day. Want me to bring anything out?"

"No. I'll be there in a minute." Was Diana freaking out? Hands on her cheeks, she was backing up into her bedroom. "Just need to get organized, okay?"

*Organized?* He had no idea what she meant. "Fine. I'll be outside." With any luck, she would not change that t-shirt.

Outside, the sun was peeking through some clouds, and squirrels chased each other in the trees. Sliding the pizza onto the table, Will sat down and leaned back on his elbows, facing the yard. Diana had a pretty little place. Small but private. Someone had obviously liked flowers enough to plant the black-eyed Susans, daisies and other plants, but it probably wasn't Diana. Weeds had sprung up and were fighting for their territory. "If you give a weed an inch," Grandma Trudie had always said, "it'll take over your whole garden. You have to pull them out when they're little rascals."

Feeling antsy, Will sprang up and started yanking away. The August sun felt good on his back. In the distance, he heard the whine of a motorboat out on the lake. He could use a little beach time, preferably with a certain beautiful blonde.

But Diana was more than that. The thistles fell from his hands, and he bent to scoop them up. Last night had been such a surprise. She was so down to earth and honest.

"Hey, you don't have to do that." Diana appeared at the kitchen door, her blonde hair in a braid over one shoulder. He was relieved that she hadn't changed from her shirt and white shorts. Flip-flops slapped her pink-toed feet when she came down the stairs. She glanced accusingly at the pile of weeds.

"Just filling the time. Pretty flowers out here. My grandmother always loved the black-eyed Susans."

"I sure don't have a green thumb. Guess that's clear." It tickled him when Diana frowned at the flowers as if they were naughty children. "What can I get you to drink?"

"Any kind of pop is fine. Let me help you."

Following her back up the steps and into the house, he took in the long legs that stretched from her cut-offs to her flip-flops. That restless feeling zapped his nerves. Maybe he was just hungry. From one of the cupboards, she took out some plastic glasses and then rummaged around in the refrigerator for the pop. Will chose one. By that time, he wanted to run the icy bottle over his pulse points. His heart had definitely revved up. Diana smelled like antiseptic ointment, which today he found sexy.

A pail and mop leaned in a corner of the kitchen. "Looks like I interrupted something."

"Nothing that I can't pick up later. How's Luanne?"

"Doing fine." They talked about the night before while she finished stacking a tray with the drinks, paper plates, napkins and some silverware. "Here, I'll take that." He grabbed the green tray while she held the door open. By this time, flies buzzed around the cardboard pizza box and he didn't blame them. His stomach growled.

Diana looked over and smiled as she flipped open the top of the box. "Sounds like you're hungry. Wow. Will you just look at this? My favorite things." Her eyes circled back to him, glowing like he'd just give her the Hope Diamond.

"Hope I got it right."

"You listened," she said in that breathy voice that made him uncomfortable in a good way.

"This is what you like right? Spinach, peppers, olives."

Her eyes widened. "Sure is. A lot of times I just forget to eat lunch." Picking up a knife, she filled both their plates.

No wonder she bordered on skinny. "How can you forget a meal? You should have three squares a day."

She shrugged a slim shoulder. "Sometimes I just get busy."

They settled back in the shade of the oak tree that towered overhead. Contentment filled him, and so did the sight of Diana. She ate with gusto. No way was this pizza going to last her for two days. The crust was thin, just the way he liked it, with lots of cheese heaped on the toppings. "This is my first Brewster's pizza," he said.

"You have a lot of exploring to do."

"Maybe I need a guide."

Her chewing slowed while her cheeks flushed. She swallowed. "In lots of ways, I'm new here too, Will."

"Good. We can take it on together." He pictured long rides up the highway, her hair blowing in the wind.

"You know what? I might take you up on that. That is, if you mean it." She shot him a shy, sideways smile. She had a sensitive side. Will knew how that felt. This wasn't the time to tell her she had spinach stuck in her teeth.

For a couple of minutes they munched in silence. Her moans of appreciation didn't go unnoticed. His body was taking them way too seriously. When she licked her fingers, he had to look away.

"Do you live in town, Will?" she finally asked. "Or out closer to your work?"

When he took a deep gulp of his soda, he found her eyes on his neck, lips slightly parted. He swiped the heel of one hand across his mouth. Their eyes locked until she looked away. "I live in one of those condos up on the ridge above Red Arrow Highway. Bowling alleys used to be there, or so I'm told."

"The pastel buildings with the white trim? The ones that are all different colors?"

He laughed. "Got it. I guess everyone notices them, although the town is full of pastel condos from what I can see. And my staff tells me that a lot of people aren't happy about it."

Diana turned reflective, the sunlight playing tag on her face.

"The book group told me that homes like this one were torn down to build those condos. All rentals now, so folks have mixed feelings."

"A sore subject with some people?"

"Yeah, like Cole Campbell. Some folks want the town to stay the same."

She'd mentioned Cole, and he had questions. "So if you don't mind my asking, how did you end up going to the Firemen's Ball with Cole? You said you were fixed up."

Diana gave a sigh as if she'd explained this too many times. "Kate's high school friends, Sarah and Chili, are part of our book group. They asked me if I would go with Cole. I knew him. We'd done some work together on the town development, so it wasn't totally awkward. There was nothing between us, but I like the women in that group. I went along with their plan to get the two back together." She dipped her head, looking embarrassed.

"But you and Cole weren't…?" He wanted everything to be clear.

"Oh no, no. We were never that way. Maybe we were both too busy. Relationships take time. That was back in the spring. My summer line was arriving at Hippy Chick. Cole was busy with new projects. Timing is everything." Her eyes clouded and he wondered what that was about.

Pushing the box toward him, she said, "Only one slice left. Take it now or be responsible for me not fitting into my jeans."

"Can't let that happen." He liked the way she looked in her jeans.

While he chewed, she chattered about her book group. He should be happy. At least he knew she wasn't interested in Cole. "Why didn't Kate just tell me?" he finally asked.

"What? Oh, you mean the dance." Her face clouded. "They were off again, on again. She didn't mean to hurt you."

"Trust me, I am not hurt. In fact, I like the way things ended up."

When she blinked her baby blues, he got a head rush.

"I'm glad, Will."

Could he put two words together after that? "Looks like we got caught in the middle."

"Maybe. Kind of stupid, really. Guess I wanted Chili and Sarah to like me."

The bare honesty of her words stunned him. "Why wouldn't they?"

Her laugh held a self-conscious edge. "I know. Crazy, right? But I didn't grow up here. Newcomer and all that."

"Odd guy out, huh?" He was trying to wrap his mind around this.

"Yeah, I guess." Reaching out, she whisked something from his face. His skin tingled. "Any regrets?"

"Not at all." Did he have crud hanging from his chin? Still, having her fuss over him was a turn-on. "I didn't really know Kate. Thing is, with my job I don't get a chance to meet many women under the age of sixty."

"What about the people you work with? Nurses and medical techs? They must drool over their handsome administrator."

She'd hit his personal hot button. "Dating the staff is a bad idea. Some administrators might do it but not me." He thought back to Indianapolis and things he would never share. Back then, he'd been young and green.

Tilting her head to one side, she regarded him with thoughtful eyes. "You've got principles, Will. Good values."

*How exciting.* Not hot. Not sexy. More like Santa Claus or the Easter Bunny.

~.~

Her comment came from her own past, and she didn't want to go there. "So, Luanne's better today? Poor thing looked so terrified last night."

"Settling in. Of course, she has the usual confusion. That's just the stage she's at with her disease." But his eyes seemed troubled.

"How about the staff? Do they know why it happened?"

He sucked in a breath. "All of the exit doors are alarmed, and none went off. That's a problem. I have to go over protocols with Jan and see what happened."

"Being responsible for people's lives can't be easy." Her mind ran over the possibilities. "Do you think someone on staff left the door open?"

Will flicked at the last crumb on his plate. "More likely, a staff member took a smoke break outside, which isn't allowed. Like most facilities, we're non-smoking."

"Sounds complicated and tricky."

"It's disappointing. Certified nursing assistants in small rural areas like this aren't easy to find. Training them takes time. Besides that, I really like my staff." He opened both hands as if he hoped a solution would drop into them. "A lot of the women are single mothers."

"And you hate to fire them?"

He grimaced. "Exactly."

She felt touched that Will confided in her. How she wished she could help. Tucking the empty plates into the cardboard box, she closed the carton. "I sure don't envy you. Back in Chicago, I had to fire a worker for taking money right out of the till. Made me mad, but more than that she let me down. I'd trusted her."

Will's expression smoothed. "So you know the feeling. Dealing with employees can be hard sometimes."

She enjoyed his interest. Diana had no one to talk to about business issues. "Maybe. I've never had any complaints from employees. Well, except for the girl who stole from me in Chicago. I'm just glad we're closed Sunday and Monday."

"You can't work all the time."

"How many hours a week do you put in?"

Will gave an easy-going chuckle. "Couldn't even tell you. I'm always on call, like last night. In a way you are too, right?"

"But the work you do affects lives. My shop caters to women's whims."

"Don't sell yourself short." His hand covered hers. Heat that didn't come from the warm picnic table cascaded through her body. "Clothes seem pretty important to women."

She stared at their hands, suddenly wanting to feel his on other parts of her body. *Snap out of it.* "Oh, ah, come on, Will. Doesn't even compare with helping seniors in their final years."

The topic had turned serious. Next to the work Will did, her own career seemed frivolous. "Sometimes I wish I were a teacher or a lawyer."

"Why, in heaven's name?"

"Oh, I don't know." Slipping her hand from his, she rolled a napkin into a tight tube. "I'd help people more. Be taken seriously."

"Come on. Running a shop is no picnic." Amazement crossed his face.

"Trust me, owning a shop called Hippy Chick is not taken seriously." Why was she being so open with him?

"You mean by men?" he said quietly.

"Right. Men."

"Then you haven't met the right man."

Well. That look in his eyes gave her shivers. Looking down, she picked at her pink nail polish. "All I know is you're a great guy, and Gull Harbor Care Center is lucky to have you. But I have to be honest, I hope my grandmother and aunt can stay in their own home."

"In Newtown, right?" He grinned and the mood lightened.

He remembered. "Exactly. Where people know them."

With a sigh, Will stretched his long legs out to the side. His muscled calves made her glad he'd worn shorts. "That's why I came to Gull Harbor. There's a family feeling in this town, don't you think? Isn't that why you left Chicago?"

She swallowed hard. Sure, they were being honest with each other but her past? No way was she sharing that. Bryce Williams had been a huge mistake. No one in town knew. Diana wanted to keep it that way so she chose her words carefully. "At first I thought Chicago was so exciting. The restaurants, the shops. But after the recession hit, I wanted to start over somewhere else. My grandfather's inheritance made that possible. I was ready to leave the big city." *And the biggest mistake of my life.*

"That's true for a lot of people, especially when you come from a small town." Looking thoughtful, Will propped his head on one hand. "A lot of learning to do, right?"

"Right." And she wanted to start with him. Would his thick hair feel coarse or soft? She flattened her hand on the table.

Will was still processing. He was a guy who probably read the *New York Times* every Sunday and had deep thoughts.

An idea flashed into her mind. Maybe it was foolish. After all, her background was in merchandising. "You ever have volunteers at your facility?"

"Yes, of course. Are you saying you're interested?"

She played with one of her curls. "Don't look so surprised. I don't have any training, but yeah I'd like to come."

"Great. I'll have Beverly call you. She's the activity director." A grin tweaked the corner of his mouth. "You have training in one key area. I know the residents would love it if you shared that talent."

"Really? What's that?" She couldn't even imagine.

"You're a great dancer, Diana. We hold Sunday dances. Okay,

mainly because I enjoy it. But turns out the residents enjoy it too, and the exercise is good for them."

She loved the idea. "Well, if you think I'd be a good fit..."

"I don't think so. I know so." They shared a silly smile. Up above, a cardinal called to its mate.

Diana liked him too much and too soon. This was just how she'd felt when she met Bryce. Amazed and hopeful, like she was back in high school and Bob Harley had just passed her a note.

Will checked the sky and frowned. "I was going to ask if you wanted to go to the beach, but it looks like we might get a little rain."

She glanced up, almost grateful for the gray clouds. "Maybe another day?" A day when her bug bites would be gone. No way did she want to put on a bathing suit today. Too revealing. Too soon.

Jumping up, Will checked his phone. "Probably just as well. We're due for a visit from the state any day now."

She put the pizza box onto the green tray. "A visit?"

"Yep, and it's not as friendly as it sounds. They come to check up on you. What happened last night might bring them sooner. The long term care field has a lot of regulations. Can I help you with that?"

"No, I'm fine." Her goosebumps were becoming chronic and she rubbed her arms.

Standing to his full height, Will stretched. "Then I'll be going."

"Thanks for the pizza." She followed him out to the curb.

"I owed you."

"Not really." That search for Luanne had awakened something in her. The idea that she could help someone else. Passing the pile of doomed weeds, she smiled.

Will followed her glance and came closer. He swept a lock of hair from her face and she cringed. All those red bug bites on her face. But when his lips brushed hers, she forgot everything. The slow heat swirling through her body drowned any common sense. She forgot the bites. Forgot the sleepy neighborhood. No one was around anyway. It had been so long. She sank into the kiss and softened it. He settled against his car, pulling her with him.

"Aren't there rules about this?" she whispered against the heat of his cheek. "Kissing on a public street."

Was that a groan or a growl? "Oh, Diana. I'm a boy who likes to break the rules."

# Chapter 6

Her stomach was doing cartwheels when Diana pulled up at the Gull Harbor Care Center the following Sunday. What was she doing here? Playing with the turn signal of her yellow VW, she let the air-conditioning run. She could leave. Give Will some excuse later.

Will had called her once since the weekend and the conversation had been short. The state inspectors had arrived, and he sounded tense. After his parting kisses, her feelings were jumbled. She was almost glad an afternoon storm nixed going to the beach the day he'd brought over the pizza. Risk was involved here. Uncertainty curled at the edge of her mind. Why had she ever mentioned volunteering at the place where he worked? What if she totally messed up?

Then she saw the old fellow sitting at the door in one of those old metal chairs. No way. Wearing a winter hat with flaps, he was the spitting image of her grandfather. In fact, Grandpa Stan used to wear a hat like that when he shoveled snow. Watching him heft the snow from the walk like it was cotton, she'd press her nose against the cold front window. She missed him so much. Those Sunday mornings when he made chocolate chip pancakes had been so special.

Spotting her, the old guy waved. That settled it. Diana turned off the car and got out.

Her long wraparound skirt fluttered in the August breeze as she walked toward the glass doors. "Hi," the man said as she approached.

Pushing her sunglasses up, Diana smiled. "Looks like you picked the best seat in the house."

He checked out her hands. "Did you bring any doughnuts?"

Oh, boy. Hadn't even started and already she was coming up short. "Nope. Sorry. No donuts today." But if she came back, she'd be carrying a bakery box.

Squinting up at her, he rocked back. "My name's Harold."

"Hi, Harold. I'm Diana." He was so darn cute.

"You're pretty."

"And you're handsome, Harold." One day he had been. "See you later, okay?"

"Sure thing, Miss. Sure thing." He adjusted his hat and attempted a wink.

When she got inside, the young woman at the desk looked up.

"Hi, I'm Diana Prescott and I have an appointment with Jan."

Probably about eighteen years old, the girl straightened. "I'll get her for you. You may have a seat."

Diana smiled at the formality and sat down. It only took a minute before Jan came striding down the hall. A no-nonsense woman with iron gray hair, she wore hospital blue pants with a short top. Her hand reached out. "So glad to see you again, Diana. I'm Jan, the head nurse. Bev isn't here today. Thanks for helping us that night with Luanne."

"How's she doing?" They began walking down a hall that smelled of baking bread, with an antiseptic underpinning.

"To be honest, I'm not sure she even remembers that night."

Diana wondered what the consequences had been for the staff, but it wasn't any of her business. She didn't want anyone to think Will had been discussing the incident with her.

"Have you worked with seniors before?" Jan asked as they approached a multipurpose room.

"Only my grandparents. My grandpa's gone now."

"Sorry, Diana. Maybe that's why you've come? In any case, plenty of folks here of your grandparents' age will be thrilled to talk to you." Stepping over to a small table, she worked with a CD player like the one her grandparents had given her for eighth grade graduation.

Slipping off her purse, Diana left it on one of the card table chairs set around the perimeter of the room. Beyond them stretched a long table with a punch bowl and trays of cookies. Sunlight poured through a wall of windows, and older people with shy smiles filtered into the room.

"Gonna play Elvis today?" one of the women called out.

Jan nodded with a smile in Diana's direction. "Of course. Everyone has their favorites, as you'll soon see," she added in a lower tone. A stack of CDs sat next to the player. "We haven't graduated to using a playlist yet. That might be hard for some of them to understand."

"My grandmother and aunt still listen to an old plastic radio."

"Then you know how it is." Jan flipped through the CDs, pulling out a couple.

Two older men came timidly through the door with their hair slicked back, or what little they had left.

"What do I do?" she asked Jan, running her hands down her skirt.

"Just dance. Talk with them." The mellow sound of Elvis singing "Only Fools Rush In" filled the room as Jan nodded to the men approaching. "They'll be pleased to have a new partner. Dance with the women too. We're kind of short on men, and the ladies love to get out on the floor."

"Yes, of course."

"Tim." Jan beckoned to a man wearing a red bow tie. "Would you dance with Diana? Kind of show her the ropes?"

The old man's shoulders straightened. Tim barely came up to Diana's chin, but that didn't matter. He knew how to dance, and he guided her around the floor to "Love Me Tender." Gladys was her next partner, and she filled Diana in with all kinds of information about the food, her roommate, and Will. Next was Arnold. By that time, Jerry Lee Lewis was doing a whole lot of shaking. Arnold just stood facing her, swinging his arms. She did the same and it seemed to work.

During a pause, she spotted Harold standing in the doorway, that old leather hat perched on his head. She beckoned to him and moved to the side. A slower song came on by Nat King Cole. "Will you dance with me, Harold?"

"Sure thing, Diana." Her grandmother would not approve of a

man keeping his hat on in the house. But for Harold, that hat was obviously a necessity. "Have you lived here a long time?" she asked, while they did a slow, jerky two-step.

"Um hmm." Lips moving, he seemed to be concentrating. It took a while for her to realize he was counting. For the rest of the song, she said nothing, not wanting to disturb him. When another song started, Harold once again showed up at her elbow. But so did Will. Wearing a white polo shirt, he looked unbearably handsome.

"Can I have this dance with Diana, Harold?" Will asked.

"Yessir." Could Harold's smile be any broader?

She shivered when Will took her in his arms, so tall and strong.

"Cold?" he asked.

"Nope. Far from it."

Giving her a secret smile, he swung her into an upbeat rhythm. What a contrast to the last time she'd danced with him. At the Firemen's Ball, she'd been trying to help out Kate and Cole. The dance had been an obligation. Not this time. Far from it. She could hardly keep up with him.

"Whew!" She clutched her chest when it was over. "What a workout."

Combing back his damp hair, he gave her a rueful smile. "Too much for you? Sorry. It's been one of those weeks." They strolled over to the punch bowl and he handed her a cool cup, which she instantly drained.

"This was really nice of you, coming today," he said, tossing back a glassful.

"I said I would, didn't I?"

"Yes, yes you did." His eyes twinkled. "So I guess you're a woman whose word means something. Good to know."

She flushed under his approval, grinning like a kid in high school. Visitors arrived, drawn to the main room by the music. When Tim asked her to dance again, she was very aware of Will's eyes on them. Would he be at this dance every Sunday? She didn't want him to think volunteering was just an excuse to see him. The air, full of Brylcreem and White Shoulders, lightened when he disappeared. But he popped in one more time toward the end. Johnny Mathis was crooning "Wonderful, Wonderful" when Will appeared at her side and held out his arms. *Shoot me now.* Her thoughts were definitely X-rated while they danced. This song was slow and dreamy, and that's how they danced. He cupped her right hand to his chest, and she could feel the beat of his heart.

"Talk to you soon," he said when the song ended. All eyes were on them, not that it seemed to matter to Will. Stepping apart, they could have been talking about the weather when he said, "Just know, Diana Prescott, that right now, I want to kiss you silly."

She sucked in a tight breath.

His brows lifted. "And that's just for starters."

"What's next?" How did she manage to squeak out the words?

"Wear that blue top you had on that night at Brewster's, and you'll find out." His lips barely moved.

"Oh, really? The one I could hardly keep up?" She was thinking of giving it to Goodwill.

He smiled as if she'd cracked a joke. "Exactly. We'll see where it goes."

"Right. Okay." She watched him walk away and then turned to Jan who was wearing a big smile.

A few seconds later, she wandered to the front door, only to realize she'd forgotten her purse. Head down, she trotted back to find Jan deep in conversation with Will. "Forget something?" she asked when Diana scooped up her bag.

"Yes. Yes, I..." She was having trouble talking and just slung the darn purse over her shoulder.

"I'll walk you out," Jan said, with a glance back at Will. "How do you think it went today?" she asked on their way down the hall that sparkled under the overhead lights.

"It was fun. The people here are so sweet."

Jan chuckled. "They loved it! A new face...and a pretty one at that."

Diana flushed with pleasure. "See you next Sunday, then?" she asked at the door.

"Terrific." Jan surprised her with a tight hug. "Thanks for giving us your time, Diana."

"Glad to do it." The truth was, the dancing filled a need she didn't know she had.

The sun blinded Diana when she pushed through the door. "See you later, Harold."

He perked up. "Bye, Diana. Thanks for dancing with me."

"You're welcome." Her spirits lifted.

He rocked back in his chair until his head touched the brick building. As she pulled out of the parking lot, she checked her rearview mirror. He was waving, and she tooted her horn.

On the way home, she thought about the commitment she'd made. Sunday and Monday were her only free days. But what else was she going to do, weed? Grandma Kit and Grandpa Stan had always been involved in volunteer work. As long as she could remember, they were down at the Hope Mission on Thanksgiving. For what seemed like forever to a little girl, they ladled out food. After everyone had been fed, they sat down and ate with the people her grandparents called their guests. "It's right to give back," her grandmother told her. "Some people aren't as lucky as we are, so we should share our good fortune. Besides, if I'm going to fix this meal for three people, I might as well cook for five hundred, right?"

As Diana grew older, she wondered if keeping so busy on the holidays kept her grandparents from missing their daughter, who remained a post card on the refrigerator.

On Wednesday afternoon, Will called her at the store. "Feel like a picnic tonight?"

"I have to work until seven."

"No problem. I've got plenty to do here."

"What would you like for the picnic?" Her mind flew ahead. She could stop at Clancy's.

"Since I'm the one with a huge kitchen, I'll take care of that."

Impressive. She drifted through the rest of the afternoon and closed the shop ten minutes early to get ready. The day had been hot and airless. Streets were empty and baking in the sun when she drove home. Most families were probably still down on the beach.

At home, she took a quick shower but felt sticky while she worked on her makeup.

Will's smile when she opened the door rewarded her. "Don't you look pretty?"

"You look pretty great yourself." But she wasn't talking about his clothes. It just felt terrific to see him.

"Like the top." His eyes sparkled with mischief.

"Ah, huh." That uptick of her heart? The deep urge to wrap her arms around his neck? Not good signs.

She grabbed a visor and sunglasses and they were off. They parked at the public beach on Townline Road. Handing Diana a small cooler, Will lugged a picnic basket from his trunk. Their footsteps rang on the wooden stairs on the way down. She came to a halt on the platform. "Oh, Will. It's so perfect." On either side, the beach stretched to the horizon, and the water reached for the setting sun.

With a sigh, she kept going. When they reached the sand, they kicked their shoes into the beach grass and put some distance between them and the family groups. Will spread a blue blanket on the beach.

The sun glanced off the waves that washed the shore. "So beautiful." She sank onto the blanket, feeling the warm sand beneath its surface. "I should come down here more often."

"Why don't you?"

"Just forget about it, I guess." She wasn't about to admit that coming down here alone wouldn't be as much fun. "I like your shorts. You look good in cut-offs. Different."

"Different?" He flipped open the cooler. "What does that mean?"

"Nothing. Usually I see you in work clothes." She wasn't about to tell him that when she met him, she felt he had that Boy Scout quality about him. The kind of man she'd never been drawn to before. History had taught her she better change her plan.

She peeked into the cooler. "No beer?"

"Not today. If we got busted by the cops, it would look bad." There was a question in his eyes.

"Makes sense to me."

Will turned back to the basket. "Now let's see what Maria fixed for us."

Will's cook did him proud. Ham sandwiches were thick with soft slices of Swiss cheese, paper-thin tomatoes and crisp lettuce on caraway rye bread. Some packets of mustard had been thrown in. Bags of chips were tucked next to decadent-looking brownies.

"Jan really likes you," Will said when they were halfway through the sandwiches.

A breeze had picked up and Diana brushed the hair from her eyes. "I like her too."

"She thinks the dance sessions will be good for you and the residents."

How could she explain it? "I just wanted to help after that night with Luanne."

Dusting crumbs from his fingers, Will settled back on his elbows. The setting sun burnished his profile. He had an aristocratic nose, but a playful breeze tossed his hair into reckless curls. He flattened them with one hand. No gel for this guy. "We could use more volunteers. Especially on weekends. Some of the families come to visit but some don't. Kelsey, our receptionist, tells me that Harold has a major crush on you."

"He's such a sweetie." Her heart warmed, thinking about the eccentric keeper of Will's gate. "Why does he wear that hat in all this heat?"

Snapping off a piece of sea grass, Will ran it through his lips. "Some people have their own private security blanket. It's harmless."

"Does he have family?"

"Yep, one daughter. He sits at the door waiting for her. She lives on the East Coast."

That did it. The bag of doughnuts grew in her mind.

"I think what you're doing is generous, Diana. What more can you give anyone than time and attention, right?"

"It's just one afternoon."

"There are a million other things you could be doing that would be a lot more fun." Narrowing his eyes against the setting sun, he glanced over. "I think I underestimated you."

"In what way?"

"Now don't take this wrong. At first, I thought you were just another pretty face."

"Wow, is that a compliment or an insult?" She worked at keeping her tone playful.

Rolling to face her, he squeezed her hand. "You're so beautiful."

"And you're so handsome."

"Haven't we had this conversation before?" His lips twitched. "Thanks, but in my book, looks aren't enough."

She didn't believe him. Lifting her hand from his, she adjusted her sunglasses.

"Didn't you say you only have a couple days off a week?" Snatching another tall blade of grass, he tickled her inner arm. The stroke felt delicious. He had so many tricks to bridge her barriers.

"Huh...?" She'd completely lost him.

Will grinned. "Sunday and Monday. Those are the days the shop is closed, right?"

She pulled her attention back. "Yes. Sometimes I go back to work in the evenings. Just think. I could be back in the stock room right now, unpacking the fall merchandise. What fun, right?"

"Fall? Hard to think about that."

"When it comes to clothes, women plan ahead. I try to think of ways to get their attention. They can buy sweaters from me or from some Chicago boutique."

"Chicago." Will's eyelids had a sexy way of drooping. "So you gave up on the big city. Smart girl. What made you choose Gull Harbor?" Gulls shrieked overhead, as if calling a warning.

She'd discovered a good way to avoid an embarrassing question was to ask one. "I could ask you the same thing. Why Gull Harbor?"

A lazy, seductive smile played along his lips. "I already told you. Here I'm close to the Michigan woods. Sounds like you could have set up shop anywhere."

She choked. This wasn't the time. Not yet. "Did you know your eyes are the color of the sky?"

"How poetic, Diana." He ran his fingers over hers. "You have beautiful hands. My grandmother would call these piano fingers."

"Never played in my life." Will's comments took her by surprise. These weren't the slick lines she'd heard so often. Made her want to inch closer. Feel his lips again. Some of the families had left. But now a new crew was tromping down the steps, probably to watch the sunset.

Desperate for a distraction, she peered into the picnic basket. "What else is in here? I think I smell watermelon."

"Really?" Sitting up, Will crossed his legs under him. Suddenly the sophisticated, self-contained administrator looked like a little boy. Opening the plastic bag, she held it out and he dug out a slice. The smell of watermelon filled the air, pure summer. In seconds, they were gulping down juicy slices, spitting out the seeds and shaking the juice from their fingers. "Okay let's have a contest." Will sat up straighter. "Who can shoot the seed the farthest."

"You're kidding me?"

"Not at all. I'm challenging you. I'll go first."

"You're on." He never ceased to amaze her and she liked it. Taking the next bite, he chewed carefully before sucking air in through his nose. The seed popped from his lips and flew about eight feet. "Not bad. Your turn."

This was turning out to be the weirdest date ever. Diana tried. She really did, but her watermelon seed fell pathetically short. "Have you been practicing?"

"Absolutely." He grinned boyishly. "This is what I do in my spare time out back of the care center. We have contests."

"Really?" She wouldn't doubt it, but he seemed to have a thing about his professional image.

Will shook his head. "No, not really. Let's just say, Beanblossom was a really quiet town where there wasn't a heck of a lot to do."

"Did you and your friends get into a lot of trouble?"

"My father kept a pretty tight eye on me."

"You were lucky."

The longing in her voice came from the heart. Taking her sticky hand in his, Will laced his fingers through hers. "You deserved better, Diana. Good thing you had your grandparents. They sound terrific and sure did a good job."

"I owe them both a lot. But the reality is, I'm an illegitimate child. A bastard." She'd gotten used to joking about it. That was the only way she survived in school. The sympathy in Will's eyes made her jump up. "Think I'll rinse off my hands.

She dashed for the lake, Will trailing behind. It didn't take long before they were splashing each other like a couple of kids. The lake felt almost bathwater warm, and before long they were drenched. He looked good with water dripping from his hair, molding his T-shirt to his chest. Self-conscious, she was aware that her blue top was heading south. He watched her tug it up and then swirled his eyes up to hers. The night was pitch dark now. Down the beach, a group was starting a fire. When Will kissed her, he tasted of watermelon.

"How yummy," she murmured, leaning into him.

"Oh, yes you are." He smiled, teasing the seam of her lips with his tongue until she opened. She wanted him so badly. They explored until frustration drove them back to the blanket. Hands linked, they stretched out flat on their backs and stared up at a million stars.

Maybe this was it. Maybe this was the time for the truth. "Will, I..."

Buzzing black flies descended and she shot up to a sitting position. It had taken her a week to get rid of the mosquito bites. "Ouch." Ducking her head, she waved them away. Grabbing her hand, he pulled her up. "Run up to the car. I'll be right there."

So she left him, and that moment of truth, down in the sand. Feeling cowardly but relieved, she was quiet all the way home. She felt way too good with Will. What was she doing? Caring brought risk. He might just walk away when he knew the truth about her past.

That hand on her knee? Felt so nice and she wanted to enjoy it just a little while longer.

# Chapter 7

Standing on Carolyn's porch, Diana hesitated. Truth was, the book group still felt uncomfortable. Despite the shared confidences and jokes, she felt like an outsider. Maybe it was just a matter of time. She'd only joined the group a few months ago, and some of them had gone to high school together. Shifting her quilted handbag to the other shoulder, she rang the bell. Chili's raucous laugh inside was unmistakable and made her smile.

"Hey, girlfriend, come on in." Carolyn opened the screen door. Pretty with a shy smile, she taught English at the local high school. Her hug smelled like fresh lemons. "Good to see you."

"Yes, Diana," Chili called out. "Come and save me! They're ganging up on me."

"As if you ever need saving, Chili." That would be the day. A fan whined overhead while Diana dug today's book from her purse. She hadn't even made it through the first chapter of *The Scarlet Letter*. "Sounds like you're having fun."

"We're celebrating." Chili lifted her glass. "*Una boda!* Cole finally popped the question. We're headed for a wedding, thanks to you!"

"Small. Very small," insisted Kate, eyes glistening with excitement.

"Wow, really?" Did weddings happen this fast in Gull Harbor?

Amazed and pleased, she felt good that she'd had a part in all this.

"Help yourself to a margarita, Diana." Carolyn gestured to a pitcher in the center of the low table.

"Gosh, that didn't take long." Grabbing a glass, Diana poured and sat in the empty rocker. "Let's see the ring. Glad to be of help." Marriage. Would she ever reach that point? Every time she talked to Grandma Kit, she asked if Diana had met someone.

All eyes were glued to the sparkling marquis diamond twinkling on Kate's left hand.

But Chili's attention swerved back to Diana. "Anything to report on the Will front?"

Choking on her drink, Diana coughed. "Nope. Not really." Thursday she'd noticed a big bag of weeds at her curb. Only one man could have done that. His low-key sweetness was a major turn-on.

Eyes narrowing, Chili tilted her head. "And why don't I believe you, *amiga mia*, eh?"

Carolyn came to Diana's rescue when she swirled in from the kitchen carrying a huge bowl. The smell of summer cucumbers filled the room.

"Cucumber dip!" A cry went up and Chili's interrogation was forgotten.

"Can someone grab the chips in the kitchen?" Carolyn asked, slanting a look in Diana's direction. God bless that girl. Carolyn knew Diana needed a break.

"I'll get it."

Order was obviously the rule of the day in Carolyn's kitchen.

Spices were alphabetized in a rack on the wall. Her old-fashioned sink was free of dirty dishes, a metal sink strainer standing ready. Sometimes Diana felt embarrassed at how she let her dishes pile up. Spotting a basket brimming with potato chips, Diana swept it up.

So Kate and Cole were getting married. It amazed her that an engagement still had the power to hurt. The pain went way back like a stubborn splinter. How well she remembered the days when she hoped for a ring. What a fool she'd been.

But she was way past that now. When she returned to the group, a cheer went up. The book discussion was temporarily forgotten. She scanned the room. "Where's Phoebe?"

"Sick. Couldn't come." Carolyn plunked a stack of napkins on the table. "While you were gone, we were talking about how great it feels to get out at night."

"With no children and no husband," Chili hooted, poking a finger in Kate's direction. "And some day you will feel this way too. Just wait."

The glow in Kate's eyes indicated she wouldn't mind a bit. Diana had the weird feeling that the group was advancing beyond her.

Feet on a hassock, Sarah lounged back. "Any night I get to escape my two ruffians is a good night." Her mother lived with Sarah to help care for her boys while their dad was stationed in the Middle East.

Grabbing some potato chips and a generous scoop of the dip, Diana took her seat. Escape from a family? Tonight she wasn't leaving anything behind but the silence of her bungalow or the tiny back office.

"Kate, where's Mercedes tonight? I thought you were going to bring your sister," Sarah said between mouthfuls of cucumber dip.

Kate shook her head. "She's not much of a reader. She likes to do things not read about them. And she's still adjusting to being back in Gull Harbor."

"Not easy after being in New York," Carolyn said. "Bet she misses the big city."

"And we are a scary group, *verdad?*" Chili looked around for confirmation.

"Funny, I thought I saw her at Mangy Mutt the other night with..." Carolyn began and then seemed to have second thoughts. The entire room seemed to lean forward.

"Yes?" Chili said. "Do I have to wring this from you?" When Chili made a strangling gesture with her hands, the whole room laughed. But the fiery girl was probably capable of it.

"Mercy, isn't it warm in here?" Carolyn jumped up. "I should turn the air up."

The air-conditioning was probably on and an overhead fan churned, but the room still felt warm. Carolyn took the other rocker. "Now let's get down to business. What did you think of the *The Scarlet Letter.*" She held up a dog-eared copy of the book that had put Diana to sleep one night. "Did you even read it?"

"Too old-fashioned." Chili always got right to the point.

Carolyn didn't look offended. "Okay that's a fair statement. Anyone else?"

"I couldn't get through the language, Carolyn. I'm so sorry." Kate shook her head.

With a deep sigh, Carolyn turned to Sarah. "How about you."

Sarah wrinkled her brow. "Not enough sex. You know with Jamie gone, I have to fill the void somehow." Diana joined in the laughter.

But Sarah wasn't finished. Between bites of cucumber dip, she kept talking. "This whole idea of wearing a big red A on your chest for adultery seems barbaric. Lord knows there are a few women who would be walking around Gull Harbor with one instead of their expensive gold jewelry." She rolled her eyes.

Diana squirmed in the rocking chair.

"What are you saying?" Kate turned to Sarah. "Out with it, girl. We want details."

Smoothing a hand over a top streaked with what looked like cinnamon, Sarah leaned into the circle. "Some men like to spread their donuts around, if you know what I mean. They'll bring a blonde in one week and a brunette the next. One woman wears a ring, the other doesn't."

"*Caramba!*" Chili pressed a hand to her chest. "Anyone we know?"

Fingertips to her mouth, Sarah made a locking motion. "Nope. Lips are sealed. My bakery would go belly up if people ever heard I'd made comments about their, er, companions."

The room turned quiet. Diana tried to settle her drink on top of some magazines and nearly spilled it. Silence dropped like a winter blanket until Carolyn broke the mood. "Back to the book. Sounds like this wouldn't interest my students, right?" She tossed the paperback onto the table.

"Oh, honey. Certainly your bag of tricks holds something more interesting to keep kids from texting each other during class." Sarah chortled while she loaded her plate with another round of chips.

"I have to get my book order in next week." Carolyn rubbed her forehead. "They need my list."

"What about the *Bridges of Madison County*?" Kate said, looking around. "We all liked it. Lots to discuss in that one."

"Not enough sex in it for me." Sarah's cheeks were getting pink.

"Well, kids have to learn about that sometime." Carolyn turned thoughtful. "At least *The Bridges of Madison County* is more current."

Diana's grandmother would call Carolyn an unclaimed treasure. Like Diana, she'd probably been too busy with her work to marry. "I don't think the students need me to teach them anything about sex," Carolyn said slowly. "From what I can see they take care of that themselves."

The group exploded. While a hearty discussion of shifting values erupted around her, Diana picked up her glass. With this discussion, she was walking through a minefield. The icy drink was making the nerves in her teeth explode.

"Okay. Too depressing." Kate clapped her hands. "You're talking to a woman in love."

"That's right." Sitting next to Kate on the sofa, Chili patted her friend's shoulder. "And I am so glad Ignacio and I were able to help with this. We're going to miss you at that flower stand."

"Any date set?" Carolyn asked.

"The weekend after Labor Day." Kate wore a dreamy expression.

"So soon?" Diana was shocked. Could a woman have that certainty after a few months?

But not too long ago, she'd wanted marriage so badly. With the wrong man, of course. The cucumber dip was having a field day in her stomach.

Chili waved reservations away. "*Es cierto.* When it's right, it's right. Besides, they go way back. High school debate club. They know each other. So we have a wedding after summer ends, right?"

"Is summer ending so soon?" Sarah's face emptied. Must be hard having your husband so far away.

"Mercedes came up with a great marketing idea I wanted to run past you." Kate set her book aside. "What would you think of an evening event called Moonlight Madness. We keep the shops open until midnight, the Saturday of Labor Day weekend. You know, give women a chance to shop without their kids. The merchants and the restaurants would offer special discounts, freebies, that kind of thing."

"Great idea." Sarah raised her voice above the hubbub that broke out. "I'm with you. Free donuts and coffee. No doubt Phoebe will be on board with her hair salon."

Diana hadn't visited Phoebe's Place yet but if she ever did get her hair cut, she'd go to Phoebe. Like Chili, that girl was a riot.

"Wait until I tell Ignacio." Chili's dark eyes danced. "We will offer something. Tomatoes. Whatever is in season then. Maybe a small bouquet of late summer flowers."

"Not much time to get ready, " Carolyn said, playing with a hoop earring. "How can we spread the word? *The Beacher* has already gone to press."

"We need some flyers," Diana said quietly. The room fell quiet while everyone's attention pivoted toward her. "When we did this in the city, all the merchants distributed flyers. We'd post them in the stores and tuck them into bags. Strictly a grassroots operation."

"I suppose I could type something up." Kate's indecision showed on her face. She probably had so much going on with the wedding and everything.

"Glad to help." Diana could hardly believe she was offering. "I learned how to use one of the computer design programs to promote a sale. Nothing fancy but happy to do it."

The glow returned to Kate's cheeks. "Would you, Diana? So much needs to be done for the wedding, and Mercedes is not an artist. If you can come up with something, that would be great."

"Don't expect a lot..."

But Kate waved a hand. "Trust me, anything will be welcome."

Her approval rating had gone up. By the time Diana left that night, she felt useful. Over the past year, helping other people had become a priority, as if she were doing penance.

During the week after book group, she worked on the flyer when the shop was empty, sketching Whittaker Street and Red Arrow Highway and adding shops and restaurants. The change in pace felt good. Then she sent the map off to Kate for approval.

Between working and creating the map, she had no time to

answer Will's texts. At least that's what she told herself. She let the days drift past. When his messages slowed and then stopped, she felt relief followed by crushing disappointment. He didn't pop into the dance that Sunday. Indecision gnawed at her all week.

When the following Sunday rolled around, Diana stopped at the Lithuanian bakery, where Mandy Klavis was usually behind the counter. Mandy was putting what she had left on three trays when Diana arrived. The small shop smelled heavenly, all cinnamon and sweet dough. "Two sour cream donuts, please?"

"Coming right up." Mandy's worn apron told a story of hard work. Suffocating heat rolled from the back. How would it feel to work with ovens in the summer months?

"Do you handle most of the baking yourself?" she asked as Mandy rang up the sale.

"Yep. Get here early in the morning. Sometimes my sister helps but she has two kids." Mandy rolled a shoulder. So many of the businesses in Gull Harbor were family owned and run.

Red Arrow was sleepy in the early afternoon sunlight when she drove toward the care center. Will's car wasn't there and she breathed a sigh of relief. "Hi, Harold." Diana stopped at the front door. Her white bag had caught the old man's eye.

"Morning, Diana." He touched his winter cap.

"Got something for you." She handed him the donuts, and a smile broadened his whiskered cheeks.

"Thank you. You're a real nice lady." The old man blushed as if she'd given him tickets to a Chicago Bears game.

"You're welcome. See you later."

She heard the crinkling of the bag as she walked into the bright lobby, where cool air greeted her. "Morning," she sang out.

The girl at the front desk looked up and Diana glanced at her employee badge. She liked to call people by name, especially if she was going to keep coming here for the dances. "Hi, Kelsey. I'm just going back to the dance today."

To her surprise, Kelsey's hand shot out like a traffic cop's. "Wait. Just have to check with Mrs. Lawson."

"Oh, but..." She ground to a halt while Kelsey punched some buttons.

"Mrs. Lawson. A woman is here. Says she's come to see you."

*A woman?* Diana shifted uncomfortably. Kelsey hung up the phone. "You can go back. Down the corridor and to the right." Diana almost laughed at the girl's tone, as if she were guarding the White House.

"Thank you, Kelsey." After all, she had to get along with these people. When she reached the sunny recreation room, Jan was happy to see her. "Want to take care of the music today?" She nodded toward the box of CDs.

"Why not?" She started to flip through the disks. A lot of the residents liked Elvis, that much was clear. She added some of the other fifties and sixties favorites. Before long, residents filtered in. They had all dressed up for the afternoon dance on Sunday. She smiled to see the silky tops and earrings. Tim was there again, wearing his bow tie. As the music played, a lot of them sang along. Moving easily from one resident to the next, she asked about family and answered questions about herself. As time passed and

Will didn't make an appearance again, she felt disappointed. Why had she let his texts go unanswered? Was she afraid to make another mistake?

Jan joined them at the end and helped Diana straighten the music and clear the refreshment table. "The residents love having you here. We never have enough volunteers, especially for the dances."

"It's fun, Jan. I enjoy it." But the afternoon had fallen strangely flat.

On her way out, Diana stopped in the restroom. Her hair was such a mess that she swept it into a claw clip. Then she noticed her chin. Good grief. Leaning closer to the mirror, she peered at a huge red bump. Thank goodness, she always carried concealer in her purse. One dab and she was walking briskly through the foyer. "Will?"

Hands in his pockets, Will lounged against the wall. "Hey, I've been waiting for you."

"Oh you have, have you?" She was so happy to see him.

"I've got a surprise for you."

## Chapter 8

Glancing outside, Diana searched the parking lot. "Where's your car?"

"Come on. I'll walk you out." Will threw her a secretive smile.

His hand felt good on her back as Diana swirled through the door. But she caught an indignant expression on Kelsey's face. What was that about?

"Bye, Diana," Harold said with a wave as they swept past.

"See you, Harold."

"Guess I've got competition," Will murmured.

"Maybe." She scanned the parking lot for his sensible white sedan. "I don't see your car."

"Over there." Will pointed to a red Mustang convertible sitting in the shade of a huge oak tree. *What?*

"That's yours?" she squeaked.

Will drew back. "Don't sound so surprised."

"Amazed is more like it." Will and a cherry red Mustang? No way. Afraid to touch the finish, she circled the red brilliance with respect. "What year?"

" '68. My father and I fixed it up together while I was in high school. He's a real car nut. My mother always complained that his cars took up the whole barn." He obviously enjoyed her surprise. "Want to go for a ride?"

"Sure." She slid her sunglasses into place.

"Great. You deserve a treat." He opened the door of the classic Mustang. The red interior felt warm under her and she smiled at the retro dashboard.

"When did your dad give it to you?" All the gauges were old. Vintage radio too.

"My senior year. We worked on it every chance we got." He adjusted the rearview mirror. "My folks thought I was running with the wild crowd."

"Were you?"

Will looked guilty as charged. "Probably. Too much drinking in the cornfields. This car helped keep me on the road to college."

How would it feel to have parents who cared about you that much? Her grandparents had done the best they could, but there had always been that generation difference. She knew some things were hard for them to understand, like what girls were wearing back then. Shifting in her seat, she realized they might both come from small towns, but there the similarities stopped.

Turning the key, Will dipped his head as if listening to the engine. With a pleased smile, he put it in gear. "I take care with anything and anyone I care about."

Pulling out of the parking lot, he took a left. While he played with the radio, she sat back. Puffy clouds drifted across a sunny blue sky. The air felt soft on her skin. What a perfect day. Once they were on Red Arrow and the car picked up speed, the wind got serious. Tugged from her long braid, wisps of hair danced around her face. She let them go. Felt great.

Her body melted into the seat while shops and restaurants became a blur along the side of the road. There was just something so old-fashioned and charming about this two-lane highway that ran parallel to the interstate, where people saw nothing but billboards. She bobbed her foot to a Duran Duran song playing on the radio. As they sped along, she told Will about the map for Moonlight Madness. Listening intently, he asked questions. But it was hard talking above the rush of wind.

Finally, she gave up. Slouched back. Let her eyes rest on his strong hands and that old-fashioned steering wheel. Will was probably very capable. At least, that's what she'd seen the night they searched for Luanne.

*Stop it right there, missy.* No way would she fall into a familiar first-date habit when hope could make any man perfect. Before you really knew him. Before you found out everything. She'd done that with Bryce.

Some men came with baggage...and some came with steamer trunks.

So today she'd only think about Will. The sun glinted on his wind-blown hair, and he filled that pink polo in the most delicious way. What a far cry from the man in the suit she'd asked to dance at the Firemen's Ball. But she didn't know who was he, not really. She had time to find out. Maybe he was thinking the same thing.

Just when they passed through the town of Sawyer and dipped through the underpass, he slowed down. Up ahead, a big blue sign announced Culver's Custard. Diana was an ice cream freak, and she sat up in her seat when Will turned in.

"Are we getting ice cream?" She'd never been up here.

"What? You don't like ice cream?" He tapped the brakes and swung into a parking spot.

She waved a hand. "No, no. Who doesn't?"

Leaning closer, he dropped his voice as if he were sharing classified information. "I happen to be an ice cream fanatic."

"Me too." She smiled up at him. "And you never gain a pound?"

"Not really." Will pulled back. "I'd like to know what your passions are too, Diana. Your dark secrets. Every one of them."

"What if I don't have any?" She wound the purse strap so tight around her fingers that they throbbed.

"I wouldn't believe it. Not for a minute." The words were delivered with sexy intent. Or maybe she was reading too much into it. Once they cleared the side door, she headed straight for the ladies' room. "Give me one minute."

"I'll be right there." Will stationed himself in front of the counter. She felt his eyes on her while she disappeared to brush out her tangled braid and reapply her lipstick. The blemish got another coating of makeup. When she returned to the restaurant, Will stood studying the menu up above.

"So many choices, right?" She stopped to stand beside him and looked up.

Smiling, he ran a hand over his chin. "I always have the same thing."

Fascinated, she turned. "And what would that be?"

"Caramel cashew sundae," he said without any hesitation.

"Sounds delicious. I'll have one too." Because of the heat, they decided not to take their sundaes outside. When their orders came up, they slid into a booth.

"How did it go with the residents?" Will asked.

While they spooned caramel heaven into their mouths, she told him about her dance partners. How Tim had tried a new step and didn't want to give her up when Harold insisted.

"Hmm. My guys are fighting over you already."

"Not really."

"Yes, Diana. Really."

They talked about his work for a while. He asked her about the store. She probably talked too much. What guy really wanted to hear about asymmetrical blouses and mid-calf skirts? Bryce's eyes had practically rolled back in their sockets whenever she mentioned work. And he never talked about his. She'd assumed he worked for a top secret company.

Bryce. Whenever the conversation slowed, she wondered if this would be a good time to open up with Will. Get his reaction. Watch the light fade from his eyes.

Nope, she couldn't go there. Not now, on this perfect day. Swirling some caramel onto her spoon, she let the sweetness melt on her tongue. Glancing up, she found Will staring at her. What she saw in his eyes liquefied the caramel fast.

"What? What's wrong?"

"Nothing. Really. Just get a kick out of you, that's all."

Really, he was so sweet. "Thanks for bringing me."

"Hey, this was just a way to see you." He leaned forward on his arms. "You haven't been answering my texts."

Embarrassed, she hitched up a shoulder. "Just busy."

"You sure that's all?" A bit of caramel clung to his lower lip.

"Wait. You've got something there." She pointed to her own lips to show him the spot. His tongue darted out and her stomach tumbled. The caramel didn't budge.

"Did I miss it?" Will's crooked smile was darling.

"Yes, well." Fumbling, she grabbed a napkin and reached across the booth to wipe it off. The paper rasped along his whiskered jaw and his smile grew. She had the wild urge to cup that jaw with her hand. Instead, she crumpled the napkin in her fingers.

"Thank you, ma'am."

"You're welcome." She sank back. They sat grinning at each other like teenagers.

"Great caramel sauce," she finally murmured.

"The best." Will nodded. "Cashews are good too, right?"

"You bet." She picked up her spoon again. The sundae could be oatmeal for all she cared. They were together and it felt good.

After a couple more mouthfuls, he said. "You know, Diana, I'm really glad you asked me to dance that night."

"Me too. Pretty bold when I think about it."

"Sometimes you have to ask for what you want." The comment floated in the air like an invitation. All sorts of images spun through her mind. He shook his head. "Anyway, thanks for coming today...the care center, I mean."

"I like being with the older folks. When my grandfather was at Westwood, I… Well, I couldn't always get over to see him." Geez, her throat still closed when she thought about it.

Will's forehead wrinkled. "Are you saying you felt guilty when he passed on?"

"Yes. No. He never should have been up on the roof...and at his age."

"Guys are like that, Diana. Proud. My dad's like that."

"Right. Well, Grandpa Stanley was up there and he fell. Two stories." Her throat closed, remembering her grandmother's scream and the 9-1-1 call. "Thank goodness it was Saturday and I was home."

The understanding in Will's eyes flowed over her, warmer than the caramel in their bowls. "He was never the same, Will. Oh, the hip healed but something went out of him, and he couldn't take on the rehab. Didn't really try."

"Hey, Diana." Taking her hands, Will brushed a thumb over the knuckles.

"Your staff did everything they could," she hurried to add. Diana didn't want him to think she was blaming Westwood.

"That was a good group. I was sad to leave, but..." He paused.

"But you wanted to live closer to the outdoors. Was that it?"

He shrugged. "Kind of. Westwood gave me good training, but I wanted my own facility. Gull Harbor came up."

"So you moved away from home?" She slipped easily into a lighter tone.

"I liked the idea of moving to Michigan. I'm an outdoor guy.

Yes. Nothing was available closer to Beanblossom. I wanted to be in a city not as large as Indianapolis but not as small as my hometown, if that makes sense. But I still go home." He looked down. "Finished?"

"Yes." The story felt half told. They were having such a good time. In the sunlight falling through the large plate glass window, his eyes turned the color of one of her turquoise rings.

He caught her staring. "What is it?"

"Nothing. I should get back. "

"Hey, it's Sunday. Your shop's not open, right?"

His unsettling eyes wouldn't let go. "No, but I promised Kate I'd get the map for Moonlight Madness to her today."

Will jumped up. No questions. No pressure. No guilt trips.

When they got outside, the red Mustang sat waiting. Will glanced up at the sky. "Looks like rain. Funny how things can change in a minute."

"In a second, " she murmured, watching the top slide overhead. Her own life was sure different since the Firemen's Ball.

On the way back, Will seemed to be feeling mellow, while she chattered about Moonlight Madness. She hated silences. For her, they had always held secrets. People should just talk, especially couples. She remembered her grandparents sitting at the kitchen table or in front of the TV. They couldn't seem to hear each other's voices enough, sometimes shouting over the TV. But she'd seen the other side too. Diana remembered her mother's crazy, inappropriate laughter or the tense silence when her parents questioned her. Star Prescott had been a trip.

Will and Diana hadn't driven far when the rain started. Fat drops hit the windshield and thudded onto the car top. He cut his speed.

"I bet you're careful with this car, right?"

Shifting down, he shot her a sideways grin. "And my passengers, especially you."

"Aw, Will." Sometimes he touched her in the sweetest way.

By the time they pulled off onto Greenwood Road, the shower had blustered past toward Michigan City. The air felt fresh. "Looks like visiting hours are over." Not many cars in the parking lot at Gull Harbor Care Center.

"People can visit anytime." Will pulled up under some weeping willows. "Good for the residents." Turning the car off, he pivoted to face her.

"Thanks for the sundae, Will. It was fun."

"Have you visited any other ice cream shops around here?"

"Not really. Work takes up most of my time." Or was the shop just an excuse? Going any place alone had never been comfortable for her.

"Mind if I help you explore?" Laugh lines fanned from his eyes when he smiled.

"We are talking about ice cream, right?"

He ran a finger up her bare shoulder and a tingle followed that path. "Why don't we leave it open? The exploration, that is."

Fall was looking interesting. "Works for me."

"I've got enough work. Sounds like you do too. This is for pleasure, okay?" All she could do was nod as Will's eyes coasted down her arms and circled back to her face. "God, you're so beautiful, Diana."

Will tasted like caramel when he kissed her. She'd always liked caramels.

"So, does this mean you're going to answer my texts from now on?" he teased, massaging the back of her neck.

"Guess so." Watch for them was more like it.

Angling in, he kissed her again. She could feel his smile turn serious. The kiss unleashed crazy feelings and left her trembling. But when she stumbled from the car and waved good-bye, she felt someone watching. Harold? No, Kelsey stood at the glass-plated door, hands on her hips. With a quick jerk, she scurried back to her desk.

What was that about? But the girl's stare was long forgotten by the time Diana reached home.

She was too busy remembering Will's lips. How they'd felt. How *she'd* felt. And why was she still shivering?

# Chapter 9

Diana's shoulders ached from dragging the metal display rack outside. Hanging her merchandise out front brought people into Hippy Chick. Fifteen minutes later, she was on the phone with a vendor when the overhead bell rang. Checking the security camera, she didn't recognize the woman. Ending the call, Diana hustled to the front.

"Can I help you?"

The pretty blonde was holding out a tie-dyed skirt with a puzzled frown.

"That's one of my favorites."

Tucking the skirt back on the rack, she turned. "Diana?"

"Yep, that's me."

She held up a flyer. "I wanted to thank you for helping with Moonlight Madness. I'm Mercedes, Kate's sister."

"Of course." Mercedes was as beautiful as Kate but in a different way. More edgy. Stylish. "I've heard about you."

"That sounds ominous. What have you heard?"

"No, I didn't mean it that way." Diana held out a hand. "So nice to meet you. I'm glad to help with Moonlight Madness. All the shops need more promotion."

"You do good work. Do you have an art background?"

She only wished. Art had been one of the fields she considered before she quit school and opened her own shop. "Let's just say my background is a mixed bag."

Kate's sister glanced around. "So, what's your plan for Moonlight Madness?"

"Thirty percent off skirts." She still had margin left after that.

"Great. Sounds good." Apparently, her offer met with Mercedes' approval. Diana liked her no-nonsense approach.

"Want to try something on?" Looking over the skirts, Diana grabbed some from the racks in greenish-brown colors that would probably look fabulous on Mercedes. "Let's see, you must be a small. Extra small?" Kate's sister was rail thin.

"What? Oh, no." Already backing away, Mercedes shook her head. "Not today. I don't have time."

*Well, all right then.* Diana slid the hangers back onto the rack, feeling like her stock had just been kicked to the curb.

"At least, not right now."

While Mercedes tried to save herself, Diana did an inside eye roll. "Today I have to work my way up Red Arrow with these flyers."

"Ah, huh. Right." Having lived in Chicago, Diana knew a city girl when she saw one. She'd seen the tortoiseshell headbands, tasteful gold earrings and Jimmy Choo sandals before. The only time city girls came in to buy her merchandise was when they were on vacation. Impulse buys.

Mercedes edged toward the door. "Ah, I should hit the road. So nice meeting you, Diana. And again, thank you."

Diana followed Mercedes out into the sunlight. "Stop in again when you have more time. Are you going to join Kate's book group?"

Mercedes looked stricken. "No, I don't think so."

Diana took her laughter back inside. So Kate's sister wasn't into books? Or maybe she just didn't have time right now. Wasn't easy to move to a new city. The screech of brakes brought her flying back to the window. Mercedes had her head down on the steering wheel. "Everything all right?" Diana called out.

She couldn't hear the answer, but Mercedes backed up and put on her left blinker. Not many folks in Gull Harbor drove luxury cars, especially not one that matched their name. Diana liked Mercedes. Should she call her for lunch? Maybe after Moonlight Madness.

Around noon, Diana was straightening stock. Times like these, she wished she could afford to have Rachel work more often. The bell rang behind her, interrupting her thoughts. Was this Kelsey from the care center, sauntering into the store? Diana's heart about stopped when she saw what the girl was wearing. The blouse with embroidered neckline and sleeves sure looked like the one Diana had sold to Will not too long ago.

"Hi, Kelsey. Can I help you?" Drawing closer, Diana couldn't help studying the blouse. Yes, this was a soft cotton with the blue and green pattern stitching.

Smiling, Kelsey ran a hand down one sleeve. "I'm just looking."

Her hair was long and dark, the kind of dark that came from a bottle. But Diana wasn't one to criticize. She hadn't been born with blonde hair, that's for sure.

"Let me know if you need anything, Kelsey. Sizes. Colors—anything like that." How did this girl end up with the gift Will had bought for his sister?

"Sure will." The girl gave her a coy smile.

Diana's heart froze. Did Will even have a sister?

Retreating to the jewelry counter, Diana put sets of earrings and necklaces together while she kept an eye on Kelsey. A delicate silver chain tangled. Diana started to sweat. Not wanting to turn up the air, she flipped on the overhead fan.

Hangers screeched as Kelsey pushed through the clothing. When Diana heard a hanger snap, she closed the jewelry display case and walked over. "Sure I can't help you?"

"Oh no. I just thought I'd stop by. See what you have." Kelsey traced the neckline of the blouse with one green-tipped finger. "A friend of mine shops here."

"Oh, really? He buys things here?" Too late, Diana realized her mistake.

Kelsey smiled. "Oh, yes he did." Her hand went to the long sleeve Diana knew was soft cotton. The comfortable blouses had quickly sold out, and she meant to place a new order. But the summer was almost over. Time for heavier fall merchandise. Relief washed over her when Kelsey turned toward the door. The sunlight spilling through the glass outlined her perfect figure. Oh to be eighteen again, although she wasn't much older.

"Well, have to get back to work. I'm on my lunch hour, although my boss never minds if I take more time." Her mascara-caked eyelashes batted. The girl should let them dry between coats.

A burning started deep in Diana's stomach. She'd bite her tongue off before she gave this customer the usual "stop in again." Watching Kelsey climb into an old sedan with some sort of beads hanging from the mirror, Diana was glad the shop was empty. As she turned toward the back, she stepped on one of the pins Will had dropped that first time he stopped in. Stooping, she picked it up, thinking about the excitement of that day. She sure hoped she was wrong.

Since the Sunday outing, she'd obsessed about Will. What he wore. What he said. What she wished he'd say. He seemed too good to be true and maybe he was. Maybe she was attracted to men who lied with honest eyes and convincing stories.

She'd thought he was different.

Kelsey? Really?

Going into the back, she cut open a box of fall clothing that had just arrived. Carefully slitting the top, she pulled out pieces in rich fall citron and dark velvety browns. With quick, jerky tugs, she ripped off the plastic protection. For the next hour, she changed all the mannequins. Summer styles were relegated to the sale rack. The front window was filled with fall russet and olive green. As a final step, she changed the stance of the mannequins until they had a jaunty don't-mess-with-me attitude. Perfect.

She was so into it that she almost didn't hear her phone ping. A text message popped up.

"Want to stop in Oink's tonight? Explore?"

Sinking onto the window platform, she stared at the screen until it blurred. No way was she dodging this issue. How should she answer? Customers interrupted her and she slipped her phone into the pocket of her skirt. The burning in her chest, where her heart should be, seared through to her backbone. Might as well deal with this now. When the women were all tucked into fitting rooms, she slipped behind the counter and jabbed at the phone. "Your receptionist stopped in today. She was wearing that blouse you bought for your 'sister.' See you at 7:30."

She pressed Send. Maybe he wouldn't even show up. Her past drew her back into a recurring nightmare. In the dream, she wandered in a dense fog, unable to find the address on the slip of paper in her hand. By the time she flipped the closed sign on the door, she was thoroughly disgusted. This time she wasn't going to take it. This time she was nipping it in the bud.

How she hoped Will had an answer.

~.~

Will stared at his phone. What was this? He'd been checking last month's figures when Diana's text finally came. He could hardly wait to see her tonight...but the deal about the blouse? Then it hit him. The phone slipped from his hands and thunked onto the desk. Right, he'd left that Hippy Chick bag with Kelsey.

Since Sunday, he'd thought of little else but Diana. How she smelled. How she felt. Now this. She sure didn't sound happy. No way was he letting this snowball. Tackling problems head on had always been his approach, so he called Jan. "Can you send someone to the front desk to sit in for Kelsey for about ten minutes?"

"Sure. Is she sick?"

"No, not yet." But he shouldn't get ahead of himself. He hated it when people jumped to conclusions.

"I'll send Felicity down."

When he came to Gull Harbor Care Center, Will had quickly become friends with Jan Lawson. If anything, she was the older sister he didn't have. She'd shown him the ropes. Gave him insights about the owners. Helped him avoid making mistakes and always had his back.

Next call went to Kelsey. She picked up immediately. "Kelsey, Mrs. Lawson is sending Felicity down to relieve you for a minute. Come to my office when she gets there."

"Sure, is anything wrong?"

"Not really. Just want to talk to you about something."

He could almost hear her gulp. While he waited, he stared out at the courtyard. His office faced the back. The scene of family barbecues and parties, the broad space held a gazebo and a huge grill. He'd have to ask Raymond to fertilize the flowers. They were getting leggy, as his mother always said at the end of summer.

"Hi, Will. You wanted to see me?" Kelsey stood in the doorway, one hip propped against the frame. Why had he asked employees to call him by his first name? Today that familiarity felt problematic.

"Come on in, Kelsey. Have a seat."

Was she wearing the blouse he'd given her? He'd never really looked at it. His eyes had been on Diana the day he bought it.

The girl slid into the chair across from him. The long top almost totally covered her mini skirt, especially when she crossed her legs. All that cleavage. Leaning forward, she caught his glance and fingered the low neckline. His eyes shot up to her face. "Everything going okay at the main desk?"

"Oh yes. Fine. I know how to do my job." She recrossed her legs. Yes, definitely a postage stamp skirt. He had to talk to Jan about their dress policy.

Will cleared his throat. "Kelsey, I thought I should explain about the gift I gave you a while back. It was a spur of the minute thing. I stopped in at a friend's store, a very good friend. And I wanted to buy something to support her."

Kelsey's full lips pressed into a straight line. "Right. So?"

Perspiration prickled along the back of his neck. "Since my sister's birthday and Christmas are such a long way off, I thought it would be foolish to save the shirt until then. It's a summer top, right?" He was so out of his league here.

"Of course it is. Don't you think I look pretty in it?"

Will's sweaty palms gripped the arms of his chair. "The blouse looks very nice. But I wanted to clarify that it was not purchased with you in mind. I could have given it to Jan or Beverly." *And I really wish I had.*

Clearly, Kelsey wasn't happy. If Will could dial back time, he'd handle that pretty little bag differently. But he hadn't been thinking. He'd been feeling.

"But I like it," Kelsey whispered. "And I like you, Will. A lot."

Good God, it looked like she was getting up from her chair.

When he made a motion for her to sit down, she leaned over with an expectant smile.

This was worse than he'd imagined. What signals had he missed? Maybe this was how Russ Crafton, his administrator in Indianapolis, had started on the slippery slope. Small gestures that could be misunderstood. For Russ, it had led to a relationship that eventually got him fired, and rightly so.

"And I like you too, Kelsey. But I want you to see this top...blouse...whatever, for what it is. If I gave you the wrong idea, I apologize."

Cheeks bright red, Kelsey folded her arms across her chest.

"Would you like some water?" He kept a small refrigerator in his office to help him get through busy days. She sat down again with a plop that echoed through the office.

"Some water, please."

"Sure." Opening the refrig, he breathed in the cold air. He heard Kelsey take a tissue from the box he kept on his desk. Oh, great. Was she crying? When he turned with the bottled water, Kelsey was stabbing at her eyes.

Stomach twisting, Will handed her the bottle. "Do you have a boyfriend, Kelsey?"

Hands playing with the white cap of the bottle, she shook her head. What could he say to restore some sense of dignity for this poor kid? She was a pretty high school graduate working as a receptionist in a long-term care facility. Must be about as exciting as watching paint dry.

"I mean, I don't have a boyfriend anymore." Her nose was

running and dark stuff dribbled from the outer corner of her eyes. He reached behind him for another tissue and she took it. Outside the sun was shining and the crunch of gravel reminded him that folks were arriving for lunchtime visits. But he wasn't going to rush this.

Kelsey balled the tissue in one hand. "I had a boyfriend all through high school. But then he decided he liked my best friend Melissa better and…" She was off, running through a painful list of hurts. Will would give her all the time she needed. Keeping eye contact, he settled back until finally she wrapped up. "That's it for me."

So young and so much pain. Was this what it was like after high school for girls? "Kelsey, for what it's worth, you're a pretty girl. Someone else will come along." But he could read her mind. *How?*

She sniffed. He forged ahead. "Have you thought of going back to school?"

Her cheeks puffed out. "Why would I do that? I hated school."

Will counted to five. "Sometimes technical colleges can help you figure out what to do with your life. What about the two-year college in Berrien Springs? See what kind classes they're offering. Maybe you could be a legal secretary, go into information systems or human resources." Her eyes brightened a little.

It took lots of self-control not to check the clock on the wall. Time spent with an employee made the facility run more smoothly. The last thing he wanted was for Kelsey to end up like his sister. By the time she left for the reception desk, she'd gotten herself together. Will gave himself a mental high-five.

"What did you say to her?" Jan asked later when she stuck her head in the door.

"Just encouraged her to go to school."

"But Will, she's an excellent receptionist."

Tucking his hands behind his head, he leaned back. "We can always find another receptionist. I like to think about the futures of our employees, especially when they're as young as Kelsey."

"You're too good." Jan shook her head.

"You say that like it's a bad thing."

"It's not. How did you get to be so kind, Will Applegate?"

"Don't you have work to do?" His chair thumping to the floor, he reached for some census reports.

His VP of Nursing laughed at him. "I love it when your face gets all red. And so does she, probably." Jan wiggled her graying brows.

"She who?" Heat flamed in his face.

"Oh, I think you know who." With a final wag of her finger, Jan took off. Her white shoes squished softly on the tile floor.

Sounded like his heart felt right now.

# Chapter 10

Diana wanted to see the look in Will's eyes when he tried to explain. Men did not buy personal gifts for employees. Not without a reason, that is.

She heard the rumble of the vintage Mustang while she was still dabbing cream blush on her cheeks. Thank God, her blemish had faded. Taking a pencil to her lip line, she filled it in, blotted then applied a finishing coat. Did her lashes need more mascara? Diana held up her magnifying mirror. But remembering the heavy hand of Will's receptionist, she screwed the mascara closed. The doorbell rang and she swept everything into her makeup bag and went to answer the door.

Not going to rush. Not going to be nervous.

Sure. Right. She opened the door.

"Hey, beautiful." Will kissed her on the cheek. "Don't you look pretty."

"Thank you." Her white jean shorts were set off by an aqua peasant top, and she'd swept her hair into a thick braid. Will gave it a tug when she turned to grab her purse, but she wasn't feeling playful. Will seemed to get the message.

"Oink's is only three blocks away," Will told her when they got to the car. "Would you rather walk?"

Her eyes flitted to the red convertible. "And miss this?" She might be upset but she wasn't crazy.

Laughing, he opened the door. "I totally agree."

"Mercedes Kennedy stopped in today," she told Will during the short drive.

"Kate's sister? Was she shopping?"

"She wanted to thank me for the map." Sliding down in the seat, she let the cooling air bathe her face. "We might have things in common. You can tell she's lived in a big city. Has that certain edge."

Pulling up next to the ice cream parlor, Will laughed. "What? So you big city girls stick together? Sounds dangerous."

How she hoped she was wrong about Will. He was such fun. As they entered the ice cream shop, suspicion clawed inside her chest. She hated it.

"Whoa." She wasn't prepared for the wild collections crammed inside. Craning her neck, she stared up at the ceiling. Whisks and sifters. Can openers and old-fashioned signs.

"Kind of crazy, right?" The blast of cold air inside made her shiver. Standing behind her, Will rubbed his hands up her bare arms. How she hoped he had an explanation. One that was true. Like the Will she thought she knew. "So, what'll it be?"

Skin prickling, she eyed the list of offerings. "Such a long list."

"Take your time." He leaned against the display case, studying her.

"What? You already know what you want?"

"Yep. Guilty as charged." But he didn't look at all sorry. "I've been here before, and I get the same thing every time. Creature of habit."

"Coconut almond fudge." She hadn't eaten dinner. "And what's your choice?"

"Pistachio...with chocolate sauce."

"But they have a caramel sundae here." She pointed.

The fellow waiting on them stood ready, scoop in hand.

Will tilted his head with a crooked smile. "I have a favorite at every ice cream shop. That's just how I roll."

Tonight that comment hit her the wrong way. Was that like a woman in every port? Every town? She fell quiet. When Will gave her a curious look, she got busy collecting napkins.

Since the small waiting area kept filling up with parents and tired children, there was no chance for a private conversation. Ice cream in hand, they sat at one of the small tables and talked about the upcoming Moonlight Madness. As the conversation dragged on, she started to wonder. Maybe he'd never mention Kelsey. Maybe he'd hope she'd forget. Disappointment curdled the ice cream in her stomach.

"How about a walk on the beach?" Will asked, after they chucked their bowls into the trash.

"Sounds good." Uncertainty battled with the hope in her heart.

When they pulled out of the parking lot, he breezed right past Whittaker Street. Head swiveling, she pointed. "Where are we going? Isn't the public beach back there?"

"You'll see, " Will said, stepping on the gas. "Let me surprise you."

With the top down, the wind caught her hair, whipping it into the night. Diana let her head rock back on the seat. When they reached Bridgman, Will turned left at the light. "Ever been to Weko beach?"

"Nope. Never even heard of it."

"Girl, what have you been doing?"

"I haven't lived here that long. It was tough getting the new shop up and running."

"You had no one to help you?" He seemed to be turning this over in his mind.

"No one." Up ahead, the road fanned into a parking lot. An orange ball, the sun was setting over the lake. "Will you just look at this?"

Like an old drive-in movie, cars had pulled up for the sunset. Some families were stretched out on blankets or collapsed in beach chairs, kids tired and cranky. He parked and looked over, his expression unreadable. "Walk?"

"Sure." The beach looked inviting. Sleepy waves brushed the shoreline as if exhausted by a long day of pleasing tourists. If Will didn't say anything about Kelsey, Diana would. She wanted this cleared up and soon.

Taking her hand, Will fit his strides to hers. "I had a talk with Kelsey today."

"You did?" He sure didn't beat around the bush. She liked it.

"You sounded upset, and I wanted to get things straight." He frowned, and she tried to imagine how awkward that conversation might have been.

The man had *cojones*, as Chili would say.

"Well, I couldn't tell her the truth."

"Which was..." She held her breath.

Stopping, Will turned her to face him. He wore that crooked little boy smile. She'd known another man who tried that approach, so she waited. Held her breath until she felt she might burst.

Placing both hands on her shoulders, Will gave her a level look. "The truth was and still is, that I was so crazy to see you that I pretended to shop. Stupid, right?"

Wonderfully stupid. "You mean you don't have a sister?"

"I do but we're not close. I wanted to connect with you again so I stopped in. Came up with some story and bought the shirt."

"Blouse," she supplied, feeling a delightful release in her chest.

"Right. Whatever. When I got to the facility that day, I just tossed her the bag." He shook his head. "My bad. I wasn't even thinking of how that would look. The sh...blouse had served its purpose, and I didn't know what to do with it."

He tucked a strand of hair behind her ear. Gulls were circling overhead in lazy circles. Relief made her woozy.

He'd leveled with her. She should do the same. This was the time to tell him. She opened her mouth just as a small boy nearby tossed handfuls of bread crumbs in the air. The birds went wild. For a second, the beach felt like an old Alfred Hitchcock movie, filled with flapping wings and screeching. She ducked. Laughing, Will cuddled her to his chest, sturdy and warm. He pulled her away from the fray and they kept walking.

"But Will, a woman makes an assumption when you do

something like that. Give her a gift."

"Never crossed my mind. I was too dazzled."

"So what did Kelsey say?"

He blinked. "Thank you. She said thank you."

She gave him a light sock on the arm. "No. I mean what did she say when you talked to her today."

"Oh, that." She watched his face shift into administrator mode. This had not been an easy conversation for him. "I guess I confused her. She's so young, Diana, just out of high school."

Diana knew how that felt. "Kelsey's lucky. You're not the kind of guy who'd take advantage of her." Her faith in him grew.

"I'd just never do that." She could tell he was struggling. "Diana, the administrator I worked for in Indianapolis had an inappropriate relationship with an employee. That was one of the reasons I left. Russ never knew where to draw the line."

"What happened?"

Hands laced together, they kept walking, their feet leaving soft impressions in the wet sand. "I don't know the details. And I don't want you to think his relationship with a young aide affected patient care. I didn't see that at all. But still...it wasn't right. Something I would never do."

Will kept walking, still processing. She liked to watch him.

"I think it would be good if she went back to school. I know Gull Harbor is a great little town, but there's a whole wide world out there."

She smiled up at him. "You are so wise."

"Great. Just what I want to be," Will said in a resigned voice.

"A wise old man."

"Who said old?"

He was closer now, bending his head until she saw the slight chip in his front tooth, stubble on his cheeks, and the lips she was about to kiss. "Mature maybe," she whispered.

Cupping her head in his hands, Will covered her lips with his with slow certainty. She'd never felt so precious. But there was a question in that kiss. Her hands rested on his muscled forearms. With a sigh, she pulled him closer.

"Oh, Will." What was a man's honesty worth? He'd given her such a gift tonight.

Grandma Kit had always advised Diana to "wait until a man shows his true colors." Were these his true colors? She sure wanted to think so. The light stubble on his chin felt welcome. His hands skimmed her sides until they settled on her waist and tugged her closer.

"What is it?" Will peered down at her through the gathering darkness. She was glad her eyes were hidden.

"Nothing. Come on. Let's go back."

As they approached the pavilion, the sustained trumpet note brought her to a halt.

"The veterans play taps every night." He squeezed her hand. "You'll like it." Walking higher onto a dune with sea grass tickling her bare legs, they finally plopped down together in the warm sand. Had she ever felt so moved? Two retired servicemen played taps while the sun dropped from the sky. There was such purity in the notes. They rang true in her heart. She didn't want to ruin it.

# Chapter 11

The night of Moonlight Madness, Diana was ready. She'd asked Rachel to work with her that night, just in case it really got busy. Some of the stores weren't sold on this idea, but why not give it a chance? Mercedes and Kate had worked so hard on this promotion. She'd set out chocolate chip cookies from Sarah's bakery and small bottles of water. Her sale racks were clearly marked. Yellow and green tie-dyed skirts wouldn't sell in October. Diana wanted them gone, and if her thirty percent off sale ate into her profit a little, she was still fine with it. As the evening wore on, more and more people poured into the store. To her excitement, many were new customers.

"You've got the right idea," Mercedes said when she stopped in around nine. Diana was glad there was a lull so they could talk. "Your markdown is a lot more tempting than the ten percent some of the shops are offering."

"So, you're coming back for that tie-dyed skirt you missed last time you stopped in?" Diana teased. She enjoyed Mercedes' blush. The New York girl wore a lot of black, and that hadn't gone unnoticed in town, where bright summer colors reigned.

Playing along, Mercedes pulled an especially colorful green, pink and yellow tie-dyed skirt. "What do you think? Does this look like me?"

"Have to be honest. From what I see, you're, well, a little more subdued."

"Guess you can't take the city out of the girl, even when the girl's left the city." Mercedes gave her a knowing smile. "You're not from here, right?"

"Nope. I grew up in a wide spot in the road called Newtown. Indiana. Ever heard of it?"

Mercedes shook her head.

"How about Kokomo, Indiana?"

Even when she wrinkled her forehead, Mercedes was beautiful. "Is that near Indianapolis?"

"You got it. I couldn't wait to get out of town."

"I guess a lot of us wanted to spread our wings. But now that I'm back? Having people know all about you can be nice. Comfortable. You don't have to fill in the blanks." Mercedes stopped sliding the hangers. "Not all of them, at least."

Diana's palms were suddenly damp, and she wiped them on her long, blue skirt. If her grandmother knew her Chicago story, she'd be mortified. That was one blank she never wanted to fill.

"Well, I've got to check on Phoebe," Mercedes said, making her way through the displays toward the front door. "You're coming to Kate's wedding, right?"

"Wouldn't miss it. See you there." Diana had been relieved when Will mentioned it to her. She didn't want to go alone.

Customers continued to trickle in, the yellow map in their hands. Diana and Rachel dashed back and forth, checking additional sizes in the stockroom, clearing fitting rooms and ringing up sales. The event had brought new faces through her door, and they quickly snapped up the summer stock. It felt good to be a part of it, to feel she belonged, that she'd contributed something. The time passed quickly.

As she closed up that night, she felt the town settle around her. Soon the summer people would pack up and head back to Chicago. Gull Harbor wouldn't see much of them unless they came for a Notre Dame football game or were into cross-country skiing. That seemed to be how the town worked.

But now with Kate at the PR helm and Mercedes adding her expertise, the winter season might be busier. She felt hopeful.

That Saturday night, she had dinner at the Mangy Mutt with Will. Watching the sun set from that upper patio was magical. The rich scent of the lake rolled over them as they dawdled over their drinks and fish tacos. Later, they strolled down to the public beach and walked north to get away from the people. Hand in hand, they splashed through the shallows. Will grabbed some rocks, asked her to make a wish, and then taught her how to skip them over the ripples on the water. He won, of course, with four skips.

"Girls from Newtown don't learn how to skip stones," she said in her defense.

"Neither do boys from Beanblossom." Drawing her closer, he kissed her forehead. When had she ever felt so content? For a while, they sat up in the sea grass, breathing in the damp lake air. "I wish I could hold on to summer," she murmured.

"Do you? Why?"

She swept one hand toward the water. "This is all so perfect. You're so perfect."

"Hey, I'm not going anywhere, okay?" Tipping her chin up, he kissed her. He tasted so good. Hooking her arms around his neck, she giggled and pulled him down to the sand, still warm from a long sunny day.

His lips inflamed her. Before long Diana felt warm and rumpled and breathless. When they were both gasping, Will drew back. Sucked in a slow breath. "Winter will be good for us but in a different way."

"How?" She wanted details. Reassurance.

"Well, let's see." He glanced around. In the darkness, a night breeze rustled through the tall sea grass and whispered over the sand dunes. "You can't make out on ice floes. That's for sure."

"Don't remind me." Remembering how the jagged ice built up to rim the lake in Chicago, she shivered. Same lake. Same climate.

"I'll keep you warm. I promise."

Now. This was a good time to tell him. The words were on her tongue. But she just couldn't. Why ruin this perfect date with a confession that could destroy all this? Just a few more days.

That night she slept soundly, but in her dreams, she was pushing against a wall, terror ripping across her chest. Something outside wanted to come in. The door bulged with the fury of the force outside. She woke up in a sweat and turned the overhead fan on high. But it was a long time before she got back to sleep.

On Sunday, she drove to the care center for the dance. Labor Day weekend and the place was festooned with red, white and blue flags and banners. A holiday mood filled the halls. When she danced with Tim, he told her about fighting in Desert Storm. She couldn't tell if any of what he said had really happened. Jan mentioned that Tim suffered a brain injury in the war. "Those explosives," she'd said with a quick shake of her head.

That day Harold, dressed in a red plaid shirt but still wearing his winter cap, insisted on dancing with her twice. Afterwards, Diana sashayed over to the shyer ladies to form some couples and send them spinning onto the floor. Only Luanne remained seated, plucking at the blue flowers on her dress. Oh, it took some coaxing but soon Diana was guiding her gently through some simple steps, while Luanne hummed to the music and smiled.

When Will didn't show, she told herself it didn't matter. She'd see him at the picnic the next day. After they straightened up, Jan walked her out. When they passed the front desk, Kelsey ducked her head. Diana hoped someday the two of them would feel comfortable together. What Kelsey had done was awkward but innocent.

"See you tomorrow, Jan," Diana said when they reached the door.

"Diana...?"

She turned back.

"Thanks for giving us your time. The residents really like you. They can feel your kindness and that matters. You care."

Diana didn't know what to say. This felt important, as if she were really touching lives. "I enjoy coming. You've got a great group."

When Monday arrived, she helped Will at the barbecue grill. "Sure you want to do this?" he asked, eyeing the glowing coals. "Gets pretty hot."

"Come on, I won't melt," she laughed. "I'll take my turn. I enjoy it."

"You're amazing, you know that?" Leaning over, he kissed her. She could feel herself glowing.

That evening a bus took the residents down to the beach for the fireworks. Will and Diana joined the outing. They sat on canvas chairs, their feet in the cool sand while colors exploded overhead. The brilliant bursts and streaks left her breathless. Or was that Will rocking her world by just holding her hand?

The drive back to her place was quiet. As soon as he parked the car, they turned to each other. The hot kisses and exploring hands felt so good but she called a halt. Other words on her lips, Diana didn't invite him inside. She wasn't quite there yet. But when she closed the door behind her, the yellow bungalow felt empty.

~.~

Kate's wedding on the beach the following Saturday was beautiful. Standing high on a dune with Will, Diana decided she'd never been in a church that felt more sacred than this sandy stretch. Carolyn and Phoebe stood near them, and the hairdresser teased Will unmercifully about being enough to handle three women. If she ever got her hair cut, Diana looked forward to spending time with Phoebe.

Kate looked absolutely gorgeous. Her dress flowed with the

breeze while she waited to walk across the sand to meet her groom. Hard to believe that this had happened so quickly since the Firemen's Ball. Obviously, Cole and Kate were adults who knew what they wanted. From what she'd heard, this flame had been burning since high school. Longing knotted deep inside, and she took a deep breath. Her grandmother had always told her that good things come to those who wait.

The setting sun turned the clouds a rose color when the short wedding procession started. First Sarah and then Chili, followed by Mercedes. Their bridal party all wore pink dresses in different styles and shades that seemed to match the sunset. Mercedes was looking pretty hot in a strapless design with a beaded bodice that twinkled in the fading light.

When Natalie, Cole's daughter, stepped forward with her basket of rose petals, murmurs rippled through the guests gathered in a semi-circle. Diana didn't know if it was Natalie or Prissy, their Great Dane, who caused such a stir. Dancing along beside Natalie, the huge dog tried to catch the flowers she scooped from a white basket. The two soon had the whole crowd chuckling.

Then it was Kate's turn. The crowd settled. Even the waves washing ashore sounded softer, slower. Cole was just a dark outline against the sky, the groom waiting for his bride. Diana blinked back the tears prickling in her eyes. Sometimes she wished she weren't so sentimental, but she couldn't explain the loneliness sweeping over her. Then Will took her hand. She wound her fingers around his, and the isolation she'd felt drew back like a retreating wave.

With steady steps and bare feet, Kate moved across the sand.

Her eyes found Cole's and their glance made them one. Diana could feel their connection. They made such a good couple. So much had changed for them this past summer. When Kate had joined the book club, she'd looked exhausted and shaky. Here to help nurse her mother, who'd suffered a stroke, she'd just gone through a painful divorce. Then she ran into Cole, her debate partner in high school. Things moved pretty quickly after that. Diana smiled to herself, remembering her part in their romance.

Glancing to the right, Diana noticed Finn Wheeler, owner of the Mangy Mutt. His eyes were glued to Mercedes. There'd been rumors about the two of them, and she wondered how that would turn out. She'd be pleased if Mercedes ended up in Gull Harbor. Diana wanted to get to know her better. Somehow, she thought they might have things in common, and she'd always believed in her instincts.

Well, almost always.

Cole and Kate had written their own vows. Although she strained to hear them, the waves had picked up and only the occasional word drifted back. The expressions on their faces told it all. Would these heartfelt promises last forever? Did difficulties strengthen love, as the minister had stated?

At the end, Cole kissed his bride. Applause broke out and he invited the group to the party at his place just up the road. Blotting tears and shrugging out of sport coats, the wedding began to break up. "Ready to leave?" Will asked.

"Yep. Can we ask Carolyn and Phoebe to ride with us?"

"No problem," Will said, pointing to the road. "This way,

ladies."

The four of them jumped into the red Mustang. Will stood with his hand on the door, eyeing Phoebe and Carolyn in the back. "Top up or down? I don't want you to ruin those pretty hairdos."

"Are you crazy, Will Applegate?" Phoebe howled. "In this hot hunk of motor vehicle? Let it rip. I want the whole world to see us, messed up hair and all."

Giggling, Carolyn settled back while Diana tied on a scarf.

"I'll be the envy of every man in town," Will said, pulling out onto the road. The ride got interesting when Phoebe broke into a raucous version of "Here Comes the Bride." Diana felt her cheeks color, glad that the bride and groom were in another car. When they reach Cole's house, they parked along the road. Darkness had fallen and crickets sang in the damp grass. Her heels sank in the sandy road as they walked to the house.

The A-frame was filling up fast, and she made a beeline for the restroom. Her headscarf hadn't helped a bit. It took her a while to detangle her hair and fix her makeup. Phoebe and Carolyn soon drifted off to circulate. Will guided Diana through the densely packed crowd his hand at her waist. The summer heat held and she fanned herself with one hand.

Just then a waiter swung past with a tray full of champagne flutes. Will handed one to Diana and took another for himself.

"So how did you like the wedding on the beach?" Will asked.

"It was beautiful. Perfect for them, right?"

Will had maneuvered her into a corner of the huge deck. "What's *your* perfect wedding?"

She choked. "I haven't thought about it."

And if Will swallowed that, she had a piece of Florida swamp land he might be interested in. He threw her a look of disbelief. "I thought all women started planning their wedding at the age of, oh, ten?"

He had that right. She bolted back a gulp too fast and sputtered.

"You okay?" Will rubbed her back until the spell subsided.

When the buffet table opened, they joined the line, filling their plates and making small talk with the other guests. Sometimes people would ask questions about their loved one at the care center. The interruption never bothered Will. His patience astounded her.

"Penny for your thoughts," Will ask later as they danced on Cole's deck. She could feel his heart beating, and her own struck the same rhythm.

She wasn't about to tell him she was wishing this could last forever. "Nothing."

"Ah, huh." His eyes roved over her face. "Hey, beautiful," he whispered. "You look troubled. Want to talk about it?"

She shook her head. "Just tired after a long week, I guess."

"How are things coming with the Sunday dances?" He hesitated. "What I mean is, do you plan on sticking things out?"

"Of course." She tossed her head higher.

Will tugged her close. "I never doubted it. That's you. Feisty and beautiful."

Oh, if he only knew. He was humming something in her ear that sounded like "I Only Have Eyes for You." She was grateful for the slow songs that kept him close. When he dropped his hands to her waist, she looped her arms around his neck while they swayed. It would be so easy to get comfortable with Will. He was such a good man, maybe too good for her, considering. Even though he rarely saw his sister, he came from a loving family where people supported each other. Could there be a future with him? Or would he politely backpedal? The thought sent a blade of fear slicing through her. Maybe it was time to find out.

Her head began to spin and she rested it on his chin. "Hey, you okay?" Will pushed back. She swallowed and nodded her head, nestled deep into the crook of his neck so he couldn't see her face. She willed herself to breath. His hand left her waist to soothe her back.

"What are you doing?"

"Nothing." The hand stopped.

"I'm sorry." She was feeling way too prickly tonight, and it wasn't fair to take it out on him. Her life held so many secrets, crammed in her past like a sealed closet. Maybe it was time to open that door.

The music changed gears to something faster. She could feel the boards of the deck pulse under her feet. Will rocked out until she could barely breathe and her side ached.

When he asked if she was ready to leave, she nodded. Lordy, she'd gotten so relaxed she felt like a wet noodle. Together they said goodnight to Kate and Cole, wishing them the best. The newlyweds were headed to Mackinac Island for their honeymoon. Carolyn and Phoebe both gave them a nod. Mercedes was nowhere to be found. Had she seen Mercedes huddled in the corner with Finn Wheeler?

Will had the top down on the convertible, and the breeze rustled through her hair as they drove to her house. "Everything's so quiet tonight," she said.

"People might be packing up and getting ready to go home. Back to school. Back to work."

"Ugh. There goes my business. Off to the big city where fashion reigns."

"Do you miss Chicago sometimes?"

"Yes. But when I signed my lease, I committed for five years. Foolish, I know."

"You can break a lease if you want." Reaching over, Will squeezed her hand.

"I don't really want to go back, Will. Not to Chicago anyway."

"I hope you don't leave."

She liked hearing that. But uncertainty danced across her nerve endings. "Time will tell. Right now, I don't have any plans to leave Gull Harbor."

"Good." He squeezed her hand again and their fingers entwined.

When they pulled up to her house, the street was dark and quiet. Trees formed a rustling canopy overhead. Should she ask him in? Sliding his back against the car door, he peered at her in the darkness.

"Come here, beautiful."

She tucked her body into his, winding her arms around his

neck. His kisses tasted like barbecue sauce, and his body felt all man.

"You smell like the beach," she giggled.

He sniffed her hair. "And you don't."

"That's hair spray."

"I don't care." And his kiss proved that.

Good thing Mrs. O'Donnell across the street went to bed early. Diana wanted him so bad that her entire body ached. Some tender, precious parts were calling. "Will?"

He answered with a hard, deep kiss that made her forget the sleepy side street. Diana wanted to invite him in but she wouldn't. Not tonight.

"We should stop," he said at one point.

"Go ahead. Try." She teased his lips with her tongue until he sighed and surrendered.

Finally, they broke apart and strolled hand-in-hand to the door where a light gleamed. The katydids seemed to be the only witnesses to their goodnight kiss.

"Talk to you soon," he whispered, backing toward his car.

"Soon." Diana watched him drive away. Then she closed the front door and leaned her head against it. Later, she couldn't even remember how she'd gotten into her sleep shirt. The look on his face, the feel of his body sent her into hot, troubled dreams where she tumbled restlessly all night.

# Chapter 12

Will didn't want to rush her. Sure, she drove him crazy. He'd never wanted a woman the way he wanted Diana Prescott. But he was a patient guy. His father had taught him to hunt. They would sit in that blind out in the woods until his feet and hands were numb from the cold. Still, they waited. He was more than willing to wait for Diana. What Will really hated were the times when she shut down. Kept him out. What was that about?

September turned cold. The summer people went home. Diana kept coming to the dances, dazzling everyone with her charm. Jan couldn't say enough good things about her. Will chuckled when he heard that Harold dogged Diana's steps when she was in the facility. "He can't get close enough to her," Jan said.

Will knew just how that felt. He began spending more time at the office on Sundays, making up things to do until he could drift down to the dance and whisk her away in his arms. How pathetic was that? The sound of her voice, the scent of her perfume—he wanted it all and more. Diana stoked his heat. Small gestures, shy looks. This was crazy and he sure wasn't used to it.

So why was she holding back?

"Want to go to Tabor Hill Winery next weekend?" he asked, walking her to the yellow VW when she'd finished on Sunday.

"They have a jazz fest that's part wine tasting. Should be fun." Leaning against her car, he framed her beautiful face with his hands.

"Sounds wonderful." She smiled up at him and then looked away, nipping her lower lip. There it was again.

"I want to kiss you. You know that, right?"

She laughed. "So why don't you?"

He checked back where Harold sat grinning. "Because we have an audience."

"Maybe Harold's our chaperone." She rested her hands lightly on his hips under his jacket. "You're so tense."

"And you're such a tease."

He could have kicked himself when she dropped her hands. "I don't mean to be. Oh, Will. It's just that..." When Diana shook her head, her long hair shimmered like the golden maple leaves dropping from the trees.

"Got you in a compromising position, have I?" He backed off.

Her attitude came back. An eyebrow went up, arched and elegant. "Don't think you won't pay. Only one scoop of ice cream on your cone next time. I could go for some ice cream right now."

"Oh, I want to give you more than that."

Her lips opened and closed, as if she'd given her words a second thought.

This parking lot conversation was going nowhere. He wanted to see her before next weekend. "Look, how about going to Brewster's tonight? We can stop for ice cream later."

"Right, sure." She gave him a confused look but then smiled.

"Great idea. Pick me up in two hours?"

"You bet." A look over his left shoulder confirmed that Harold's eyes were glued to them like yesterday's oatmeal. A frustrated recklessness overcame him. Angling his body so Harold saw only his back, Will gave her a kiss that ended with her pushing away.

"Will?" She blinked up at him. "Tonight let's talk, okay?"

"Sure." But her words had felt heavy and ominous. Standing in the parking lot, Will watched her drive away. A chill wind chased the yellow leaves over the parking lot, a dry scraping sound. Jamming his hands in his pockets, he walked to his car.

~.~

Getting dressed that evening wasn't easy. Her hands shook as Diana tried to fasten her necklace with the silver starfish. She couldn't put this off any longer. It wasn't fair to Will. Besides, she wanted to know. Could she put her past behind them...or would she then face a future without him? One way or the other, she had to know.

The steamy urgency today decided it for her. Did she want Will? In the worst way ever, and she knew he felt that way too. But she'd pushed him away. Any other man would have moved on by this time. But he wasn't a guy who'd count dates or press the point. Almost too good to be true, in the light of her dating experience.

The fall wind rattled the windowpanes. She pushed her airy, sleeveless tops to the back of the closet. Instead, she decided on a violet-blue turtleneck with black jeans. After Labor Day, she just couldn't wear white. Even as a little girl, she remembered her grandmother tucking her white shoes away after the holiday weekend.

Will always commented on her eyes, and she spent extra time on them that night. Three different shades of brown with a light brush of violet on top. While she wielded her brushes, she rehearsed her speech. But her hands shook and she smudged her eyeliner. Grabbing her cold cream, the kind her grandmother used, she started over. What if she said her piece, and he was totally turned off? Disgusted. Tears brimmed and she didn't have time to do her eyes again. Tipping her head back, she carefully blotted below and above the lashes. She wouldn't blame him. She was running out of time.

Fastening her necklace just wasn't in the cards tonight. Her hands shook so bad that she had to give up. Two spritzes of perfume and the doorbell rang. When she opened the door, Will grabbed her and brushed his lips across hers. Then he kissed her deeply and she melted.

"I needed that," he whispered, easing back.

"Me too." She cupped his face, breathing in his heat.

With a groan, they sank into a kiss that reached into deep, damp places. Finally, she pushed away, lips throbbing. "Guess that would shock the hair right off Harold's head."

"Harold's bald."

"What? No way." Grabbing her purse, she stepped out the door and Will pulled it shut.

"That's the truth. But I think his reliance on that hat runs deeper than a hairline." Will took her hand and they walked toward the Mustang. She only saw his white sedan when he went to work.

They talked about nothing and everything all the way to Brewster's. "Let's get a table in the corner," she said as they stepped up to the reception desk. Five minutes later, they were at a small table that was private and perfect. She waited until after they ordered a pizza and their drinks arrived. The pear vodka had never tasted so good or been needed so much. Now was the time. She could lose it all right here and pressed a hand to her heart.

"Hey, you okay?" Will leaned toward her, his eyes almost navy blue.

"Sure. Just icy vodka, that's all."

"To us." Will raised his glass. He looked so happy.

"T-to us," she managed to say. If there would be an "us," she'd know soon. Heart galloping, she set the glass down.

"Honesty's so important in a relationship..." she began and then stumbled.

Will frowned. "I am being honest, Diana."

So much for all her rehearsal. "I meant *I* have to be honest with *you*."

"Oh." Suddenly wary, Will sat back.

"My past relationship..." Might as well dive right into it. "He was married."

Will's jaw tightened. She felt him pulling away and a rock lodged in her throat. "I-I didn't know, Will..."

Giving his head a quick shake, Will focused. She waited, taking in every nuance while emotions played over his dear, handsome face. But no judgment darkened his eyes, just curiosity. "So, he told you he was single?"

She rushed on. "He came into my shop. Said he was looking for something for his sister." They exchanged a glance. After all, hadn't Will done the same thing? "We talked. I showed him some things. He said he was in Chicago for a meeting but he lived here, in Gull Harbor. And his sister had a birthday coming up."

Will's face had paled. "Does he still live here?"

"I don't think so. As it turned out, this was his second home. The place was sure big enough to be their main house." All those rooms with ceiling to floor windows. She'd been more than impressed. Later, that all seemed so shallow.

"What an ass." Reaching over, he squeezed her hand. "I mean the guy, Diana. Not you."

"I know." Disgust curdled in her stomach. "I was so stupid. A small town girl, not that being naive excuses me. At the very least, I should have googled him."

"Did you love him?" The guarded Will was back.

She chose her words carefully. "I loved who I thought he was. We dated for a year. I should have questioned those lunches. Some weekends he would pick me up at my shop on Saturday evening and bring me here. Now I realize those were times when his wife wasn't in Gull Harbor. During the summer, he took me away on long weekends. His wife was probably here with their children. His job was very demanding, so it was easy to lie."

"The guy had kids?" The disgusted tone was back.

"Yes, but I thought he was divorced at the time. He came on so strong, bringing me roses and you know, expensive gifts." How embarrassing to admit it.

"A real lady killer. I'll never bring you roses again."

"You won't?" Could this get any worse?

"Don't take it that way. I just meant there must be other flowers. I sure don't want to be lumped in with this guy. What a terrible experience."

She began shredding her cocktail napkin into thin strips. The whole story had to come out now. "I trusted him. We talked about the future. The recession came. My shop in Chicago wasn't doing well and my lease was up. I had some of my grandfather's inheritance left, so I came up to Gull Harbor during the week and rented the space I'm in now. What a goof I was. He had a birthday. I thought my news would be a big surprise."

"Bet he was thrilled."

She cringed, remembering the terrible scene. "Furious was more like it. He went ballistic. Told me I was naive and stupid, that of course he was married. He thought I knew that." The confession brought back bad memories.

Taking her hands, Will gently pried open her fingers and wiped away the torn up mess. "Don't be so hard on yourself. Sounds like he had you snowed. He lied."

"He was right though, Will. Sometimes I think I just fell off the turnip truck." How it hurt to admit it.

"Not naive. Honest. Trusting." The words soothed her like a healing balm. "There's a huge difference."

Then his expression shifted. "Why didn't you tell me this

sooner?"

"I was so afraid..."

"Look, the guy took advantage of you. He's a predator. You have a sweet, innocent side and he could see that." His nostrils flared.

"You make me sound like a child." Did she even want to hear this from Will? "Maybe I am that kind of woman. Easily taken. Maybe my mother has rubbed off on me."

That's what killed her.

His thumb stroked softly over her knuckles. "You are not your mother. But you are a small town girl. Like me, you grew up far from the city, where it's easier to take on a new identity or be anonymous. You weren't city-wise."

She threw him a rueful smile. "Those corn fields could get pretty crazy, Will."

He chuckled. "Don't I know it? I told you that was why my father gave me that car. He didn't want me smoking pot, much less get into the other stuff. I'm just saying, it's easier to deceive someone in a huge city like Chicago. But coming back here? That was risky of him. Has anyone ever recognized you? You know, restaurants. Places like that?"

She looked away. "We didn't go out a lot. Ordered in most of the time... From what the girls in book club say, things happen here too." She was thinking of Cole Campbell's first wife. There were plenty of rumors about her.

Lines appeared between Will's eyes. She hated putting them there. "And it's over? You have no contact with him."

"Yes. Over and done." If she ever saw Bryce Williams again, she'd give him more than a piece of her mind. "I tried to call him again once, just to read him the riot act, but the number had been disconnected."

Will's mouth twisted. "It was probably a throw-away phone. The one his wife never knew he had."

"How stupid I've been." All the while, she'd felt so sophisticated, coming from Chicago to Gull Harbor on weekends. "I'm sure not perfect and this proves it."

"No, you're wrong. You are perfect, Diana. Untouched in a lot of ways."

"That's crazy." But she liked hearing it. If anyone was perfect, it was Will. Didn't he come from a solid family who loved him?

Now he plied her with praise. A weighty load slowly slipped from her shoulders. If she were a balloon, she'd float to the ceiling. The best part was, she'd told him everything, holding nothing back. But he still looked at her like she was one of those fancy desserts in Brewster's case, and he wanted to devour her. Slipping off her sandal, she ran her bare foot up one of Will's legs, felt the short hair above his ankles. Didn't take much for her imagination to go into gear.

Glancing around, he gulped visibly. She was being so unfair...and loving it. "Okay, enough. Either cut that out or we're leaving. Fast. You're perfect and hot, and it's time we do something about that." Will raised a brow, as if wanting to be sure they were on the same page.

"What's on your mind?"

"Nothing I can say out loud without a snoopy waiter dropping his tray." And he glared at the bus boy hovering nearby. Grabbing his tub of dishes, he hustled toward the kitchen.

"Are you really hungry?" Will asked.

"Yes, but not for food." Pizza was the last thing she wanted.

"Right. That does it." Flagging their waiter, Will asked him to box their pizza. When the box arrived, he settled the bill and she jumped to her feet. They tried not to run as they headed for the car. On the short drive back to her place, their hands did the talking.

Inside her bungalow, he slid the box into the refrigerator and hoisted her onto the island. She could feel the cool granite through her jeans. The sensation melted under the heat of his gaze.

This was feeling very bad, which was oh, so good.

"We're going to take this slow," he promised in a hoarse whisper. But his kisses weren't slow. They were hot and hungry. If she didn't whisk off her sweater she just might burn up. So she tossed it to the floor. His eyes narrowed. "Oh, Diana. Babe, you *are* perfect."

She could hardly breathe while his eyes traveled over her as if he were memorizing every curve. She sucked in a breath while he kissed the parts he seemed to like the most. Thank God he was wearing a polo shirt, easy to pull over his head. "What a great look. I like you messy." Smiling, she smoothed back his hair.

"Good. Let's keep that in mind. The messier the better."

Laughing, she plowed her fingers back into his thick curls and mussed up what she'd just fixed. Impatience made her hands shake.

Lifting her carefully, Will swept her into the cool darkness of her room.

"I've wanted...you...so...badly." Now that her confession was behind her, she realized how much she needed him.

His gravelly chuckle just about undid her. They took care of the rest of the clothes. "I was beginning to think you were planning on joining the convent or something."

Now that made her laugh. She pushed him back onto the bed. "Trust me. I'm bad material for a nun."

Leaning back on his elbows, he leveled a challenging look. My, he was quite an eyeful. "Why don't you show me just how bad you can be?"

So she did.

# Chapter 13

Autumn ripened. The leaves began to turn the most gorgeous shades of gold, citron and russet brown. Diana wished she had a coat in those colors. She'd twirl and spin until she was dizzy. That was her life right now. The weather had been playfully warm. Soft breezes seemed to caress her body, leaving her skin extra sensitive. Or was that Will?

She couldn't stop thinking of him. Wanted to spend every minute with him. The words he whispered, like "perfect" and "beautiful," rang in her ears every day. He'd accepted her past. Diana's confidence soared.

Truth was, she'd doubted herself big time after Bryce, and she'd brought that caution to her relationship with Will. The incident with Kelsey wouldn't have set her off if she hadn't been so disillusioned. Now? She approached everything with more certainty. When it came time to choose the spring lines, she made bold choices. Picked out silky styles she'd never tried before in colors like Tequila Lime and Desert Sunset. Tops that clung and skirts that moved with her body. Will teased her about hiding her figure under flowing skirts and blousy shirts. She'd never thought of it like that. Now she chose differently, with him in mind.

"You're beautiful just the way you are," Will told her.

"Absolutely perfect. Why would you want to hide...all that?"

The rapid change in her life left her dazed. She daydreamed about Will constantly, toppling mannequins, jamming her register, and even forgetting to lock up one night in her rush to meet him.

"You're a mess," Rachel told her with a pleased grin.

"Yeah, what's your point?"

She was a mess. Absent-minded. *In love.* The words pulsed in her mind like a neon sign.

Even her book club teased her. "*Chica!*" Chili's eyes narrowed as Diana lounged on the sofa, yawning after a late night with Will.

"What?" She straightened, wondering what she'd just missed.

A giggle rippled Chili's full lips. "*Que pasa?* What's going on with you?"

"You do seem different, Diana. In a nice way." Distracted, Sarah burned her finger, swirling a bread chunk in the hot cheese dip. Any meeting at Chili's was bound to be hot.

Kate gazed at her over the glass of apple cider. "Yeah, something's changed. Want to talk about it?"

Diana pulled herself erect, almost spilling her chardonnay. "Nothing. Just...nothing." But she couldn't help the Cheshire grin lifting the corners of her mouth.

"What are you keeping from us?" prodded Sarah gently.

With a quiet smile, Kate leaned her head on one hand. "A man has to be involved. And I just bet I know who."

"Anyone want more wine?" Carolyn waved a bottle, no doubt a kind attempt at distraction.

"Maybe you need a wild streak in your hair, like Mercedes,"

Phoebe threw in.

"Right. Perfect for Mercedes but not for me." Diana had been amazed when she bumped into Mercedes at the deli counter in Clancy's. The green streak was wild. Will would be shocked and suddenly his opinion mattered. But maybe she'd misjudged the guy. Two months ago, she'd pegged Will as definitely on the reserved side.

But maybe not. The last couple of weeks had shown her a different side of Will. Why, he might be excited by a fun slash of color in her hair.

Where had this man dropped from? What she'd felt for Bryce was nothing compared to the feelings that now held her hostage. Did she love Will?

Kate was laughing, and Diana struggled to focus. "Yeah, Phoebe, I think you strong-armed my sister into that streak."

Phoebe was eyeing Diana with a wicked eye. "Why not give it a try?"

"Oh, I couldn't change my hair." Twirling a thick strand around her finger, she thought of how Will had tugged her down onto the sofa last night. Yes, maybe she loved him. Anyway, she sure loved how he made her feel. She'd flipped over onto his chest and tickled him with her hair until he begged for mercy.

"*Chica, donde estas?* Where are you?" Chili snapped her fingers in front of Diana. "Your head is in a cloud, no?"

Flustered by all the questions, she wondered why she'd even come tonight. She hadn't read the book. But she dearly loved these women and the special bond they shared.

"So, how's it going with Will?" Kate tried again, oh, so casually.

Diana's mouth turned dry at the images flooding her mind. Nothing she could share, for sure. "Fine." She grabbed her wine and sipped, then choked and coughed until her eyes started watering.

Patting her on the back, Carolyn smiled. "That good, huh?"

"We're just dating," she finally gasped.

*Sure. Right, Missy. That position last night was "just dating"?*

"Lucky you." Carolyn made a face.

"Carolyn, you could be seeing someone if you made an effort," Phoebe said. "Join Matchmakers online. Cast a wide net."

"Right, and drive all the way to Kalamazoo for a date? You try it. I don't have the time."

"Well, there is that. And speaking of the supply of men in Gull Harbor, is Mercedes dating Finn Wheeler?" Phoebe turned to Kate, who arched her brows and made the tick-a-lock motion with her fingers on her lips.

"Ah, hah!" Chili exploded. "You're holding out."

"Not my story to tell." Kate turned to Carolyn. "But certainly there are some men around to date."

Carolyn lifted a shoulder. "Seems like every man I know is under eighteen."

"Oh, I don't mean your students." Chili wagged her head. "That's a definite no-no."

"Absolutely."

"Still, I hear younger men are more virile." Laughing, Phoebe fingered her glass.

"Now, how would you know that?" Kate turned toward her friend.

The meeting went downhill from there, every comment more outrageous. Diana loved their carefree spirit. In Chicago, she'd worked such long hours that she didn't have time to develop friendships. And then she met Bryce. For obvious reasons, he never encouraged her to spend time with anyone but him. But that chapter of her life was closed. Will had helped ease the pain and shame.

Feeling relaxed, Diana leaned back. Her eyes fell on Kate, sipping a glass of cucumber water. "Hey, Kate, no wine tonight?"

Silence fell over the room like a soft blanket. "Kate? Your turn. Are *you* keeping something from us?" Sarah leaned forward from her beanbag chair.

Kate's face glowed. "I'm pregnant."

The place went up for grabs. Lots of hugging and jumping up and down. Laughter and tears. Life just galloped along in Gull Harbor.

"I wanted to be sure. So I took the test." Kate rested a hand on her flat stomach. "Natalie's so excited, and so is Cole of course. But don't tell anyone yet, okay? Natalie overheard us, or we wouldn't have said anything yet."

Chili lifted her glass. "To Kate and her *bambino. Buena suerte, eh?*"

They all clicked glasses, followed by more excited planning. Chili brought out more cheese dip, and they forgot all about the book discussion. Talking about pregnancy and babies was way more fun.

Babies. Sure, she'd dreamed about marriage and children with Bryce. What a wasted effort. Now Diana let her mind wander into a nursery with circus wallpaper. The smell of talcum powder seemed to fill the air.

Was she crazy? Trying to rein in her emotions, she turned her attention back to their chatter about stuff going on this fall. Will had mentioned a few events to her. On chilly nights, people made bonfires on the beach and roasted marshmallows. He wanted to go apple picking and drive north along the highway to see the yellow and red leaves. The facility always had a Fall Festival. She was looking forward to all of it...with him.

That night the book group broke up later than usual. As she drove home, Diana fell into comparing Bryce to Will.

Never again would she give herself so cheaply.

If there ever was another time.

If she ever needed to enter the dating pool again. Mercy, she sure hoped not.

The next day Diana and Will drove north and picked apples. When they got home, she made applesauce, the kind her grandmother used to make, rich with cinnamon and nutmeg.

"So you're a domestic goddess too?" Will asked after he sampled the applesauce straight from the pan.

She looked at him. "You know I'm not."

"My Grandma Trudie used to make this." He waved a spoon at the pan.

"Really?" Taking the wooden spoon from his hands, she kissed his sticky lips. "You never talk much about your family."

Will skated a finger down her cheek. "I want you to meet them. Maybe over the holidays if you can swing it?"

"We could go to Newtown to see my grandmother and aunt before heading over to Beanblossom." Her mind spun ahead, but wasn't he paving the way?

"You bet. We'll have a great holiday." Will's lips moved to her neck, and she turned woozy as he whispered, "Can't wait to meet your grandmother and Aunt Ethel. Bet they're both gorgeous like you."

"They're a lot older. You're tickling me." Not that she was complaining.

"Oh, you'll always be beautiful, Diana. Dignified. A matriarch. Age won't matter."

Chuckling, she snuggled back into his warmth. He could sure conjure up a wonderful future. Because of her last experience, she hadn't mentioned Will to her family. She knew there'd be questions, and she didn't want her grandmother or aunt to jump ahead. Now Will's warm certainty melted her reserve.

Phoebe and Mercedes began to stop in the shop more often. Diana felt her social network broadening, and her roots sinking deeper in this town. The fall came in unseasonably warm. The night she hosted the book group, they threw open the windows for what felt like the last gasp of summer, smelling of the lake and campfires on the beach. She'd made a hot clam dip, and Carolyn helped her toast bread rounds for scooping. Conversation soon left the book and focused on Kate's morning sickness. Spying Diana's calendar on the refrigerator, Chili plied her with bold questions.

But she played stupid about all the W's scrawled in so many blocks. They were seeing each other a lot. Looking up, she caught Carolyn's eyes and winked. Could life get any better?

Every weekend she had plans with Will, and they continued to visit other towns. Saugatuck, South Haven and Holland became more than dots on the map. She couldn't eat enough burgers with caramelized onions or would never tire of blue moon ice cream, especially when it dripped from Will's lips.

The warm weather held. He scheduled picnics for the residents, and Diana helped out where she could, cutting buns, carrying salads from the kitchen, or even working at the grill. Harold tagged after her whenever she showed up. It was kind of cute. The residents made her feel wanted.

"You work magic with these guys," Will told her teasingly as they set up the grill for the Fall Festival. The Musak Man was scheduled to play tunes from the 40s and 50s. Will was so sensitive about having music that residents recognized. Looking around at the picnic tables decorated with pumpkins and squash, she'd never been so happy. Will looked adorable working over the hot grill in a white apron and hat. He never worried about how he looked ... and that made him very hot.

Spatula in hand, he turned to her. "Happy?"

Hugging him, she nodded. "Very." Could life get any better than this?

Just then a surge of people flooded through the french doors from the main room. Will waved to them. "Here come the folks from the St. Joe Senior Center. We invited them for the day, but I never heard back. Guess they took me up on it.'" He glanced at the empty serving trays. "We'll need more food."

Diana broke away. "I'll run in and get more burgers and fries from Maria, okay?"

When she reached the kitchen, the cook was already pulling cases from the freezer. "I'll just take these burgers and hot dogs out to Will. Could you watch the fries?"

"Sure, no problem." Diana had watched Maria do this a hundred times, and she peeked into the bubbling oil. Looked like they'd need more than this. Cold air blasted her when she yanked the freezer open. Slitting open the bag with a knife, she hoisted the icy sack on one shoulder, just as she'd seen Maria do. Diana was positioning it over the open vat when the heavy bag shifted. Fries poured out in one icy mass.

The bubbling oil hissed and erupted like a volcano, spitting fiercely. Diana screamed when the pain seared her arm and face.

~.~

Harold came stumbling toward Will, waving his arms. This couldn't be good. "What's up?" He steadied the older man with his hands. Harold's lips worked but he could hardly get the words out. "Diana, she's hurt. You gotta come fast. She's hurt real bad."

Will dropped the spatula and ran. A couple of the aides fell in behind him. He heard Diana's screams before he saw her, and his heart nearly stopped beating. When he reached the kitchen, she was sobbing, working the faucet at the sink, and trying to get her face under the cold stream. One look at the oil on the floor and his heart contracted.

"Sweetheart. Hold it. Ease it back." She could blow the skin right off her arm. His first aid training had taught him that much.

Jan arrived. "Call 9-1-1," Will murmured. Ripping a dish towel from the counter, he soaked it in cold water and applied it to her face. "There, there, sweetheart. It'll be all right."

"I wanted to help," she sobbed, breaking his heart. "I only wanted to help. Oh, Will, my face."

## Chapter 14

*Please let this be a nightmare.* But it wasn't. Diana's face and arm throbbed with pain. And she'd done this to herself. Will wouldn't wait for the ambulance. Thank God he bundled her into his car and drove her to the hospital in Michigan City. Holding cold compresses to her face and arm, she fought the tears and battled total panic.

In the ER, the staff took over and her last glimpse of Will showed a man on the edge. And she'd brought him to this point. How could she ever have been so foolish? When she told the nurses what had happened, they exchanged a look. "What?" she asked. "Am I totally stupid?"

"It's still barbecue time," one woman finally said. "Almost the season when people dunk a whole turkey into hot oil. We see this a lot."

Then the doctor bustled in, quick and efficient. Gave directives to the nurses and tore a prescription off a pad. Although the nurses dressed the wound and gave her painkillers, Diana's arm and hand screamed with pain. This wasn't going to be a short fix. The arm was one thing. She could always wear long sleeves. But her face?

"You're lucky," the second nurse told her when they were alone. "Hardly anything on that cheek. I've seen a lot worse."

Diana turned her blurred vision to the plaid privacy curtain. No doubt the plaid had been pretty once. Fresh and spotless. Now a rip in the upper corner marred the surface. A tear dribbled slowly down her right cheek.

"Would you like some water?" the nurse asked.

"No, I'm fine."

But she wasn't. Her pulsing left cheek told her how terrible she looked, all bandaged up. She'd been showing off, proving herself part of the team. Totally stupid.

"How are you?" Will asked when they let him enter.

"I'm sure I'll be fine."

The glib words might work with the nurse but Will knew her better. "No, I mean how do you *feel?*"

"Oh, Will," she groaned. She didn't want to talk about how she felt. Didn't want him to see her like this.  "Go back to the care center. The party's still going on and you should be there."

"Don't be silly. I'm staying." He settled into the blue plastic chair next to the bed. "As soon as they discharge you, I'll take you home. Should I call someone in your family?"

Diana gave a sharp jerk of her head. "No. My grandmother and aunt would both freak out."

Will shot her a strange look. Right. His super supportive, perfect family would be there for him as fast as they could make it from Beanblossom.

When would the pain pills take hold? Her nerve endings felt shredded. Grabbing a handful of the crisp white sheet, she tried again. "I don't want to worry Grandma Kit. She'd want to come up, and there's no need for that." The thought of her grandmother and Aunt Ethel trekking up Highway 31 in their ancient Saturn terrified her. Now, that was something to worry about.

Will squeezed her right hand. "You're so independent. So brave. But you're not alone in this."

"I know, Will. And I appreciate your support." She patted his hand to reassure him.

"I feel guilty as hell. If I hadn't mentioned that we needed more food, if I'd stopped you from running back into the kitchen..."

Slipping her hand from his grasp, she pushed away. "Don't. How could you know I'd do something that stupid? My poor judgment is to blame." The words mocked her. She seemed to hop from one mistake to another. The last time, she'd wound up dating a married man. Now she'd destroyed the one good thing she'd inherited from her mother. Her looks. In the past, she could always count on her appearance.

Why wouldn't he leave? While they waited together, she felt imprisoned in the closed area that was too bright, had a lot of scary machines and smelled like medicine.

Eventually she was discharged. A pearl gray dawn greeted them as they drove up an empty Red Arrow Highway. Along the road, the yellow and red leaves were stripped from the trees. The only greenery was provided by pine trees, and everything else looked so bleak. Once home, Will set her up on the sofa with a TV remote. "I think you should move in with me for a while." His blue eyes swam with concern.

"Absolutely not."

"Please, let me take care of you."

Her throat felt like a grapefruit was wedged in it. "I can handle it, Will."

She used to love feeling his eyes on her, but now his constant attention annoyed her. When he reached over to brush a lock of hair from her eyes, she grabbed his hand. "Please stop." He winced and she loosened her hold. The poor guy looked like he didn't know what to do and she felt awful. Will Applegate—the administrator who set protocols following state and national guidelines—was at a loss. She desperately wanted to come to terms with the accident on her own, the way she'd always handled everything. Finally, Will left.

Alone at last, Diana fell into a deep sleep and dreamed she was caught in a hall of mirrors. Distortions laughed at her, the faces twisted. When she woke up, her hoodie clung to her body, damp with perspiration.

Thank goodness her shop was closed on Monday. Getting up, she dragged herself to the refrigerator but when she opened the door, the cold air made her wounds throb. Slamming it shut, she searched her cupboards until she found a can of baked beans. But she couldn't work the opener with one hand. In the end, she ended up eating white bread, dry and tasteless. Agonizing, she wondered if she'd chased Will away.

When he rang the bell that evening, she felt so glad. Sitting next to her, Will filled her in. "I talked to Rachel. She's going to cover some hours for you. Chili too."

"Chili? But Will..."

He started to reach for her hand but she tucked them both into her lap. "Ignacio's vegetable business has slowed down with the change in the weather," Will explained slowly. "They have tons of cousins here to help. Chili insisted she has time. You just take care of yourself, okay? That's what she told me. Well, it sounded something like that." A shy grin teased his lips, as if he were inviting her to see the humor. But she didn't.

"Thank you." The shop had to remain open. She needed the revenue and should be grateful. But she didn't like to accept help from anyone.

Whipping out his phone, Will pulled up his calendar. "Let's see. We have an appointment with your doctor tomorrow."

"You called Patty Jordan?"

"Yes, the ER doc said you should be checked out by your physician."

Was this man amazing or what? "You're so sweet, Will. I didn't even hear him say that."

"Totally understandable. That's why I'm here." The kiss on her forehead sent warm comfort coursing through her.

"Will, about the Sunday dances. Can you tell Jan I won't be there? Not right now."

"Sure thing. She'll understand but you will be missed." Turning her slightly, Will began to massage her shoulders. "You're so tight, Diana. Does this feel good?"

"Don't stop. Please." *And don't leave. Don't let me be stupid and push you away.* His thumbs worked at the tense knots until he was satisfied and moved to another muscle. "You're really good at this."

"Probably feel even better with warm oil," he whispered close to her ear.

Desire pooled in her lap with liquid heat. How incredible. Just when she thought she'd never feel desirable again. But when his lips brushed her neck, she pulled away. No way was she getting into anything physical right now.

"Just checking my patient," Will teased.

"Sure. Right. Back to the Sunday dances. You understand, don't you?" She just couldn't face anyone right now. But that massage had felt mighty good.

Will left a short time later. She needed time to process, and maybe he saw that. Seemed like ages since she'd dare imagine a future for her and Will. Those were the days when he greeted her with, "Hi, beautiful."

The next day, Patty Jordan examined her burns. Diana really liked Dr. Jordan. With her athletic walk and snappy manner, she exuded confidence. When she peeled back the bandages, she looked over the damage thoughtfully. Then she taught Diana how to care for the injuries. "You'll need your...friend out there to help you with the bandaging at first."

Patty was having trouble defining Will, sitting in the waiting room against his objections.

"I think I can manage."

Lips pursed, Patty fingered the stethoscope around her neck. "He's worried about you. Always helps to have some support."

"I know that, but right now? I want to handle this myself."

Diana still hadn't asked the most important question. "Am I going to have s-scars?"

Bless her heart, Patty didn't glance away. "This will take time. Try not to imagine the worst. Let's just see how things heal."

"Do you want me to take you into Chicago?" Will asked on the way home. "Loyola has a good burn center."

*Heck yes.* But she couldn't do that to him. All that traveling back and forth. The thought of being with strange doctors in a city where she'd been humiliated just didn't feel good. Besides, her insurance was an HMO, and a Chicago hospital would be out of network. No, she wanted to stay with Patty Jordan's quiet confidence. "That's not necessary, Will, and I don't want to take you away from work."

"Jan is filling in for me." They'd reached her house and he parked. Turning, he searched her face, and she shrank from the scrutiny while a cold wind buffeted the car.

"Don't." Will put a hand gently on her arm. "Please don't pull away."

"I'm not. It's just that, you don't have to do all this."

"Oh, yes, I do. I want to." His eyes overflowed with compassion. She'd seen this expression so many times, only then it was directed at Luanne or one of the residents who needed his care so badly.

"You're not responsible. You don't have to take charge. I'd like some private time. Dr. Jordan said this would heal. That the burns might leave some lightly discolored spots, but I'll be fine." Those weren't Patty's exact words and maybe Will knew that.

"This isn't about responsibility, Diana. This is about...love." Even he looked surprised by his words. "I love you, Diana. You're all I think about."

*Not now.* Uncomfortable, she backed against the side door until the handle bit into her back. Sure, she'd hoped he'd say these words someday...but not when she was like, well, this.

"Maybe what we had before was physical attraction," she finally said. The accident had changed all that.

"That's crazy, Diana. You couldn't really believe that." His chin squared. "Trust me, I know how I feel."

This was not how she'd pictured it. Sure, she'd been cherishing similar thoughts. Will Applegate was the real deal. Caring, kind and hot. But now?

"This is where you say, I love you too." His eyes blazed.

Nausea churned in her empty stomach. "But I can't." He was on her left side. No helping that when he drove. Nervous, she pulled a hank of hair over her bandaged left cheek. "I have a lot to work through."

Jaws clenched, he looked beside himself. "All right. You need time. But I'm here, whenever you need me."

She'd heard him say these words before at the facility and they left her cold. He was trained for situations like this and was treating her like one of his residents.

"Thank you, Will." She cracked open her door and gave it a heave with her right hand.

"Let me get that." Jumping out, he came around to help her. The path to her door felt long. The black-eyed Susans that had been so bright and beautiful in August were now shriveled sticks.

Silence shrouded them when they climbed the steps. Inside her mind a tiny voice clamored, telling Diana to bury herself in Will's arms, accept the help and love he offered. But she couldn't. Not at this stage, when she didn't know how she'd end up. It wouldn't be fair.

"Want me to call Brewster's and pick up a pizza later?" he asked, playing with the keys in his hand.

She shook her head. "Not hungry, but thanks." Why hadn't she gotten her keys out in the car?

"Everything I've read on the Internet says you have to eat a lot of protein to create new cells."

"I'm not your patient, Will."

A nerve twitched in his cheek.

# Chapter 15

Now she'd hurt him. The disappointment in his face twisted something deep inside. "I'm sorry, Will. You've been so sweet. Could you go to Clancy's and grab something from the deli? You know, easy to eat?" The thought of facing people and answering questions terrified her.

He was at the door in two seconds. "Sure. Be right back."

"And Will? Could I ask you one more thing?"

Eyes bright with his mission, he pivoted.

"Could you leave it at the back door?"

His smile collapsed. "Sure. Fine."

"It's just that I have to take a nap and..." *And I'm a total mess.*

Lifting his hands palms up, he said, "You don't have to explain. Whatever you want, Diana."

"Thank you. I really appreciate everything you're doing."

Inside, she didn't get far. That sofa looked so inviting, pillows punched in all the right spots. Shrugging out of her jacket, she slumped onto the soft corduroy. Hoping for sleep, she just wanted to forget. When she woke up, it was pitch black outside. Took a minute to figure out where she was. Then the dull pain reminded her. With a sigh, she leveraged herself up and dragged herself to the back door for the groceries. The bag handles bit into her skin.

Served her right for being such a butthead. Wrenching the refrigerator open, she stacked the plastic containers inside.

Why was it so hard for her to accept help? The rest of the week was spent in front of the TV, where she could lose herself in shows about abandoned storage sheds and junk pickers. As the hours slipped by, she had to remind herself to eat. Changing the dressing was no picnic, and she tried not to look. But how could she help it? The wounds were seriously ugly, but they didn't show any of the red flags Dr. Jordan had mentioned.

Will called every day, and she always found an excuse why coming over was a bad idea. Shaking her depression over what had happened, and the uncertainty of her future, was almost more than she could handle. But when Saturday rolled around, she relented. This was silly. She was punishing both of them. The pizza he brought from Brewster's was the first good thing she'd eaten all week, spinach and roasted red peppers with lots of cheese. His arm around her, they watched TV. When he began to ply her with questions—how do the burns feel, has she been putting the ointment on—Diana gave an obvious yawn. Will got the message and soon left.

The following day she visited Hippy Chick and found the shop neat as a pin. Rachel and Chili had done a great job. When the afternoon rolled around, she wondered if the residents at Gull Harbor Care Center missed her. About now, they should be whirling around the dance floor. Missing the group terribly, she was tempted to drive over there. But she didn't want to frighten them with these bandages. She buried herself in posting invoices that afternoon.

Going back to work the next Tuesday was a relief. Rachel stopped in just before closing. "Wow" was her only response when she saw Diana. "Does it hurt?"

"Not that much." No, the pain was buried deep inside, in a place Diana could not reach.

Book club was coming up. "I haven't had time to read the book," she told Phoebe when she called that evening to remind her. Her scalp itched like crazy, and she poked at it with a pencil while they talked.

"What does that have to do with anything, hon?" Phoebe chortled. "We hardly ever talk about the book. You know that. Carolyn will pick you up. It'll do you good."

"Well, I'll see." Trying to grapple with the phone and the pencil, she dropped both.

"What's going on over there, girlfriend?" Phoebe asked when Diana came back to the conversation.

"Sorry, I was just messing with my hair. It's driving me crazy." Her attempt at a laugh failed miserably.

"I'll be right over."

"Don't you dare." Let Phoebe see her like this?

She heard Phoebe suck in a deep breath. "Diana, I'm coming with all my supplies. As a friend. You don't have to change. You don't have to put on makeup. This is me, Phoebe, and I want to help you."

Okay, now she felt really foolish. Her resistance folded. "Great. See you soon."

Besides, what was her option? Ask Will to shampoo her hair? A week ago, that might have felt sexy. Now? No way. She was holding him off again, not answering his texts. Oh, she knew how frustrating this was. Their evening phone calls were a lifesaver for her. She loved hearing his voice, but she didn't want to face him, not after last Saturday. Besides, she'd liked that shoulder massage way too much. No way was she getting intimate until these injuries looked a heck of a lot better.

So she was soldiering on alone. Washing her hair with one hand had been a disaster. The spray had shot all over the kitchen. She cleaned off her counter next to the sink and waited.

True to her word, Phoebe soon bustled in, bringing a carton of her homemade minestrone soup. "First we eat then I do your hair, okay?" Phoebe cackled. "If you don't eat, you can just live with your hair, got it?"

The threat made Diana smile. But her left cheek protested.

"So how's the shop coming?" Phoebe asked as she ladled steaming soup into bowls. The aroma awakened Diana's hunger.

"You mean beside the fact that Rachel looked at me like I was Frankenstein?"

"You don't look that bad. No visible stitches holding you together." Phoebe opened a bag of oyster crackers.

The air seemed to lighten. Dark moods never lingered around Phoebe. Lifting a spoon, Diana started to sip. "Hey, this stuff's good."

Perched on a stool, Phoebe waved a spoon at her. "You'll get over this. Besides, who's perfect? That's not life. Perfect would be boring."

"Maybe." She'd have to think about that. Diana had spent her life aiming for perfect. Her mother had a little dressing table with a flowered skirt. She'd spread out her cosmetics on the tabletop. After she took off, the dressing table became Diana's. Her grandmother bought special lamps for it.

When the soup was finished, Phoebe assembled her arsenal of products on the kitchen counter and went to work. She had Diana bend forward while she shampooed her hair. Under Phoebe's capable fingers, she groaned. "This feels like heaven and smells wonderful."

"Thanks. The shampoo is my own concoction, lots of lavender and shea butter. Think I might market it."

"Heck, I would." Even the conditioner smelled heavenly. "What are you going to call it?"

"Orgasm," Phoebe said with no hesitation.

When Diana laughed, the bandages on her face pulled at her skin. "Stop," she said. "No more of that. Laughing hurts my face." Still, inside the laugh felt really good.

Wrapping a towel around Diana's head, Phoebe stepped back. "Didn't they tell you to take those bandages off once in a while? When my brother got burned working at a gas station he gave it some air."

"Yes, every three or four days and I do. But I sure don't want them off all the time."

By the time Phoebe gathered her supplies together to leave, Diana felt like a new person.

"Carolyn will pick you up tomorrow for book club," Phoebe said at the door. "Six forty-five. You be ready or I'm coming to get you myself."

"Oh, I don't know." Was she ready for that raucous group?

"No excuses now. They're all asking about you." Giving Diana a careful hug, Phoebe said, "Remember, we're all in this together. They want to know you're all right."

The words eased their way into Diana's heart. How lucky was she to have friends like this? "Thanks. Truth is, I'm getting cabin fever."

"You know this group will blow the doors right off," Phoebe said with one of her sassy grins. Joking around, Diana had forgotten for a second that she was scarred for life. Her friend left. Feeling better, Diana straightened up, tossing deli containers and junk mail into the black plastic trash bag hanging on her right arm.

Then she passed the mirror and that horrible bandage stared back at her. Her skin had been so smooth. But there wasn't much she could do about it. What did Grandma Kit always say? "No use crying over spilt milk." She was making a life for herself here in Gull Harbor. The past few days, people had shown her nothing but support. Time to look forward instead of back.

The following evening, she pulled on her jeans and an aqua hoodie with bell sleeves that could fit over the bandages on her left arm. She'd planned to change her dressing the next day but one glance in the mirror and the plan changed. Her generous use of eye makeup showed on her bandage.

With only fifteen minutes before Carolyn arrived, she rushed to set out her supplies. Diana was peeling the dressing from her arm when the bell rang. *Rats.*

"Sorry I'm a little early," Carolyn said when Diana opened the door. "I stopped at Clancy's but the shopping didn't take that long."

Closing the door on the chilly November breeze, Diana said, "I decided to change my dressing. Actually I could use some help." It wasn't easy to apply the tape with only one hand.

"Sure. No problem." Slinging her shoulder purse onto the sofa, Carolyn followed Diana to the counter where fresh gauze and tape were laid out, along with the ointment.

"I hope this doesn't gross you out."

"I'm a big girl, Diana. And I teach high school, remember? You wouldn't believe what the seniors pull their last day of class. Does it hurt?"

"A little." The bandage stuck to the fine hair on her arm. What hurt more was just looking at the huge blisters that had formed. "Ugly, huh?"

"Yeah, but it's temporary."

"Don't know yet. It'll never be the same. *I'll* never be the same."

After rinsing the soap from her hands, Carolyn twisted the water off. "Nothing ever is. Just as long as the important things stay the same, like the people in your life. How has Will been through all this?"

"He's been great. Wants to help with everything." Diana blew out a breath, and Carolyn handed her a clean wet towel. First she blotted the skin with warm water. Then she went over it with a dry towel, being oh so careful. "Look, I know this could be worse. I could have been caught in a terrorist bomb blast or crushed in a hurricane. My house could have burned down or flooded with river mud. Those disasters happen around the world, and I feel terrible for the people involved. But..."

Okay, so she was turning into a whiner.

"This is your personal disaster," Carolyn said softly. "And I totally understand, but you're not allowed to make it into a catastrophe. Got it?"

Diana exhaled. "Got it." Carolyn's sensible approach was definitely what she needed right now. She applied the ointment carefully, and then Carolyn helped her tape on the gauze.

Her face was next. The cheek stung as Carolyn slowly peeled back the tape. "Not bad. You're lucky."

Hope in her heart, Diana dashed into the bathroom. The reflection in the mirror crushed her. "It's huge." Like her arm, the skin had blistered.

Coming up behind her, Carolyn frowned. "The half-moon is dime-size. Some people would pay for a tattoo like that."

"On their face?" Diana sputtered. "Come on, Carolyn. I look totally disgusting." Her hands shook as she went through the cleansing ritual, anxious to have the burn covered again. From the half-moon, as Carolyn called it, three small dots dripped in a graduated line.

"Burns take time, right?" Carolyn said softly. "Didn't you ever splash yourself with grease or oil when you were growing up?"

"No. My grandmother didn't even want me near the stove. I never learned to cook."

"If you can read, you can cook." There was that common sense again. "Anyway, I spattered myself plenty growing up. You learn to have respect for oil and fats. The scars fade."

"Wish I'd known." She tucked the gauze and ointment in a drawer. No using fussing about this any longer. "Have I made us late?"

"Nope. Come on. Let's go." Waiting at the front door, Carolyn jiggled the doorknob.

"Do you think I look all right?" Diana looked down at her jeans. Carolyn was wearing a mini skirt over tights. "Those black boots are to die for."

"You look fine. Sometimes you sound like Mercedes. This is Gull Harbor, not Manhattan or Chicago. But you might want a jacket over that hoodie."

Diana snatched a green quilted vest from the closet, and Carolyn helped her pull it on.

"What you need is a night with the girls," Carolyn said as they headed up the highway to Phoebe's place in the woods.

"I think you're right." Getting out felt good. Work was one thing but this was fun with friends.

Laughter and conversation met them when they burst through the door at Phoebe's. "You came!" Chili called out. "See I told you, this is one tough *chica!*"

Nothing had changed with the group. They were rowdy and fun. Sarah had brought a baby book, and Kate was looking through names. This early, Kate didn't know if the baby was a boy or a girl, but Sarah was already planning a baby shower. Plans were going full steam ahead.

As the evening unfolded, Diana relaxed. How amazing. Her book buddies accepted her just as she was and didn't pester her with questions.

But it wasn't the girls Diana was worried about, it was Will. The sweet, steady man who hadn't called her beautiful since that terrible Sunday.

# Chapter 16

By mid-November, the bandages were off Diana's arm. But the pink scars itched, and her arm and hand looked like they'd been splashed with Pepto Bismol. She wore long sleeves now, with ruffles if you could find them.

Her face was another thing entirely, and Diana left that bandage in place, religiously changing the dressings and hoping for a miracle. The half-moon plus three small dots beneath her left cheekbone were still horrifying. "The markings will fade," Dr. Harris, the dermatologist that Dr. Jordan had recommended, told her on her last visit. "There might be a scar, Diana. But nothing major. It will shrink and fade with time."

She left the office feeling relieved but still kept Will at arm's length. When he suggested going up to St. Joe for dinner or to the restaurant at Tabor Hill Winery, she always had an excuse. No way was she appearing in public or facing Will across a table. At work, her hands were always on display, and she learned to live with it. She kept her face bandaged.

Desperate to find a solution, she even made a trip to Phoebe's Place one evening. Sitting her down in the black vinyl chair, Phoebe had fussed until Diana wanted to scream. "Nothing is going to work," she finally groaned.

Squeezing Diana's shoulders, Phoebe made eye contact in the mirror. "Look, you are a beautiful woman. Sure, I can cut your hair into something shorter that will swing more, but it will never cover your cheek, darlin'. You're going to have to learn to live with this. It's not as bad or big as you think."

Diana gently fingered the bandage. "Darn thing itches like crazy."

"Do you mind if I take a peek?" Phoebe asked softly.

"Okay," Diana whispered, settling back in resignation.

Padding to the front door in her flip-flops, Phoebe changed the sign to Closed before returning to peel back the bandage. Diana studied her reaction. Phoebe's full lips formed a plump bow. "You probably don't want to hear this, but it's not bad and could be sexy."

"*Sexy*. What are you smoking?" Sometimes Phoebe was totally off the wall.

"Why not let this baby have some air? I think what's itching is the latex from the tape. Did you ever have trouble wearing Band-Aids when you were growing up?"

Diana thought back to the Sleeping Beauty Band-Aids Grandma Kit bought for her when she fell on the playground. The ones that drove her crazy. Phoebe could be right. Diana skated one hand lightly over the angry raised areas that bracketed the actual scar. "That might help but... " The thought of exposing this ugly mess made her stomach churn.

"What did the doctor say?"

"She said it would fade in time."

Phoebe shook her head. "You don't want to mess with that darlin'. We gotta learn to play the hand life deals us."

But Diana's face had been the one area of her life where she felt like she held a full house. The one thing that worked for her.

The smile faded from the hairdresser's face. "Look, lady, where is that sassy gumption I've seen in you? You are gorgeous, and that isn't to going to change."

"Oh, I think it already has." Diana thought back to the "Hi, beautiful" that she never heard anymore from Will.

"I have a cousin who does summer stock up in Saugatuck." Phoebe tapped a finger against her lower lip. "Mickey uses some kind of heavy makeup she swears will cover anything. One of the actors has a port wine stain on his face, and he uses it offstage too."

Hope fluttered in Diana's chest. "Really? Where can I buy it?"

"I'll find out, but I still don't think you need it. Shit happens, Diana. And there's nothing we can do about it." Her eyes turned distant, like she was thinking of the past. Phoebe never talked about herself. She was too busy fixing everyone else's problems.

Driving back to her bungalow that night, Diana tried to put the whole thing in perspective. Thank goodness Phoebe had noticed the welts. Maybe latex free bandages would help. She wasn't ready to take the covering off entirely.

November darkness shrouded the road ahead. How she wished she could dial summer back to those first carefree days with Will. But Phoebe was right. Some things you just can't change.

When Will called later that night about the weekend, she put him off.

"I'm hosting my book group next week," she told him. "Haven't read a page and have to look over appetizer recipes. So sorry." How lame was that? He knew she hardly ever cooked.

Will must be watching football. She could hear a crowd roar in the background and wished she was there with him, eating popcorn the way they had during Monday Night Movies. "Please don't push me away," Will finally said.

"I'm not," she said softly. Oh, how she wanted to feel his comforting arms around her. But not when she still looked like this.

"I miss you. Don't let what happened separate us."

His words clutched her heart and twisted. "I miss you too, but I need some time, okay?"

"Your looks don't matter to me, Diana. We have so much more than that."

She didn't believe that for a minute. Still, she squirmed with uncertainty. "You're a good man, Will, but I just..."

The hiss of his breath cut across her nerve endings. "I never should have let you go back into that kitchen. We had to declare the accident, you know. State will be back."

That put a whole new spin on it. "Oh, Will. I'm so sorry." Had she ruined his professional life too?

"It's all right. I can handle the state." He paused. "But I can't handle not seeing you. I want us to be fine."

What could she say? They'd been so good together before the accident. He'd accepted her past mistake, even made her see it differently. But now this.

After they hung up, she picked up her electronic reader. Three pages later, she couldn't remember what she'd read. Who would she be without her good looks? The question haunted her.

Growing up, life hadn't been easy. She'd been teased plenty about not having a father. Things only got worse after her mother skipped town. "The girls are jealous because you're so pretty. You know I don't give out false compliments," her grandmother told her, braiding her hair. "Pretend it doesn't bother you a bit. You're going to have a bigger life than Monica Lewis or Betty Sue Page."

The very next day, Monica and her friends cornered Diana in the bathroom and snipped off her braids. Junior high had been the pits.

Furious, her grandfather had visited every parent. The bullying stopped but the friendships never developed. Well, those girls back in Newtown were now saddled with a slew of kids and husbands who hung out at the Dew Drop Inn every night. Diana was the girl who'd gone to school in Indianapolis, the Big City, as everyone called it, as if there wasn't another one in the entire country. Jaws must have dropped when her grandmother told everyone about Diana's store in Chicago.

But now this. She'd survived her past. Would she let this defeat her now?

Lying on the sofa that Saturday night, she tried to concentrate on the mystery for book group. She read the words but nothing registered. Finally, she gave up. Her body and soul ached for Will, and what they'd had before this happened.

Under the stark light of the bathroom mirror, she ran the flat of her fingers over the pink splotch on her cheek. The welts were going down. Afraid to risk anything, she bathed the cheek in cool water and then dried the scar and covered it with ointment. What would happen if she didn't bandage it? Maybe it was time to find out.

Over the next couple days, the swelling seemed to ease. The half-moon remained. If customers noticed it, they said nothing.

The night of book group, she heard the girls giggling on her front porch before they even rang the bell. Diana threw open the door.

"How's the patient?" Kate asked, giving her a hug.

"Guess I'll live."

"I'd say so. Atta girl." Pulling back, Kate studied the burn. "Sorry that happened, Diana."

Chili crowded Kate out of the doorway. "*Ah, caramba. Pobrecita!*" She almost choked Diana with a ferocious hug then held her at arm's length. "Not so bad, eh?"

"I think she looks sexy with that half-moon," Phoebe chimed in, bringing up the rear.

"Trust me, I do not feel sexy." But it felt good to talk about it, just like taking off the bandages.

"How are you feeling, Kate?" she asked, hustling into the kitchen area and bringing back the brie wrapped in phyllo dough, still warm from the oven. What a relief to find this easy recipe on the Internet, her kind of cookbook.

"Tired." Kate fell back on the sofa. "Mercedes came into the office last week and found me sound asleep on the plans for the Holiday Walk. Guess I was snoring." They all laughed.

Returning to the kitchen, Diana grabbed the bowl of bread rounds. "That's normal, right?"

The bell rang and Sarah charged in, her hair a mass of frizzy curls. "What did I miss?"

"Me complaining about feeling tired," Kate said with a yawn. "And this nausea. When does this stop? I can't even look at a cheese crown. That's serious."

The bell chimed again and Carolyn stepped inside. "Hey, how are you doing, lady?" She hugged Diana. "Need any help?"

"Want to open the wine?"

"Excellent." How lucky she was to have this group. Carolyn followed her into the kitchen area, where Diana handed her the opener.

Carolyn's eyes skimmed her face. None of the women looked at her arm. "Is it improving?"

"Yes, but it's not disappearing," Diana whispered.

"Gotcha." Carolyn got to work on the wine.

As usual, they discussed the book for about fifteen minutes and then moved on. The conversation focused on the expectant mother, which suited Diana just fine.

"And what about you, Diana?" Sarah finally asked. "How are you doing?"

Setting her wine glass on the coffee table, Diana swept back the hair over her cheek. "Getting used to it. What do you think?"

"Looks like it's coming along," Kate said.

"Burns probably fade." Sarah reached for more bread and Brie. "My cousin burned his arm, and in a few years time, you could hardly see it."

*A few years?* Diana cringed.

"What was Will's reaction?" Kate asked softly.

"He's being, ah, great about it." Not the time to let everyone know she didn't want to see Will. Lordy, she missed him in so many ways. It wasn't just the sex. She missed his smile. His great sense of humor. And she missed dancing with him on Sundays. Jan had called to say she could return when she was ready. She wasn't ready. Not yet.

"Will's a good guy," Chili spoke up. "He's not a man who'd feel differently."

"Oh, no. Of course not." She waved the concern away with more confidence than she felt.

"Not at all."

"No, never." Their chorus of encouragement rang in her ears. Brave words but Diana wasn't so sure. Once upon a time, Will had told her he loved her. Would he love the woman she was now?

# Chapter 17

From the streaked windows of Hippy Chick, Diana watched the freezing rain drill down on Gull Harbor. Absolutely nothing was happening. The holidays were coming and business was slow. Before the weather changed, a few women wandered in. But they were just looking. Not even Thanksgiving and people were saving their money for Christmas gifts. Kate was doing a great job with her promotions, including her Holiday Walk, planned for mid December. She couldn't wait to see Santa and his sleigh at the end of Whittaker.

"Are you coming home for Thanksgiving?" Grandma Kit had asked when she phoned.

"Wish I could, Grandma. But that's my busy time. Maybe after Christmas?" She couldn't let her grandmother see her like this.

"Oh honey, of course. Don't worry about Ethel and me. We're fine. I may not be able to work down at Hope Mission anymore, but church is having a big party..." and she was off. Grandma Kit had always been resilient. She would never lay a guilt trip on Diana for not making it home for the holiday.

The rain was turning to snow. She sure hoped the salt trucks got out. The ring of the landline was a pleasant distraction.

"Hey Diana. It's me." She sank onto the stool behind the

counter. How she missed him. "I'm picking you up, and we're going for ice cream."

"But it's freezing outside."

"All the more reason to get out."

"I'm fine. Really."

"I'm not." His sigh made guilt stir in her chest. "I want to see you."

*See* her? See her scars? "I miss you too." By holding him at bay, she was just delaying the inevitable. If her face was going to change things between them, she wanted to know now.

"I'll pick you up at your house at seven."

"Where are we going?" She glanced out at the bleak street.

"You'll see."

His playful tone made her smile. "Always so mysterious."

"I promise you'll like it." The words stoked a heat deep inside. She knew what she really wanted and it wasn't ice cream. Then she touched her face and felt the stiff half-moon. She'd have to hustle him right to the car so they didn't end up in the bedroom. "All right. I'll watch for you."

Closing up shop that day didn't take long. She'd had plenty of time the past few days to fold, straighten, and clean the glass counters until they sparkled. Once home, she ate a quick frozen dinner and then surveyed her closet. The cold weather made her choice easy. Her violet sweater had a deep turtleneck that she could tug up around her face. Black jeans were a staple, as was her black leather jacket. The knee-high boots were easy to slip on.

Now for hair and makeup. Phoebe had come through for her

with the website for theater cosmetics, and Diana placed an order. But the pancake makeup hadn't arrived yet and that was a problem.

Facing herself in the mirror, she played with her hair. Definitely needed bangs. "Sorry, Phoebe, I know you might not approve but I'm short on time." She began to snip, and hair showered into the sink. Wasn't too hard to shape the bangs longer on the sides. Not perfect but not bad.

When Will rang the bell, she was ready but her stomach churned with anxiety. Hand on the doorknob, she sucked in a breath. The hammering of her heart told her just how much she cared about Will. This wasn't Bryce, whose callous dismissal disillusioned her those last weeks with him. No, this was sweet Will.

She loved him. Her heart thudded in her chest. Yep, the L word.

"Diana? You in there?" Will rang the bell again. Now or never. She opened the door. How it tore at her heart to see that tentative smile on his face, like he didn't know if he'd be welcome.

"Hi, Will."

She was already in his arms when he said, "Hey, beautiful."

Diana stiffened. Oh, she'd wanted to hear those words, but now they did sound strange.

He pulled back. "Anything wrong?"

"No, nothing." Twisting from his arms, she grabbed her jacket and followed him to his car.

Seemed like forever since they'd taken a trek up Red Arrow. His hand fell to her knee so naturally. But those carefree dates in the

Mustang, with her hair blowing in the warm breeze, were past. Now Will drove his sensible white sedan.

"No Mustang?"

He shook his head. "They're predicting snow."

"Ah, protecting your pride and joy?"

"You got that right. I take care of things and people I care about, remember?" His voice trailed off. "Or I try."

She looked over at his clenched jaw. "You did, Will. You did."

"Like hell. Diana, I..."

"Shush, shush." How long would he blame himself?

Salt had been sprinkled over the road, and it rattled against the tires. The headlights bounced off the slick road. Was ice forming as the temperature dropped? Summer seemed so long ago. In the car, she couldn't keep Will on her right side and she felt exposed. Dry heat blasted from the vents, and she could practically feel the scar tighten. She tugged at the collar of her leather jacket. When they got wherever they were headed, she'd find a ladies' room and apply more ointment on her scar to keep it supple.

She squirmed in her seat. "Where are we going?" The rain had stopped but the car was buffeted by strong winds. Winter was closing in on them.

"Almost there." Dusk was falling when he pulled into a place called the Beach Bucket.

"I've never been here." Through a large glass window, she saw a man turning out the lights.

"Damn, I should have called. He must be shutting down early because of the crummy weather." Jumping from the car, Will hurried her into the shop where the owner was packing up. "Ready to close?"

"Not quite. How can I help you?"

The smell of warm chocolate filled the air, a lot more enticing than the case of frozen ice cream. "Is that hot chocolate?" Scanning the area, she ran smack into a huge mirror. The pink scar screamed at her. Had the cold air made it darker? She tugged at the deep turtleneck.

Will walked over to a tall, stainless dispenser. "Got any left?"

"Help yourself. I'm about to throw it out."

"I'll take you up on that." Hands on the display case, Will studied the huge containers of ice cream. "I'll have the maple bacon ice cream in the hot chocolate." He turned to her.

"Um, pistachio?" She tried to focus. The man plopped a scoop of ice cream in each cup and handed them to Will and Diana.

"Hot chocolate is in the dispenser against the wall." The man pointed and Will did the honors.

"Is this your secret recipe?" she teased while a mouthwatering aroma rose from the concoctions he was creating.

"Yep. Wait and see." Will handed her a cup. The warmth felt good in  her hands. "Want to sit in the car?"

"Sure." Braving a ferocious wind, they said good-bye, pushed through the door and climbed back into the car. Will turned on the motor and the heat blasted. Her skin would dry but she pushed the worry away. For a few minutes, they sipped and gulped. It felt so good to be with him. When Will ended up with whipped cream on his nose, she swiped it off. They sat and talked about nothing in particular. After they finished, he gathered the cups and braved the wind to dump them in the trash. He dodged back inside, bringing the cold air with him. But the chill didn't last when he kissed her.

"God, how I've missed you," he murmured.

"Me too." But while their kisses kicked up a notch, her left cheek began to itch. "Think I'm getting overheated."

His chuckle stirred something low in her belly. "You aren't alone with that."

"Oh, I didn't mean that."

"Well, I did." Eyes sultry, he brushed her lips until she couldn't resist. He tasted so good, like hot chocolate and bacon. For just a few minutes, they were back in the early fall when every day felt like a gift.

Now it wasn't summer. A cold wind whistled outside and it felt like a quarter was pasted to her cheek.

Finally, they pulled apart. "What are your plans for Thanksgiving?" Will asked.

~.~

Now what? Will felt Diana stiffen. Tugging at the neckline of her sweater, she looked away. How could he help her see nothing had changed? The marks on her face would be shrugged off by a guy, even considered macho. But it was different with a woman, and he felt terrible that he'd helped cause it. He was determined to work through this, but she sure wasn't making it easy. So far, Diana hadn't gone back to the Sunday dances. Jan kept asking about her.

"I'll probably be here for Thanksgiving," she finally said. "Kate has pulled together a promotion for a Black Friday sale, so I have to be in the store. Business has been down this month." She dropped her eyes.

"Couldn't Rachel take care of Hippy Chick for a couple days?"

Diana shook her head. "She's going into Chicago to visit her boyfriend."

A Thanksgiving Day feast was planned for the care center. But he didn't know how she would take that, kind of like returning to the scene of a crime. Besides, he wanted her to himself. "I've got an idea."

She was playing with her hair.

"Why don't I cook dinner for you?"

"Oh, Will. You don't have to do that. Aren't you going back to Beanblossom?"

"No, I always stay at the facility for holidays. Cooking this meal could be good practice." What was he saying? Any cooking he did was in the microwave.

"I don't know, Will." She pulled away.

How could he peel her from that damned door? "I don't want to be alone for Thanksgiving."

She cocked her head to one side and he held his breath, hoping she didn't overthink this. After all, he had two hundred residents ready to celebrate the holiday with him. Before, that had always been fine. Not anymore. But Diana felt so distant. He hoped putting plans on their calendars would bring them together.

"Sounds nice, Will. Thank you." Frowning, she pulled at her lower lip. "Hope I have the right pans. I may have to call my grandmother."

He wanted to whoop. "I'll take care of everything." Brave words.

"What fun." Her face had brightened.

When they reached her door that night, he stood helpless, hands at his side. Would she give some signal. She half-turned toward him. "Thank you for tonight."

Heck with this, he put his hands on her waist. "Everything okay with us, Diana?"

She hitched a shoulder. "Sure. I'm just, well, in recovery mode."

"Does it hurt?" He'd never had a burn and had no clue how she was feeling.

"Not much. Pulls a little. But this might be the best that it gets, Will. Right here." Lifting her chin, she pointed to her cheek.

He raised a hand to push back a wisp of her hair. "You know you'll always be beautiful to me."

Her eyes filled. What had he said? She stiffened when he pulled her close to cuddle on his chest. Finally, she sighed and settled in. The smell of her, the feel of her body put him on overload. When they kissed, heat surged through his body. Wanting her so badly, he let his hands wander lower. But she wasn't having it. Hands flat on his chest, Diana reared back. "I'm, ah, a little tired."

"Sure. Right." Stepping back, he knew he had to give her space. Thanksgiving was next week. They'd have that time together, and he'd make it count. He had a lot to prepare for and he wasn't thinking about food.

# Chapter 18

Diana spent Thanksgiving morning cleaning while she watched the Macy's parade on TV. Keeping busy helped keep her sane. A lot could go wrong this Thanksgiving.

What if Will looked at her in the daylight and couldn't handle it? The heavy grease paint had arrived, and she watched three YouTube videos to learn how to use it. Still, what if they got cozy and it ended up all over, well, everything? She couldn't coat her entire left arm in the stuff.

When she closed up shop on Wednesday, she'd gone straight to Clancy's for her Thanksgiving dinner supplies. Cans of green beans, mushroom soup, and cranberry sauce made an impressive pyramid on her kitchen counter. She'd rearranged them at least four times before Will rang the bell.

When Diana opened the door, Will stood clutching an enormous pan, the top covered with foil. Hair upended and cheeks flushed, he looked like a wild man. A very attractive wild man.

She threw the door wide. "That looks heavy. Don't drop it."

"I've got it. Happy Thanksgiving." When he tried to kiss her, she turned just in time. His lips landed on her right cheek, the huge bird a cold lump between them.

She glanced down. "Did you thaw it?"

"I kind of forgot and left it in the trunk all night. Think it'll be okay?" After stamping the snow from his boots, he stepped inside. "I did take it out of the plastic wrapper this morning and covered it with foil. My mother always did that."

If his mother did it that way, it must be right. "Here. Let me take that." She held out her arms.

"Absolutely not." After toeing off his boots, he shuffled toward the kitchen island. "This is too heavy for you."

Diana shut the door against a leaden sky. "Are we supposed to have snow?"

"With some accumulation." Free of his burden, he settled his eyes on her and smiled. "You look pretty."

Self-conscious, she ran a hand down the soft white cashmere sweater. "Thank you." Her hair had taken an hour to get just right.

Shrugging out of his brown leather jacket, he snatched some notes from a pocket. She was used to the administrator, the man in command. Today Will looked flustered and adorable. "What's our timeline? When should this go in the oven?"

He expected her to know this? "Soon. Right?" Grandma Kit had always handled Thanksgiving dinner. Setting the table had been Diana's assignment. Now her small, circular table held orange and brown placemats from the dollar store, along with orange napkins with napkin rings that were autumn leaves. Three wooden candleholders sat in the center. That and the cans on the counter were her contribution, along with a pumpkin pie from Mandy Klavis' bakery.

Staring at the oven, Will scratched his head. "How do I start this?"

"It's electric. I think you turn the knob."

He gave her a side-glance. "And then?"

"It goes on. You pop the bird in, right? Okay, I'm better with the microwave than a stove." How humiliating. Frozen dinners were her forte. "Maybe we should have gone out."

"I tried. Everything's closed. We can do this." He eyed the knobs on the almond-colored stove as if they were spaceship controls.

"Here. Let's try this." She pushed in the oven knob and turned it. Red lights went on. Lift-off.

"Excellent." His smile restored her confidence.

Checking his notes, he fiddled with the knob. "We might have to ramp this up a little," she heard him mutter.

"Can I peek?" She fingered the foil.

"Sure. Of course. But first, one thing." Coming up behind her, Will slipped his arms around her waist. She forgot all about the mountain of poultry on her counter. He smelled wonderfully spicy, warm and familiar. Feeling like candle wax, she leaned back on his shoulder. When he nuzzled her neck, his lips tickled. They also turned her on. Desire flared through her body. "Oh, Will."

"What is it?" Hands soft on her shoulders, Will tried to turn her, but she wasn't ready for a face-to-face.

While her feelings ebbed, she broke away. "Shouldn't we get this party going?" The kitchen drawer rattled when she yanked it open.

"Guess so." Resignation weighed his voice.

But she had to stay focused. "That is one big bird." Shuffling stuff around in the drawer, she finally found the meat thermometer Grandma Kit had given her, still in the packaging. The can opener was there too. "Is the turkey all set?"

Will stared at it woefully. "Guess so. I took it out of the bag." Misgivings curled in her stomach. Were they both out of their element?

"Where did you get that huge pan?" she asked, meeting some resistance when she tried to slide the thermometer into the bird's breast. This sure looked easier when Grandma Kit handled it.

"Clancy's. They had a pile of them."

She eyed the pan, the kind good for one meal. "My grandmother's roasting pan was big and battered with a metal rack inside."

"Right. Like my mother's." Will looked baffled. "This should work, right?"

How would she know? "Guess so. I picked up the rest of the meal." She motioned to the stacked cans. And then it hit her.

"Oh, my gosh, Will. I forgot the potatoes. I'm such an idiot."

"Hey, don't ever say that." Taking her shoulders, he gave her a little shake. "Trust me, your IQ isn't measured by whether or not you remember the potatoes. Do we have gravy?"

Will looked so darn serious, she had to laugh. They were two grown adults about to be defeated by a turkey. "Yessir. If you say so."

"Are you laughing at me?" Picking up a can opener, he waved it. "Let me show my true talents."

"Believe it or not, this is something I can do." Whisking the opener away, she worked on the cans of cranberry sauce while Will stuck the bird into the oven. The door creaked when he closed it.

"Aren't you supposed to heat the oven for a while?"

Will shrugged. "You got me. My mother usually worked on the dinner with my sister Delinda. Dad and I tended the fireplace and watched football."

She turned to him in mock horror. "Well, Will. You stinker. Thought you were the expert."

He threw her a wry smile. "Now I wish I'd paid more attention."

Coming closer, he tipped his head until his nose nudged hers. "Sorry, I don't even have a fireplace for you to tend," she whispered.

"Don't need it. We can generate plenty of heat." Nuzzling her neck, he worked up to her lips. This felt good, so good.

The first kiss had a tentative edge. Lifting one eyelid, she saw his eyes were closed. Excellent. The tension in her body released. She let his lips erase any uncertainty. Felt his hands smooth away the anxieties keeping her prickly and isolated. Today they felt just the same together. The way they'd been in September, when their love was new.

*Love.* The word simmered in her heat-fogged brain.

"What is it?" Will's eyes blinked open.

"Nothing. Nothing." She tilted her hips into his. Responding, he brought her closer until she groaned. "I really missed you."

"You did, huh?" His lips painted a trail across her cheek, halting behind one ear. Thank God for the makeup he didn't seem to notice. "Did you miss this?"

"Uh, huh." Diana quivered.

He moved lower. "How about this?"

"My neck especially."

The kissing dropped lower. "And here?"

She met his eyes. "This sweater's heavy. Can't really feel much."

Those blue eyes crinkled at the corners. "I can fix that." Cool air teased her skin when his hands tunneled under the sweater. Everything he touched turned molten.

"You're so talented." She caught one of his hands in hers. "Come on."

Smart man that he was, Will didn't resist. Her room felt dark and cool. The bungalow wasn't well insulated and tonight she was glad. "No, don't." She grabbed his hand when Will reached to turn on the seashell lamp.

"Please. Let's get through this, Diana," he whispered. "I'd like to see you."

For a second she hesitated. But after all, why did she buy this expensive makeup? Time for a test ride. "Okay."

He coaxed her with his lips. Soothed her with his hands. While he unclasped the barrette that held up her hair, she unbuttoned his shirt and worked on his belt. Oh, so gently, he lifted her cashmere sweater, and she wiggled out of her jeans. Team effort.

So nervous that she was shaking, Diana sank onto the bed. His eyes glowed in the fading light. No disgust, no recoiling. Her body calmed and the knot in her stomach loosened. When they came together, she loved the feel of his skin on hers. Breathed in his scent. Did what she could to hear him moan. After a bit, he flipped on the ceiling fan.

Here they were, just like before. Diana thought her heart would burst. Will made her feel like the most attractive woman on the earth.

The words he whispered, the way he made love to her. Nothing else mattered. Not tonight.

~.~

Will studied the whirring blades of the overhead fan. After making love, they'd both nodded off. The sex had been hot. Mind-blowing. Did this qualify as make up sex? He chuckled quietly. Whatever, it had been better than anything he'd ever experienced. Maybe love was the key to great sex.

But Diana was still skittish. Although she was in a better place by the end, he wasn't laying the love words on her just yet. She still didn't seem ready.

Asleep on her side, she pillowed her head on one hand. He brushed a wisp of hair from her face. The only thing that hurt him about the fading burns was that he'd been the cause. If not for him, she would never have been in the kitchen. But the scars weren't as bad as she thought. They didn't seem to bother her as much anymore. What a relief.

His thoughts circled back. Hands behind his head, he relived the high points of the past hour. God it had been hot. So. Damn. Hot.

Hot. Will sniffed and sat straight up. Something was burning. Kicking the sheet back, he grabbed his slacks and slowly stood up, not wanting to wake Diana.

But she lifted her head. "What is it?"

"Do you smell something?"

She drew in a breath. "The turkey. How long did we sleep?"

"I'm not sure." Damn. The floor was freezing when he sprinted out to the kitchen. Throwing open the oven door, he shut his eyes against the smoke billowing out. A smoke alarm went off with a piercing shriek.

"Oh, my God." Looking sleepy but alarmed, Diana followed, trailing her blue sheet. "Hot pads." She shook a hand toward the counter.

Grabbing the quilted mitts, he pulled the rack out. The blinding smoke stung his eyes, and the screeching alarm still rang. "Any way to turn that off?"

"Sure. Right." Yanking open a kitchen closet, she brought out a broom and poked the handle at the ceiling. When her sheet fell to the ground, he wished he could do something about that.

"Will!" She waved the broom at him. "Turn the oven off."

He did and then heaved the heavy pan onto the stovetop.

Unfortunately, the sheet was back in place. Diana peeked through the kitchen curtains. "It's pitch black outside, and it looks like it's snowing. What time is it?"

"Five thirty."

"So it's only been in the oven for ninety minutes or so, right? What happened?" They peered at the charred mess. "Don't turkeys cook slowly? I figured we wouldn't eat until seven."

"I upped the heat a little so it would cook faster." Had he ruined their dinner?

"How high did you set it?"

"High as it would go. That's how you do it, right? I did some mathematical calculations." Made perfect sense to him.

Diana was laughing, clutching her sides as his voice faded off.

"Sorry, sorry. I don't think that's how you do it." Grabbing some tongs, she dug a couple plastic bags from the bird. "You didn't take out the gravy packet. Or the neck and giblets?"

"Where did those come from?" She must think he was a total moron. When it came to cooking, maybe he was.

Holding a dish towel underneath the dripping bags, she dropped them into her trash with a look of disgust. "These are the parts of the turkey that you take out to make gravy. You can't cook with plastic in the bird."

Of course, he would have needed an ice pick to get them out. "When were they going to tell you that?"

"Hey, don't look like you won't be fed." Coming closer, she ran her hands up his bare chest. Seconds before, he'd felt cold. Her soft hands changed all that. The sheet slid to the floor again, and he moved closer. She was still toasty from bed.

"I think this is the best Thanksgiving I've ever had," she murmured, her swollen lips taking his.

"Ditto." Who cared about a burned turkey? He tripped over the sheet in his eagerness to follow her.

Wagging a finger at him over one shoulder, she said, "Let me show you what happens to bad boys who let the turkey burn."

"Is this like being sent to the principal's office."

"Could be."

Heat pulsed in his head, as well as parts farther south. Over the next hour or so, he forgot all about Thanksgiving. Diana had returned to her old self, playful and sexy. Oh yeah, this was a day to feel grateful all right.

But hours later, when the moon cast blue shadows through the skylight, his stomach rumbled. Shifting onto her side, Diana said, "You must be starving."

"I'm fine." He sucked in his gut.

Diana was getting dressed. "Come on. Let's find something."

He pulled on some clothes and they returned to the scene of the crime. Hands on her hips, Diana eyed the charred mess on her counter. It really was a mess. "What should we do with this? I hate to throw out good food."

"You sound like my mother," he said, squeezing her waist. "Do you have a heavy duty plastic bag?"

After he'd taken the black trash bag outside, they opened a couple of cans and perched on the kitchen stools. Diana dug green beans from one can while he spooned out cranberry sauce from another. Then they switched. She'd picked up Parker House rolls, and now she smeared them with cranberry sauce. He was still hungry and that looked pretty good. "Are you going to share?"

"Always." The sassy grin was back.

"Sounds like a commitment."

Her blush deepened to the color of the cranberry sauce. She

looked so darn pretty.

He never knew Parker House rolls tasted this good. "Did you talk to your family today?" Will asked between bites.

Diana nodded. "Yep. Called Grandma Kit this morning. How about you?"

"My mother called me bright and early. She loves to cook this meal. They had a ton of people coming from church."

"How about your sister?"

His stomach tightened. "Oh, no, we won't hear from her. I'd like to strangle my sister. My mother worries about Delinda and Maisy constantly."

Diana glanced at the magnets on her refrigerator. "Yeah, I know how that feels. How old is Maisy?"

"I forget. Only saw her once when she was little. Delinda married Mark when he got her pregnant in high school. They stayed in Beanblossom a while. But he was restless so they picked up and went west. Marriage didn't last but she never came back. But enough of that." He patted his stomach. Sure wished that turkey had turned out. Rolls and cold beans weren't going to do it for him.

"How about dessert?" Diana asked. "I bought a pumpkin pie from Mandy Klavis' bakery."

He perked up. "I love pumpkin pie. Got whipped cream?"

She slanted a wicked gaze his way. "As a matter of fact, I do. There was a display at Clancy's." Opening the frig, she took out the pie and cut two slices. After topping his with generous squirts of whipped cream, she handed him the plate. "Sorry about

Thanksgiving, Will."

"What's to be sorry about?" He dug into the pie and discovered the cinnamon and nutmeg seasoning was perfect. "Probably the most satisfying Thanksgiving I've had."

"Are you talking about the food?' she teased, dotting his nose with whipped cream.

"Not at all." He took one swipe at his nose and kept eating.

The wind howled outside and every window in Diana's small bungalow rattled.

"You need some grout on those windows."

"Maybe I need a handyman." She smiled shyly.

"Full disclosure. I'm not good with that kind of thing. But Gus, our maintenance man, is."

"You seemed pretty capable cutting my lawn and weeding last summer."

"Look, I was trying to impress you. Guess you didn't notice I took out some of the flowers too."

"Nope, I didn't."

"This pie is pretty good." They were both leaning against the counter, and he fed her the next bite. With a storm brewing outside, it felt so cozy inside, just the two of them. This was way more fun than sitting around a big table, stuffing himself. Not that he didn't love his family and the residents at the care center. He couldn't recall another Thanksgiving when he'd felt so right with the world. All because of her. "I love you, Diana." He could see her swallow hard.

"We don't know each other that well."

Okay, he'd take his time. "Sometimes it's not a matter of time. It's more about expectations and compatibility."

She seemed to think about that.

Will set his empty plate on the counter. "Diana, I'm getting tired of being the only one saying what I feel. Am I in this alone?" God wasn't that devastating? But he didn't believe it. Not his body. Not his heart. No way.

Her face crumpled and he felt terrible. Was she still so fragile? "Sorry. Forget I said anything." Frustrated, he opened the refrigerator and tucked the leftover pie inside.

"Are you leaving?" Wearing a woeful expression, she looked abandoned. He wasn't going to do that to her.

"Absolutely not." Snow was plastered to the windowpanes, and the wind continued to howl. No, he couldn't let her face this night alone. "My car's probably covered with snow. I think I should bunk here. What do you say?"

Her smile came slowly and the playfulness was back. "I think you're on to something. The weather here can be fearsome. Blizzards aren't uncommon."

Will wished she felt as certain about him as she felt about the snow. Ten minutes later, he didn't care.

# Chapter 19

*He loves me.* The words expanded in Diana's heart. And Will's face when he said them? The look of love. Oh, how much she wanted the same loving conviction. But right now she was scattered and he deserved more.

Even though she wasn't the same girl he'd met at the Firemen's Ball, he loved her. How she wished that in time his words would echo in her head louder than her mother's endless loop.

"Beautiful girls have an easier life. And you are beautiful, Diana. Make the most of it, kiddo." After her mother left and the years passed, Diana realized the other part of that message was, "beautiful like me." Star's looks had been the one thing her mother could give Diana without any inconvenience.

Grandma Kit and Grandpa Stan were different. They handed out compliments like Halloween treats—one at a time. Even good grades didn't win their approval as much as what she did. *Actions speak louder than words.* That was her grandparents when they rewarded her with words like considerate, polite or caring.

When she found a baby bird flopping around under a tree in their yard, her grandfather helped her fix up a box.

"Did her mama throw her out?" she'd asked, feeling so bad for the puny thing with no feathers and a huge squawking mouth.

Diana was sure the baby bird was crying for her mom. Her heart broke.

"No, sweetheart." Grandpa had smoothed a hand over Diana's head. "More than likely the storm last night knocked this little one out of the nest. Life can be like that. That's why the world needs caring people like you. Why, if you hadn't found this helpless thing, a crow or raccoon would have." Her grandfather taught Diana how to feed the baby bird from an eyedropper. She called him Chirp. One day Grandma Kit open the sliding glass door and the bird flew out. But sometimes Diana would hear a certain warbling chirp, and she knew the bird had come to say hello.

But now she was on her own. Like Chirp, she'd flown the nest. And recently she felt like she'd found a place that suited her. Friends to laugh with and a man to fill the empty ache in her heart. But so much had happened. She wanted her life to slow down. Wanted to heal, in lots of ways.

The marks on her skin continued to improve, although the cold weather didn't help. At the cottage or the store, the heat ran continually, drying her skin. When she ran her fingers lightly over her left cheek the week after Thanksgiving, the skin felt different. Harder. Her mood flattened. She wasn't Will's beautiful girl anymore. Not really.

But he didn't seem to mind. She'd been holding on so tight to what she'd always known to be true about herself. Perfection. The beautiful little girl who'd become a beautiful woman. Maybe she'd just let that go. Will still cared about her, and her friends weren't turning away. Perfection had become a burden. Leaving it behind felt like a good idea.

Work became her focus. In merchandising, the weeks between Thanksgiving and Christmas were really important, even in a beach town. Last year had been quiet, but she'd had a good November. Maybe Moonlight Magic had helped, and Kate Campbell had planned a Sunday Holiday Walk. Kind of like Moonlight Madness, shoppers would be enticed by sales and giveaways. Next to her register, Diana was going to set a basket of small, brightly wrapped boxes. Buy something and choose your Christmas treasure. She was deep in her wrapping project one day around five when Carolyn Knight stopped in.

Diana waved her back to the desk. "Hey, stranger. Good to see you. Have you read the book for next month yet?" Their choice that month included a mother and daughter relationship. Diana couldn't turn the pages fast enough.

Carolyn shook her head. "Are you kidding? Our semester ends before Christmas. Then I have to grade all those papers before I can turn in my grades." She did look exhausted with her hair springing from a topknot and dark rings beneath her eyes.

"Anything new besides work?"

Carolyn shrugged. "Nothing much. My grandmother, who lives in Santa Fe, had a bad fall. My mother wants me to go out there over the holidays."

"You must be so worried." After her experience with her grandfather, Diana knew older people sometimes needed a lot of help.

"So, you've heard about Kate?" Carolyn was good at changing

the subject.

*What was this?* "No." She watched Carolyn's smile fade.

"Oh, Diana, I thought you knew. Kate had a miscarriage."

The package slipped from Diana's hands. "What happened?"

"Who knows? They're devastated." Carolyn shivered. "I wonder if she'll be at book club."

How her heart ached for Kate. She had been so excited about her pregnancy. "I hope so. We can all give her a big hug, not that it will fix anything." Diana's recent problems seemed minor compared to Kate's loss.

"Right. Hard to know what to say." They stared at each other with empty eyes.

"I can't imagine how she feels."

"I know, she was so happy. And we were going to have that baby shower. Well, back to my exams. See you at book club, Diana." Carolyn left but the weight of her news had darkened the day. Diana was glad when it came time to turn out the lights and go home.

When Will called that night, she shared the sad news. Their relationship had settled into a calm steadiness she'd never known before. She heard from him every day. Just listening to his voice relaxed her. While he talked, she listened to her heart. With every beat, it seemed to say I love you. But he didn't say those words again, as if he were waiting.

"Poor Cole," Will said quietly.

"What about Kate? Imagine how she feels."

"Oh, I feel terrible for Kate. Losing a baby, well, I can't even imagine. But for Cole, how will he comfort her? That man's got a big job ahead of him."

Was Will talking about himself? He'd felt awful about her accident and blamed himself. How could she make it easier on him?

~.~

The news about Kate and Cole ripped through Will's gut. Sure, his job often involved comforting families. Bereavement counseling. But usually the loss involved an elderly family member who'd had a full life. Kate and Cole were just starting out. As always, Will transferred it to himself. He was just wired that way. Pacing the floor in his office, he couldn't help but wonder how he'd feel if he and Diana lost a baby.

Whoa. He stopped so fast, coffee splashed all over his shirt. "Damn." In his private bathroom, he grabbed some paper towels, which did absolutely no good. Diana and babies. Where did that come from? Wasn't it bad enough that he'd told her he loved her twice and got little response? But there was no stopping his feelings. He'd dated plenty of women but none with Diana's combination of sweetness and gutsy drive. Her story about the guy who'd lied to her turned his stomach. Made him want to fill her life with happiness. How many women would admit to that? Heck, he'd dated a woman for four months without knowing that she had kids. One night they ran into one of her friends at a restaurant, who asked his date if she was enjoying a night out, away from the kids. The fact that she had children didn't bother him. But she hadn't been honest about it.

If a woman would lie about her children, what else would she keep to herself? Will wanted the truth.

He glanced at the clock. Just past eleven and Diana would be in the shop. Grabbing his phone from the desk, he hit the speed dial button. She answered on the second ring. "Did I get you at a bad time?"

"You are always so polite. I don't expect anyone to come in until lunch hour. What's up?"

"How did last night go?" Will closed his door and sank into his chair the chair behind his desk.

Diana's sigh held a world of hurt.

"That bad?"

"Awful. Kate had been crying. We hardly even talked about the book."

"Must have been a lot of support for her." Women were so different from men when it came to stuff like this. When guys said "man up," they meant stay strong and keep quiet.

"I think being with the group helped a little. Sarah and Chili both have children. Chili had a miscarriage so she knew how it felt."

The line went silent. "Hey, you still there?" he asked.

"Yes. Sure." But Diana sounded distracted. "It must be so exciting to be pregnant. But then I can't imagine how terrible you would feel if you lost the baby."

"You'll be pregnant one day." Whoa, where had that come from? He heard her suck in a breath.

"Oh, Will, you never know." Her voice became vague and distant. She was pulling away again.

Picking up his stapler, Will wanted to use it on his mouth. He sure as hell knew what and who he wanted in his future, but Diana must have doubts.

He heard the bell chime in her shop. "I'll let you go. Call me back if it gets quiet."

"I will. Thanks, Will."

When he opened his door, Gus from the maintenance crew was pushing a huge cart loaded with decorations down the hall. Maybe dressing up the facility would help his mood. He sure didn't have much Christmas spirit this year. First Diana's accident and then Kate's news. "Hey, Mr. Applegate," Gus greeted him. "You gonna help us trim the tree?"

He smiled. "Sure. As soon as you get it up." Trimming the tree was a tradition at Gull Harbor Care Center. When he was in training, he actually visited a facility where the tree sat in the activity room all year. Lazy administrator and staff, that's how he saw it. At Gull Harbor, decorating the tree added excitement. No way would he just shove the tree into a corner and then drag it out every year.

His cell rang and Will grabbed it from his pocket.

"Hey, so your customer didn't stay long."

A cough came from the end other end of the line. "What customer? Will, it's me, your sister."

Delinda? "What's up?" Will sat down. Christmas was coming and his dear sister always used any holiday as an excuse to hit him up for cash. Their dad would not allow Mom to send Delinda any money. But Will was a softer touch.

"How would you like a visit from your favorite niece?" Her blunt approach hadn't changed one bit. Delinda got right down to brass tacks.

"You want to come visit with Maisy?" The chair squeaked when Will rocked back.

"Kind of. Wouldn't that be fun?" Her voice held that little girl tone she probably thought was cute. He braced himself. "My boyfriend Richie has planned a holiday vacation for us, him and me. Am I lucky or what? Won it in a lottery and decided to tack on an extra week or so."

"Isn't Maisy in school?" As he recalled, his niece had been a shy little tyke.

"Lots of parents take their kids out of school for vacations."

"Yes, Delinda. But usually they're vacationing *with* the child."

"No one in these parts wants Maisy." Desperation crept into her voice.

So that's how it was. The poor kid. "Where are you living now?"

"Kentucky. Up in the hills."

She'd been that close to his parents for God knows how long and never bothered to contact them. His forehead began to throb.

"Consider this my Christmas present." Her laugh held the harsh edge of too many cigarettes.

"Have you asked Mom? She might want to visit with her granddaughter."

"Right." Delinda snorted. "And hear Dad lecture me? No way."

God he was so torn. Every cell in his body told him this was a bad thing to do. But where would his niece end up if he said no? Will wasn't Delinda's first choice. She'd made that clear. "Okay, fine. As long as the school knows. She can bring her homework here, I suppose."

"Absolutely." Delinda let fly her nervous, horsey laugh. That much hadn't changed. Wasn't until after he hung up that he wondered how Diana would take the news.

~.~

"My sister is coming," Will told Diana, not a trace of excitement in his voice. They were sitting in front of the fire in his condo. "She's bringing her little girl."

"For the holidays? Terrific. How long will they stay?" She'd get to meet someone from his family.

"I don't know." Will stared into the flames.

The crackling fire threw deep shadows, and she couldn't read his expression. "You mean they're coming for a holiday visit?" Christmas was only two weeks away.

"In a way. Guess I should have asked more questions." Jumping up, he grabbed another log and opened the fireplace screen to toss it in. Sparks flew up the chimney when the wood hit the glowing embers. With a sigh, he sat back down. Poor guy didn't seem happy.

"Hey, what's up? Aren't you excited?" This was a different Will, one she'd never seen. Not too long ago, she'd thought the man came from a perfect family, upstanding citizens and all that. Far too solid and stable for a girl with no father and a mother who'd kicked her to the curb. Now? She wasn't so sure. The picture had shifted.

"Delinda's not exactly the family success story." Leaning forward on his elbows, he stared into the fire, as if it might have some answers. "I haven't seen her in a long time, Diana. She's kind of like my older sister who never grew up."

"You said they went West. Where did they go? Did your folks ever find them?"

His grimace didn't bode well. "They wound up in Vegas. But the marriage didn't last. Mark eventually took off and they got a quickie divorce."

"He abandoned them? Did she come home then?"

Will shook his head. "No, Delinda can be very stubborn. My father even went out there. But when he threatened to have the baby taken from her..."

"He would do that?"

Will huffed out a rough chuckle. "If he thought the baby was in danger, yes. He didn't find Delinda in the best of situations, but she was eighteen and stubborn."

Diana's own heart twisted just thinking about the poor little girl. She pictured dirty hotel rooms and meals at gas stations. What kind of life was that? Maybe she was lucky her mother had left her behind with her grandparents. "So what happened?"

"They argued. Delinda promised she'd give Beanblossom a trial period, just to get Dad off her back. She was supposed to follow him home. Instead, she cashed in her ticket, took the traveling money from Dad and disappeared, taking Maisy with her."

Chills chased down her spine. "Oh, my word. Just like my mom, Will. When she didn't come home from Chicago and just sent a text, my grandparents hired a detective. They found her in Florida, and Grandpa Stan went down to bring her back. But she wasn't coming back and she was eighteen."

"Trust me, you were lucky." Disgust etched lines in Will's face. "You'd never want to live through what my sister and Maisy have seen...and I don't even know the half of it."

Holding her closer, he kissed her forehead. She was fine with that as long as he didn't end up on her left cheek. Diana still kept him on her right side if she could manage it.

"You must have really missed your mom, Diana."

"Sure. As I grew up, I was convinced she didn't love me. Oh, she'd send me those refrigerator magnets or a t-shirt from whatever city she was passing through. But my grandparents were wonderful. Grandma Kit would fix my lunch every day and walk me to the bus. My grandparents never missed a parent teacher conference."

"Did she ever come back?"

"Once or twice. Mainly I think she wanted money but not me. She'd breeze in on a cloud of perfume, looking so beautiful." Her voice caught in her throat. Even as a child, she could detect her mother's hard edge under the glamour. "Don't know how she did it, but she always wound up with another high roller, as Grandpa said, a man who could give her what she needed. Paulo is her third or fourth husband. I've lost track. Their place on Ibiza isn't shabby, from the pictures." She was over feeling hurt.

Will appeared to mull this over. How amazing that their families shared the heartbreak of a lost child. They watched the logs collapse on each other in the fireplace, sending sparks up the sooty bricks.

"Do you think you'll ever have a relationship with her?" he asked.

"I doubt it. What she did to my grandparents was unforgivable. She was their only child. Grandma Kit...she's all the family I've got now. Besides, I'd have a hard time getting over all those scenic magnets she sent me."

Will's arms tightened around her and the hurt eased a little. "Magnets are easy to pick up. Kids require constant attention. You were lucky that your mother didn't drag you along."

"Right. Well, I could have gone for a vacation in one of those villas." She'd imagined that so many times over the years. Her beautiful mother would send her a plane ticket. Upon arrival, she'd tell Diana how bad she felt about the past. To atone, she'd whirl her daughter through Europe, one beautiful hotel after another.

But Diana had given up those dreams. They weren't worth having. "When I catch a gleam of platinum blonde hair or the flash of blue eyes, I wonder. But it's never her. She had the most amazing turquoise eyes."

"At least she gave you those."

Dragging a strand of hair over her scar, she ducked her head. The eyes were probably all she had left that resembled her mother.

Will's arm tightened around her shoulder. "Don't. It takes more than a pretty face to be truly beautiful. Heck, you know that, Diana."

Did she? His lips coaxed her into forgetting. When she was in a dark room with him, she could pretend she was the same Diana Prescott. Soon he had her stretched out on the leather sofa. Her whole world became Will Applegate from Beanblossom.

"What's that smile on your face?" He traced it with a finger.

"Never mind. Come here." Locking one leg around his thigh, she twisted, molding her body to his. They made love that night with feverish urgency in the flickering light of the fire.

Long after Will had fallen asleep, his news kept her awake. He was a patient man but he'd never had a child. How would he be with his niece?

The concerns stayed with her as Christmas came closer. The snow continued until the plows couldn't keep up with it. Some of the cross-country skiers came by and cleared her out of the ski apparel she'd ordered as a test. Next year, she'd order more. No other Gull Harbor store carried it.

Decorations sprang up along Whittaker Street, but she had zero Christmas spirit. For her, the holiday season held bitter memories. That's when she found out Bryce was married. By that time, she'd taken out a lease on the storefront in Gull Harbor. Bryce hadn't been excited when she shared her news and that hurt. They were supposed to be having a romantic dinner at his place in Gull Harbor that Friday when a package arrived at the shop in Chicago.

Her hands had shaken as she opened the outer box. This must be the perfume she'd mentioned to him last week. But it wasn't.

Instead, her stomach turned at the cloying scent she'd never buy. How had he gotten this wrong? The man was always jotting things in his black leather book with a small gold pen. Only later did she understand why he had to keep things straight. Maybe Diana hadn't been the only "other woman."

When she questioned Bryce as they sat at the dinner table overlooking a gray Lake Michigan, the story came out. He even seemed tearful. Yeah, right. Sometimes she wondered if he hadn't planned the mix-up. And the worse thing was, he expected her to continue but in secret. "Let's not spoil a good thing," he told her.

"But you're married."

"Of course I am. You must have known that." He'd blinked those brown puppy dog eyes. That probably worked on some women. "But it's not a good marriage, and we've been talking about splitting up..." The words stung like pebbles.

Then her anger flared. "Do you have children?"

"Of course. Two, a boy and a girl." No names. He was protecting them.

"Really. And you'd do this to them?"

After that, they'd thrown angry words at each other while below the waves thundered against the ice floes. The drive home was silent and long. She held her tears until she was inside her own apartment above the shop. Then she wrote him a long letter and sent it to his house. After she was settled in Gull Harbor, she drove past the mansion on Lake Shore Road and a For Sale sign was attached to the gate.

The following Christmas had been a year of quiet forgetting.

This year? Christmas would be different. Her life was coming together, despite the harrowing accident. She couldn't pass a window or mirror without touching her left cheek. The heavy theater makeup worked, but strangely, the thick coating reminded her of what lay beneath.

After Thanksgiving, she went back to the Sunday dances at the Gull Harbor Care Center. Everyone seemed so glad to see her. Their questions were open and honest. She felt relieved when that part was over, and residents stood in line to dance with her. Of course, Harold was first, clumsy in his eagerness and so sweet. But then it was Tim and Richard, Luanne and Edith. She maneuvered Frieda around the floor and listened to her account of when her husband took her to the Silver Lake carousel up at St. Joe, Michigan. Or Roseanne would tell stories about her grandchildren. Diana had seen the gaggle of children at the picnics.

Usually Will would ask her for one dance, but she had to hold herself so stiff with him. They wouldn't tease the way they had at the Firemen's Ball. Instead, they kept a proper distance. Sometimes it almost felt agonizing.

Diana looked forward to Delinda's arrival, but his sister hadn't given Will a date yet. Although Will didn't seem to think much of Delinda, she'd shed some light on his past.

How could she know they were opening a door to a nightmare?

# Chapter 20

Will was on the phone when Kelsey appeared at his door. He waved her in. "I know you have other customers, Zeke. But we're a living facility for seniors, and the weekend's almost here. Family visits mean a lot to my residents."

Kelsey's expression made him cup a hand over the phone. "What is it?"

"Someone to see you."

He glanced outside. Staff cars huddled under a heavy blanket of snow. A white car that screamed rental was stuck right at the entrance of the unplowed parking lot. "Zeke, I have to go. A car's blocking my entrance. Can you put us at the top of your list? Thanks."

When he ended the call, Kelsey edged closer and whispered, "She says she's your sister?" Disbelief tipped her words into a question.

His glance swerved to the car. "Yep, probably." Delinda was the kind who would just show up without a call. "Any cookies out there?"

She looked offended. "What do you think? Of course."

Her response made him smile. "Could you offer the little girl a cookie?"

"They took care of that as soon as they hit the reception desk." That sounded like Delinda. With a flutter of her hand, Kelsey was gone.

Slipping into his hounds tooth jacket, Will worked on his attitude. He'd be loving, supportive but firm. Where was she going and when would she be back? The smell of bacon and french toast hung in the air as he walked through the tiled halls. Corporate had warned him about exceeding the food budget. No problem. He just shifted some numbers from the activity budget. Covered the parties and picnics out of his own pocket. Food was the one pleasure left for a lot of his residents. He didn't care what it cost.

Two women huddled at the front desk. "Only one more, Maisy," he heard his sister say. No way could he miss Delinda's wildly curly hair, now a dull brown. When she turned, the eyes that once sparkled matched the hair. His attention shifted to his niece. This tall young woman with bright green hair and sullen features was Maisy? His steps slowed. How many years had it been? He gulped. Maybe thirteen since that Thanksgiving when Delinda stopped in Beanblossom before disappearing again. Mother and daughter were dressed in cheap-looking navy quilted jackets and stocking caps. No snow boots, just running shoes that looked soaked.

Time hadn't been kind to his sister, and her sagging cheeks couldn't even hold that smile. "Ah, here he is. And all grown up. Maisy, let's give Uncle Will a big hug."

Will restrained the urge to duck when Delinda threw her arms around him like a cobra.

"Delinda." Slipping from her grasp, he turned to his niece, munching her cookie as if it were her last meal. Crumbs sprinkled her quilted jacket like brown snow. Looking tough and resistant, she had none of her mother's brightness at that age. So young and so road weary. A fist tightened in his chest. "Hey, Maisy. Been a long time. You were three or so when I last saw you."

She huffed. "Maybe. Who knows?"

Ah, huh. This was going to feel like a very long visit. How long had Delinda said? "Want to follow me to my office so we can catch up?" Mother and daughter exchanged a dark look. Had Delinda just planned on dropping Maisy off? Anger quickened his steps. Once in the office, he closed the door behind them and took a breath. He had to keep it together.

Eyes taking it all in, Delinda threw herself into one of the wing chairs across from his desk. "Big office. You must be one of those uppity bigwigs now." She hooked one leg over the other in what used to be her coy pose. "Thanks for helping me out, Will. You're such a good brother."

The false gratitude took Will back to the years when she'd been his popular older sister, the queen of Beanblossom—at least that's what he'd thought back then. A late-night partier, she'd filled his young ears with wild tales. Now that he was older, he wondered what had drawn boys to Delinda. She'd caused his parents plenty of sleepless nights. The back of his neck prickled. Would her daughter be just like her?

Time to lay out some ground rules. He pressed a button on the phone. "Hey, Kelsey, can you take Maisy down to the cafeteria and get her a soda? Maybe give her a quick tour." This might take some time, and he wanted Delinda alone. He shrugged out of the wool jacket and rolled up his sleeves. The air vent overhead blew dry heat.

"Sure, be right there."

Maisy's mouth fell open, probably to protest, but his sister gave her a warning look. Kelsey arrived and Maisy disappeared. Putting his hands flat on his desk, Will faced Delinda. He tried to remember that they were related, but the truth was, he was facing a stranger. Sadness seeped through him. "So, what's your plan?"

She smiled brightly. "Just like I said, Willie. Gonna take in the islands with my boyfriend. Didn't think my family would mind helping me out."

He grated at his childhood nickname. "Do Mom and Dad know anything about this?"

"Hell, no." She took her time unwrapping a stick of gum before jamming it into her mouth. Eyes turning thoughtful, she began to chew. "The folks are getting on, Willie."

That was bull and she knew it. Not even sixty, their parents were spry. But they probably hadn't responded to Delinda's latest demand for money. He had. "Will. That's the name I answer to, Delinda."

The chomping stopped and his sister's eyes grew guarded.

"So where can you be reached and when will you return?" His patience frayed. "It's Christmas, for God's sake."

Delinda's caked eyelashes blinked slowly, another throwback to her high school days. "I'm flying out of Kalamazoo tomorrow.

Gonna meet up with Richie in Florida. His friend's got a boat. Great, huh? We'll be cruising for a while…"

The blood pulsed in his head.

"Two weeks, probably," she quickly added.

Fourteen days. What the hell was he going to do with Maisy for all that time?

He'd made surprise reservations at a bed and breakfast over the holidays. Diana's shop would be closed, and Jan could handle things here at the facility. They could enjoy some time alone, and he wasn't thinking of Christmas shopping or tree lighting. Since Thanksgiving, they'd gotten their relationship back on track.

Now Delinda had thrown a monkey wrench into that plan. But she was his sister. Families came with responsibilities.

"Give me your cell number so I can get a hold of you." He slid a pen and paper across the desk. "Don't you feel bad leaving your daughter at Christmas?"

Lips pursed, she made some notes and pushed the paper back. "Girl knows her mam's got to have a little fun." Her bleak eyes carried years of wreckage. His poor niece. What had she seen and experienced over the years?

"Right. Fine." He got up. Outside the snow kept falling. "Be careful driving to Kalamazoo."

"Of course I will." Jumping up, she grabbed her purse.

Leaving his office, she turned left. Dammit, she was heading to the front door. He grabbed her arm. "Delinda, the cafeteria's this way. I'm sure you want to say good-bye to your daughter." He jerked a thumb. With an aggrieved shrug, she fell into step. How had he ever wound up with this sorry mess for a sister? His parents had tried to discipline her but it had never done any good. Nausea sloshed in his stomach. Would he have any better luck with her daughter?

In the cafeteria, a group of residents played bingo, while Bev called the numbers. Maisy sat at a table, sipping a can of pop.

"Guess I'll be running along, sweet pea." Delinda bustled over and dropped a kiss on her daughter's forehead. Were tears brimming in Maisy's eyes? "I'll call you, okay, sugar plum?"

"Sure, whatever." Blinking, Maisy stared straight ahead.

"Be sure to keep your phone charged up, now."

"You gonna do the same, Mom?"

"That was just one time." Delinda's hands fell to her side. "Want to walk me out?"

"Can I take the soda?" Maisy asked Will.

"Sure. Come on, we'll see your mom to the door." Walking to the lobby, they were a sad little group. The clicking of his heels and the squeaks of their shoes couldn't cover Maisy's sniffles. How his sister could leave was beyond him. Delinda filled the silence with comments that shot from her lips like popping corn. The walls, the bulletin boards, the nurses' stations—her attention veered to anything but her daughter.

At the door, she jabbed another kiss at Maisy. When she finally pushed through the frosted glass, a frigid breeze invaded the waiting area. Even Harold had moved to an inside chair. Disgust and awe churning in his stomach, Will watched his sister brave the drifts until she made it to her rental car. To his relief, it started.

~•~

Waiting for Will to pick her up for the Holiday Walk that Saturday, Diana felt a shiver of apprehension. He'd sounded nervous on the phone. That wasn't the confident Will she'd come to know. His sister had shown up to drop off his niece. Then Delinda left. "Maisy's a total stranger." He sounded rattled. Diana was burning with curiosity.

A niece. Poor kid. An only child of a single mother. She wondered how that was working out.

After two days of blizzard-like conditions, the town was covered in a glistening mantle of snow. Diana had ordered a bright white jacket online, with a hood trimmed in white fake fur. A bright green stocking cap was another find, long enough to twist around her neck and cover her chin.

Will's car fishtailed into view and she chuckled. No way was the boy going to drive the red Mustang in weather like this. Her own car stood in the driveway, a shrouded white form.

The walk started at two o'clock, and Rachel told her she could handle any traffic at Hippy Chick. They didn't expect many customers. Diana wanted to zip through the other stores to see what they were offering. She imagined the Holiday Walk would be like Moonlight Madness. Mercedes had mentioned that Kate's spirits seemed to pick up as she threw herself into this new promotion. Thank goodness. Diana's heart still ached for Kate and Cole.

When she threw open the storm door, a blast of cold air took her breath away. She waved. Getting out of the car, Will came around and opened the door for his niece. The collar of his navy parka was turned up and he looked handsome as ever, despite the scowl. The girl who climbed out of the car almost made Diana tighten her grip on the door. A shock of neon green hair framed pouty features, and the bright sunlight glinted off several piercings. Leading the way up the walk, Will looked at her with resignation. Poor guy. What a pair. They looked like punk rock meets business casual. She leaned out the door. "Hey. Where's the Mustang today?"

"In the garage where it belongs." He stepped to one side. "Diana, I'd like you to meet Maisy, my niece."

Not looking at all pleased, the girl mumbled something.

"Great. Well." Diana stepped back. "Good to meet you, Maisy. Come on in while I grab my things."

"Wipe your feet on the mat," Will told his niece as they came through the door.

"Like I didn't know." Maisy made a show of wiping off her tennis shoes. Her feet must be freezing.

"I'll have to get a bigger mat. All this snow. Do you think it will be busy today? Rachel is holding down the fort at Hippy Chick so we can take our time..." Diana's words rattled out with a speed that brought a strange look from Will. Maisy was taking stock of the bungalow. But she quickly dropped her eyes when Diana caught her staring.

Slipping into her white parka, Diana crammed her hair under the green stocking cap and wrapped the tail around her neck. When she felt the girl's eyes on her face, she pulled the knit higher.

"Don't you just look like Christmas." Will's eyes warmed. With his niece standing right there, he gave Diana a kiss that burned through her body until she felt it curling her toes.

"Whoa, buddy." Dazed, she nudged him away. "Let's save that 'til later, okay?"

Maisy snorted.

"Must be cold out there. Your cheeks are freezing." Diana pressed her palms to his face.

"Maybe they need your hands to warm them up."

His niece's expulsion of breath filled the room. They broke apart. No use putting on a show, although from what Will said, her mother was dating someone.

"Let me get my gloves." She wrenched open the closet door. Tension crackled in the air. Will was in trouble. Sure, she'd hoped for an intimate Christmas with him, their first. But the situation had changed, and it sure looked like his niece was a handful. Diana felt sorry for both of them.

Five minutes later, they were crammed into Will's car, their breath quickly steaming up the windows. Tires whirred and squealed on the slick streets. His windshield wipers shuddered across the window until he turned them off.

"Do you think people will come out in the cold?" Diana looked at the banks of frozen snow along the street.

"I have no idea."

Maisy looked upon the snowy scene with disgust. Maybe she was used to warmer weather. "Maisy, do you have much snow where you live?"

"Not much. We live in Kentucky right now. I've lived everywhere. California. New Mexico. Florida. You name it." But it was said with disgust not pride.

"Sounds interesting." And a major upheaval. "All warmer climates, right?"

"Yeah, I wonder how those people pay their electric bill."

Diana exchanged a look with Will. The words sounded so adult, as if she were echoing her mother.

Will pulled over when they got close to Brewster's. "Well, now you're here and it's the Christmas season. The Holiday Walk on Whittaker is new this year. Should be fun. "

"Yippy do," his niece muttered.

Good thing Will didn't hear her. He was already out of the car, coming around to help them out.

Whittaker was decorated in colorful green and red holiday garb. Over the street sprinted reindeer, their flight lit with tiny white lights. At the end of the street sat a sleigh where a red-suited Santa sat ready to greet a long line of children. Elves in green costumes handed out candy canes to those who waited. All along the street, each store had someone dressed in costume to welcome shoppers.

"Hi Diana, Will?" Oscar Werner waved to them from the doorway of Sun and Sail.

"So they do this every year?" Some of the disdain had melted from Maisy's face. Without the frown, she was really kind of pretty but she had brown eyes, not Will's piercing blue.

"We have a new PR person who dreamed this up," Will said,

taking in the scene with approval. "Maybe I should have had Bev bring some of the residents down, although the sidewalks might be slippery." Blue ice melter glittered on the street.

Diana was blown away by the holiday scene. "Isn't it beautiful? Maisy, don't you think the street looks like a Christmas card."

"I guess." Maisy scuffed at the snow. Had the poor kid ever gotten a Christmas card?

Pulling Diana's arm through his, Will led the way. "Let's stroll up to Santa."

"Don't even think I'm gonna climb onto that guy's lap," Maisy said. "Probably the local perv."

Turning on his heel, Will faced her and Diana's stomach sank. "Enough, Maisy. People have worked very hard to make this a special day. I won't have you ruining it, got it?"

Amazement emptied Maisy's face, making her purple eye shadow even more obvious. "Well, don't get your shorts in a bundle. I get it, I get it."

Diana watched Will struggle. His hands clenched and opened. This was so hard, but lashing back wouldn't help. "Come on." Diana tugged on his arm. "I should check on Hippy Chick so we have to move this along."

Relief filtered through her when he turned his attention back to Santa's sleigh.

As they drew closer, Santa's hearty "Ho, ho, ho" could be heard.

Will and Diana exchanged a smile. "Cole?" she asked.

He lifted a shoulder. "I guess. Maybe Kate roped him into it."

When they got closer, Diana noticed Sarah standing with her little boys, Nathan and Justin. Both boys were practicing for their turn with Santa, ticking items off on their fingers.

"Looks like serious business," Will chuckled.

"Did you ever sit on Santa's lap?" she asked Maisy, trying to start conversation.

"Nope. Where would I have done that?"

Yep, her childhood had been pretty bleak.

"Well, look who's here!" Cheeks ruddy from the cold, Sarah clapped her hands. "My boys are getting ready to put in their order." She winked.

Was their father on that list? Sarah's husband Jamie had been overseas for almost a year, or so Kate had told her. Must be hard, although Sarah had her mother.

"And who is this young lady?" Sarah asked, eyes landing on Maisy.

"My, ah, niece Maisy," Will said. His lips worked the name like a new dish that he doubted he'd enjoy.

"Isn't that nice? Visiting your uncle for Christmas?"

"Yeah. I guess." Maisy concentrated on a parking meter. Sarah shot a puzzled glance between Will and Diana.

"Is your mother watching The Full Cup?" Diana asked, eager to change the topic.

"Of course. She was up until midnight, making gingerbread men." Sarah checked her watch. "We better get back." By that time, the boys were finished with Santa and Sarah gathered them up.

Maisy shuffled her feet. "Can we go home now?"

Will's mouth opened and then snapped shut. He seemed to be counting to ten. "And what's waiting back at my condo, Maisy? What could be more fun than this?"

Diana's heart just about stopped when the girl rolled her eyes. Will's face flushed and then drained.

"Don't you have video games or some movies?" Maisy asked in a pathetic voice.

"Video games have never been my thing. I spend most of my time at work...or at Diana's." Well, the truth was, Diana was spending a lot of time at his condo, but she wasn't about to point that out.

This continual confrontation was making Diana nervous. She took his hand. "Come on. Let's stop at the library." She turned to Maisy. "You can pick out something."

But once inside the library, Maisy wrinkled her nose. "This place smells weird. "

"Books," Diana supplied. "Do you use a Kindle?"

Maisy gave her a vacant look. "Thought you said we were going to get some movies?" Her voice held a whine that was getting old fast.

With that, Mildred Wentworth stepped from behind the desk. "Did I hear something about movies?" She waved toward a steaming dispenser and a plate of cookies. "Help yourself and then I'll take you back."

The cookies had definitely caught Maisy's interest. Not only did she take two, she stuffed more in her pockets after Mildred turned around. A chuckle tickled Diana's throat but Will's expression told her this was no laughing matter.

"All she wants to eat is sugar," he mumbled, following Maisy to the back, where Mildred helped her pick out some movies and a couple TV shows. Fifteen minutes later, they were on their way to her store.

When Diana opened the door to Hippy Chick, the place was packed. Rachel waved to her from the behind the counter, looking totally panicked.

# Chapter 21

"How's it going?" Diana murmured to Rachel, slipping behind the counter.

The girl looked frantic. "Thank God you're here. The fitting rooms are full. I was thinking of offering the stockroom." Three women stood waiting, clothes over their arms.

"Sorry, Rachel. I didn't expect this or I would have been here." Maisy wandered off and Will was quickly surrounded by chattering women.

"Pardon! Pardon me, ladies, can I have some help here please?" Shivering with indignation, a gray-haired lady dangled holly earrings in Diana's face.

She got to work. "Did you know these are buy one, get one fifty percent off?"

"Oh. Well, let me look." The woman stepped back to the case.

"I've got this, Rachel. Check out the fitting rooms, okay?" Turning back to her elderly customer, she helped her select a second pair of earrings for her granddaughter. Her attention was pulled away when two women began fighting over a pair of sunburst earrings on the turnaround display. She totally understood. The bright copper pair was a personal favorite. "Ladies? Ladies!"

While she sorted them out, she got a glimpse of Maisy sitting on a chair in the corner, eating cookies. She felt sorry for the girl. Like Diana, she'd been kicked to the curb by a mother more involved with her love life than her daughter. How sad was this?

Maybe Will wouldn't welcome her interference, but she couldn't help but become involved. The poor guy. Eyes wide, he edged toward the door, looking like he wanted to bolt.

~•~

How would he ever get through the next two weeks? Guilt played havoc with his stomach. After all, Maisy was his niece. Still, he felt like he'd been stuck with a stranger. "Maisy, can you wait to eat that cookie? You're getting crumbs all over the floor."

Her face crumpled and then flared. "I'm hungry. No breakfast."

"I told you, cereal in the cupboard." So he was responsible for this too?

"I like Sugar Crispy Pops."

"They'll rot your teeth."

Her mouth trembled. Old ladies? He knew how to talk to them. Teenagers were a whole different story. "Sorry, Maisy. I'm..." More women had pushed into the shop, bringing a wintry blast with them. This wasn't the time or the place for a heart-to-heart with his niece. "Give me a minute, and I'll take you to Rosie's for breakfast."

He must have struck a chord. Her face cleared. Nodding to a few people who had relatives at the care center, he made his way toward Diana and waited until she was through with a customer.

Pushing her hair back, she exhaled. For the first time since October, she didn't pull her hair over the scar. "I'm going to take Maisy to Rosie's. She's hungry."

"Good idea. Do you believe this?" Her eyes darted around the packed shop.

"I'll be back in about an hour." He escaped, taking Maisy with him. Ten minutes later they were seated in a booth, looking over the menu.

"So, what are you studying in school?" he asked once they'd given their order.

When Maisy blinked, the purple eye shadow was even more noticeable. "The usual stuff."

He searched his mind. "You're in high school?"

"Of course. After all, I'm fifteen." Okay, she'd gotten that tone from her mother.

He was going to be patient if it killed him. "I'm sorry, Maisy. I haven't got a clue what kids study in high school."

She shrugged. Why didn't she take off that bulky coat? "Algebra, English, social studies. A bunch of crap if you ask me."

He stiffened. "What makes it crap?"

She slid lower in the booth and started picking at her nails. "When am I ever going to use algebra? I have a calculator."

"Good point." He thought back. "I think they told us algebra helped form logical thinking."

"That's stupid."

"You might be right." Her scathing glance froze the chuckle in his throat. "So, what's your favorite subject?"

"Computer science."

What a relief to see her eyes sparkle. "What goes on in that class?"

"We're making our own website."

Things were looking up. "Sounds fascinating. You enjoy that?"

"You bet. Well, sort of." Had she realized enthusiasm wasn't cool? The waitress arrived and Maisy's eyes brightened. She'd ordered something called Waffle Sunrise. The waffle was heaped with eggs. Dousing the concoction with butter and syrup, she dug in. His scrambled eggs and toast looked boring compared to her plate.

"Coffee?" asked a waitress, sweeping past with a pot.

"Yeah." Maisy shoved her empty mug to the edge of the table.

"Yes, please." Will spoke slowly. Maisy seemed to get the message.

"Thank you very much," she said, with an exaggerated drawl.

His parents would be aggravated no end to hear their only grandchild being this rude.

"So you'll probably be glad to get back to your computer class. Finish up that website, right?"

"But I have to change schools again."

"Why?" His own heart squeezed at the dismay on her face.

"Mom's got that new boyfriend, and he lives in Florida. Bye bye, Kentucky and my class." She was trying to be flippant and failing.

"Florida. The guy she's with right now?"

"Yeah." Halfway through the waffles, she'd stopped eating.

Will hated to pump Maisy about his lame sister, so he stopped there.

"I could work on my website now if I had a computer. I have the login and everything. Most of the kids worked on theirs at home. I used to stay late and use the school computer." All this came rushing out in starts and stops that clearly expected a no. "I saw some in the library. Do you think they'd mind if I stopped in and used one?"

"Well, of course you can. In fact, you can use my laptop at the condo."

Her lips fell open in amazement. "Really? I could?"

Her gratitude was so pathetic. You'd think he'd given her a car. And it made him very sad.

Her appetite restored, Maisy took up her fork and cleaned her plate. He glanced at his watch. "Let's go back to the shop. Maybe things will have slowed down."

"Does Diana only have that one girl to help her?"

"Yep. It's a small town. Usually she doesn't have that much business."

"Maybe I'll come over and go through the shops some day."

"Great idea." Maybe this visit wouldn't be so bad after all. Somehow, he'd fill her time. She'd probably hate the care center, but he couldn't leave her at his place. If she was anything like her mother, she'd have a party going in no time.

But she didn't know anyone in Gull Harbor. Christmas and she was with total strangers. Damn, he wished his folks were up here. They might be mad at Delinda, but they loved their granddaughter.

"How was Rosie's?" Diana asked when they returned to Hippy Chick.

"Jammed. The whole town has benefited from this Holiday Walk."

"They have the best waffles ever." To his surprise, Maisy jumped right in.

Diana turned to Rachel. "Can you handle this? It's almost closing time."

"You bet. I'll spend the time straightening the stock."

She turned back to Will. "Let me just get my jacket."

Maisy was busy studying the tops. Looked like she preferred dark colors. Will followed Diana into the dimly lit stock room. Okay, he felt like a stalker but he was dying. She was reaching for her jacket when he closed the door. "Will? Whatever..."

Wrapping his arms around her, Will settled his lips over hers. He liked her eager response. Loved it when she gave him a light shove and the shelving bit into his back. This was getting better. "I'd trade eggs and waffles for you anytime," he murmured between kisses that quickly turned wet and heated.

"I know just how that feels. Oh, Will," she moaned and he had to clap a hand over her lips. A slight nip of her teeth only made the situation worse.

"You're a vixen."

"Vixen?" Her low, suppressed laugh was music to his ears.

When she eased back a little, he could still feel her luscious curves. His body sat up and begged. This room had possibilities. Dark and dim, the storeroom had a faint smell of dust, now mixed with their heat and the rustle of jackets. He wished he had more time, and that his niece wasn't waiting. Running his hands down the sides of her body, he tried to commit it to memory. "Looks like we won't have much opportunity for this in the coming weeks."

"Hope we find some. Can't we?" He loved the disappointment in her voice. "But the visit won't be long. Well worth it, to help your sister. And more important, Maisy." Pulling away, she studied him, suddenly businesslike. Her stern look brought him back to the present and their situation.

"You know she really is a sad, little thing," Diana said.

"She's not little but she is sad. And no wonder." Why had he let Delinda get away with dumping Maisy on him...especially during the holidays? All he wanted was to curl up with Diana. "I don't know what I'm going to do with her. She wants to spend time at the library. She's creating a website in her class and can use the computer. I'm sure Mildred won't mind."

"Are you kidding? She'll be thrilled."

He kissed her cheek, her left cheek. His lips just landed there, not intentionally. For the first time since the accident, she didn't cringe. Her eyes were distant as she chewed on the corner of her lip. "Maybe she could come with me tomorrow to the dance."

He choked. "Really?"

She squeezed his shoulder. "Well, of course. What are you going to do? Plunk her in front of *The Grinch Who Stole Christmas*?"

"That's thoughtful of you to help with Maisy, Diana."

Shrugging into her white jacket, she smiled. "Not a problem."

Casting a glance toward the closed door, Diana planted a kiss on him that could last a while. Oh, yeah. How he wished they could go to his place and take this to a new level. "This is frustrating," he moaned when she finally pulled away. The smoking hot kiss left him panting while she laughed and reapplied her lipstick.

"This is life."

~.~

The following day, Diana met Will and Maisy at the facility. Her breath billowed into frozen clouds when she climbed out of her car. With his coat collar turned up, Harold sat at the door.

"Hi, Harold. Aren't you cold out here?"

"Nope. Just waiting for you."

Now, that was so sweet. She was always surprised that he remembered her name. Bundled in a heavy coat with mittens, he had a scarf wrapped around his lower face, the earflaps firmly in place. "It's real pretty, the snow. Don't you think it's pretty, Diana?"

"Yes, yes it is. But if you get too cold, you come inside now, you hear?"

"Yep. That's what Kelsey tells me. She brings me hot chocolate," he said, obviously pleased by the attention. "We gonna dance today?"

"Yes, we are." It felt so good to be back on schedule. Why had she ever backed away from something that had made her feel good about coming to Gull Harbor?

"Will you dance with me, Diana. Will you, huh?"

"You know I will. See you inside."

The hot, dry air of the facility met her when she pushed through the glass doors. She'd stopped worrying about it. Too much other stuff on her mind. After seeing Maisy's heavy hand with her makeup, Diana had pulled way back. Will mentioned he liked her without eye shadow. Yep, Maisy had definitely left her mark.

Kelsey nodded at her from the front desk. "Hey, Kelsey. Are Will and his niece here?"

"In his office." She jerked a thumb down the hallways before leaning over. "That girl took half my fresh baked cookies with her."

Diana's eyes dropped to the plate, now almost empty. "Growing girl."

The receptionist rolled her eyes. "I'll say."

*One thing at a time.* Maisy needed so much. The cookies were just an emotional filler. At least, that's how Diana saw it. After the breakup with Bryce, she'd gorged herself on pastries, cookies and ice cream. But the emptiness inside lingered for a long, long time.

Hurrying down the brightly lit corridor, she wondered what she would find in Will's office. How was he doing with his niece? When Diana poked her head in, her heart fell. Will and Maisy faced each other across the desk, and it wasn't a cozy scene. "Ready, Maisy?"

The girl turned to her. "Yep." Her eyes were heavily lined in black with deep purple eyelids. Will looked like he hadn't slept.

"Let's go then." Casting a worried glance at Will, Diana headed out. "My hair's so staticy here. Such dry heat." Her hair crackled with static electricity when she raked her fingers through it. "How about you?"

Maisy's hair was piled on top of her head. "Uncle Will uses guy shampoo. No conditioner. I didn't even try."

"We'll pick some up. Anything else?"

The poor girl looked like she wanted to say more but couldn't.

"Why don't you make a list?" Diana suggested. "We can stop at Dressel's Drugstore." What had Delinda been thinking? She'd dropped her daughter off with nothing more than a backpack. Her abandonment bordered on criminal.

They'd reached the activity room. Swing jazz poured through the sound system, and Bev was urging couples to dance. Maisy sank into a chair. Diana would let her watch for a while. "Just jump in when you're ready," Diana sang out, drifting over to Harold, who had followed her inside.

The good thing about dancing with seniors was that anything was fine. They just wanted to move. After Harold, Diana chose one of the women and another woman after that. From the sidelines, Maisy watched cautiously.

"Ready?" she asked Maisy when she stopped for a breather. She pulled at her green turtleneck. A t-shirt might have been a better choice.

"Nah, not me." Maisy looked away. Maybe she was just shy.

When Will appeared in the doorway, Diana's heart turned over. He still did that to her. Dressed in his red V-neck and khaki slacks, he looked mighty fine and he came straight for her. "Want to dance?"

*Want to breathe?* She nodded.

When Will took the floor, the residents drew back. Diana wished they wouldn't do that. But from their pleased expressions, they liked Will and they enjoyed seeing him dance. Who wouldn't? The man was a bundle of energy with his pivots and swings. She had a hard time keeping up with him.

"Missed you last night," he murmured, passing her under one arm.

"I know the feeling." She had to be honest. But Diana hesitated to stay at the condo while Maisy was a guest.

Her back against Will's stomach, she felt an extra tight squeeze before he released her. By the time the number ended, she was breathing hard.

Will drifted over to ask Maisy if she wanted to dance. Diana watched with cautious optimism. Ducking her head, his niece shook her head. What teenager wanted to dance with older people? At least Will had the good sense not to press her. In time, the teen would come around. Diana had complete confidence in him. After all, who could resist his charm? With the Christmas tree in the corner, and blue and silver stars spangling the walls, the room felt so festive. But one look at the miserable teen was enough to dampen anyone's spirits. Still no word from Delinda. Wasn't she concerned about how her daughter was getting on with the uncle she really didn't know? How would that feel if your mother seemed to have no interest in you? Diana knew the answer to that question.

"What are your plans for Maisy this week?" she asked Will

when they drifted over to the refreshment table where Bev had set out eggnog and cookies.

"She mentioned the library. I'll drop her off and then come back for her when she calls. Bring her back here."

"The library's a great idea." He looked so helpless. "Do you think she'd like to spend time with me at the store?"

Relief eased the strain on his face. "You can ask her. She looked pretty happy there yesterday. You don't mind?"

"Not if she's willing. Spring stock came in yesterday. Maisy could help me open the boxes and display the new merchandise."

When they broached the subject with Maisy, she quickly nodded. "Sure. Why not?"

The store was closed on Monday, and Diana was looking forward to having time alone with Maisy. Midmorning when a cold sun was sparkling on the heaps of snow, she picked Maisy up at Will's and off they went to Hippy Chick. As they hung up their coats in the stock room, Diana couldn't help but notice the tattoos on her arms. A lot going on there. These weren't butterflies and hearts. "Have you had them long?" Reaching for scissors, she slit the first box open.

"The thorns was the first one." Maisy fingered the ring around her upper arm with her purple nails.

"What makes you choose the design?" She handed the girl a hanger.

"Stuff just happens. Or Mom will give me a little money. I saved up."

For a while, they stripped plastic bags from the filmy tops and hung them up on a rack. "I like your tattoo, Diana."

"What?" Diana glanced down at her arms. She'd pushed up her sleeves to work and had forgotten the light tracing of the burn on her arm. "Oh, Maisy. That's a burn. An accident."

Maisy's shoulders lifted. "I meant the one on your face. I'd like a little half moon like that."

Diana's fingers flew to the scar that had made her so uncomfortable not that long ago. "This is my battle scar. Me against a huge bag of frozen french fries." Amazing that she could joke about it now.

"Guess it is lighter than a tattoo." Maisy flushed. "Sorry, I can be so stupid."

"Trust me, *I* was the stupid one. Threw a bunch of french fries into boiling oil and got splattered." She handed Maisy another hanger. "I was really upset about it. Ballistic was more like it. As time passes, though, it seems to get smaller."

"You're so beautiful. Just makes you look hotter, if you know what I mean."

"Does, huh?" She pulled out the ticket gun.

Hanging up the pink top, Maisy studied it. "That's what my mom always says. It's not enough to be pretty. You have to be hot."

Diana cringed. She certainly didn't want to be lumped in with Delinda. "Being kind is probably more important, don't you think?" Was she sounding like her grandparents or what?

Suddenly shy, Maisy worked her lower lip. "I guess so. Sometimes that's hard when people aren't nice to you."

So that's how it was. The back bell rang. Since this was Monday, Diana figured it was UPS, which tied her up for a while and gave Maisy more to do. But Maisy's words stayed with her...and so did the hurt look on the teenager's face.

"You're getting a look at spring," she told Maisy when she rejoined her later. The girl had become an expert with the pricing gun.

"Spring? Man, it's freezing outside."

Diana laughed. "That's the whole idea. After Christmas, people become desperate for spring."

"So do you put these on your website." She held up a peasant blouse.

Diana stared at her blankly. "I don't have a website for Hippy Chick. Never got around to it."

Maisy looked at her as if she couldn't believe it. "My teacher says every business has to have a website to be incredible."

"You mean credible?"

"Right. Anyway, that's what Miss Franklin says."

"And she's probably right. It's just that I never have time." *Or money.* Every time she turned around, there was still so much to do. Diana slumped onto a stool.

"Do you mind if I try to build a site for you? I mean, you don't have to use it or anything. But I could use your site for my homework project."

"You would do that for me? Really?" Beneath that tough exterior, Maisy was a sweet kid. Definitely underappreciated.

"Sure. I'd do it. I mean, it won't look like Macy's or anything."

"Oh, Maisy. You're the best." Diana's hug came so naturally. At first, the girl felt stiff as an icicle. Then she melted, making an awkward attempt to hug Diana back. Hugs were no doubt something she didn't do that often.

They fell into a schedule. All that week, Maisy came to Hippy Chick to help straighten the stock or work on the windows. Around two o'clock she'd walk over to the library. "She's doing a terrific job of organizing things," she told Will when he stopped at her house Thursday night.

"Glad to hear it. She doesn't really say much when we're together. Just disappears into her room to work on the computer. Probably your site, right?" She'd told him about Maisy's offer.

"Any word from Delinda?"

At the mention of his sister, Will's face clouded. "No. She hasn't contacted Maisy or me. One week before Christmas and she hasn't spoken to her daughter since she left. This borders on abandonment."

The past week had been absorbed by Delinda and Maisy. Her tiny tabletop tree glimmered in the low light. The place felt warm and cozy now that Will was here. Every cell in her body leapt to life when he gave her a slow smile that let her know he was thinking the same thing.

"What's on your mind?" He came closer, slipping his arms around her waist. His eyes said he missed her and so did his body.

"Want a beer...or something?" she breathed.

"Definitely the *something*." He nuzzled her neck, and she felt other parts of her body leap to life.

"Or we could make hot chocolate." How she loved to tease him.

She felt his growly chuckle in the pit of her stomach. "Save it. I'm already overheated. Only one thing could cool that fire."

Cupping his face, she stroked his forehead with her thumbs. For just a second, the worry lines smoothed. Stubborn, they came back too fast. Lately he'd had plenty to worry about. First her accident, and now Delinda and Maisy. "So what do you have in mind, relaxation therapy?"

"Yeah, right."

When he pulled her closer, she moaned. "Oh God, Will."

"Yeah." His hands moved over her body with familiar remembrance. She longed to trace the same path with him.

"You're a good man," she whispered as he led her into her dark room. Her heart brimmed with love.

"Let me show you how good," he rasped, pulling her down onto her bed.

"So what are you going to do about Maisy?" she asked later when he was getting ready to leave, and she was still savoring the bliss.

He kissed the tip of her nose. "Don't worry. I have a plan." His eyes sparkled. Once again, he was the man she knew and loved.

*Loved.* There it was.

"You know what?" she said.

Pulling on his jacket, he stopped. "What, beautiful?"

This time she was ready for those words. "I love you, Will Applegate. Every bit of you from your sunny smile to your silly dance moves."

He plunked back down on the bed, as if his legs had been taken out from under him. "Aw, Diana. Finally."

She kissed him. "Yep, I love the guy who can make senior ladies wish they could adopt you. But with Maisy? You've done an amazing job coaxing your poor niece out of her shell."

"Wow. I'd say you're the one doing that." Looking dazed, he fell back onto his elbows. "So...you're finally admitting to your feelings, huh?"

"Finally feeling it, Will. So deep sometimes it hurts."

He slipped out of his jacket.

"What are you doing."

"Think I'll stay a while."

The gleam was back in his eyes, along with a love she knew would last forever. "Want to tell me about your plan?"

"Later."

# Chapter 22

Maisy and Diana were decorating the tree in Will's living room when they heard the crunch of tires on the hard-packed snow in the driveway.

"Is that them?" Maisy asked, setting down her box of ornaments.

Will looked through the blinds. "Yep, looks like Dad's driving a huge SUV. Wonder when he got that."

Peeking out, Diana asked, "Do you think he rented it? Red for the holidays? Looks as big as a fire truck."

"Maybe." Will went to the door. "He needed room for your mom and Aunt Ethel. Knowing my mother, they brought a gazillion gifts."

Poor Maisy had turned pale. "Nervous?" Diana asked.

"Yeah. A little." Maisy smoothed her hands over the black jeans Diana had bought for her when they visited the Michigan City outlet mall. "What if they don't like me?"

"Not gonna happen." Diana rubbed Maisy's shoulders. "You're their granddaughter. They already love you." How could Paul and Marianne Applegate have raised a man like Will and not be warm and caring?

But then there was Delinda. Will had left three messages on his sister's phone. No reply and Maisy hadn't heard anything either. His last-minute plan for Christmas was sorely needed. When his father included Diana's grandmother and great Aunt Ethel in the plan, she was thrilled. Paul Applegate had offered to pick them up in Newtown. "It's on the way," he'd said, although it meant making an eighty-mile loop.

Springing outside, Will helped the older ladies out of the red SUV, while his mother clucked at her husband to open the back. Their breaths formed white clouds in the cold air as they greeted each other. Will had been right. His parents trekked to the open door, laden with bulging shopping bags.

"You must be Diana," Will's mother said, plopping the bags in the front hall.

"Yes, I am." So Will had gotten his sparkling blue eyes from his father and charm from his mother. The burly guy helped his wife inside with the packages, while Will escorted Grandma Kit and Aunt Ethel up the walkway. Will and Maisy had scattered enough melter on the snow to turn the entire walkway blue.

While Diana hugged Will's parents, she was aware of Maisy hovering in the background. This must be so awkward for her. When Diana took her hand, Maisy threw her a grateful smile. "And this is Maisy. Your granddaughter."

The teenager stood trembling. So much hung on this moment. Marianne Applegate flung her arms wide. "I would have known you anywhere, honey. Can I give you a big hug?"

"Yeah. Sure." Maisy looked over at Diana as if to say, *Do you believe this?* But she hugged her grandmother back. She was getting better at the hugging.

"Just call me Paul," Will's dad said, looking uncomfortable with the granddaughter he didn't really know.

When Grandma Kit and Aunt Ethel made it inside, there were more excited introductions.

"Will you just look at that tree," Aunt Ethel exclaimed as Diana took her coat. "Kit have you ever seen anything like it?"

"Uncle Will cut it down!" Maisy said, as if this were a miracle.

"Right," Will admitted with a rueful smile. "Nearly chopped my hand off doing it."

His mother recoiled until Maisy turned to her with a very serious face and said, "He's kidding. He does that a lot."

"Hungry?" Diana asked. She'd bought a frozen lasagna and the smell of garlic permeated the condo.

"Starved," Will's dad roared while his mother bent to arrange her gifts under the tree.

"Your grandfather is not a quiet man," Marianne told Maisy. What followed was a wild evening of catching up. Of course, Diana's grandmother and aunt were very interested in Will. She could feel their eyes circling from Will to her and back again. The two women would stay in Diana's second bedroom. Luckily, Will's place had three bedrooms, so his parents could have more time with their granddaughter.

During the two days before Christmas, there was a lot of traveling back and forth. Of course, everyone wanted to see the Gull Harbor downtown. Diana's mother found the two-block downtown area "quaint," while Aunt Ethel wanted to buy everything she saw in Hippy Chick.

Will's folks were more homebodies. They spent time with Maisy, trying to catch up. Taking a hint from Will, they took her to Rosie's for breakfast. Later, Paul told Diana how excited Maisy had been when explaining the website she was building for Hippy Chick. "Very bright girl," Diana overhead Paul tell Will.

"Runs in the family," Will shot back, but his parents exchanged glances. Clearly, the situation with Delinda concerned them. Diana was grateful that they'd stepped into the picture, for Maisy's sake. She was a good kid, who deserved a lot better than what life had doled out so far.

When Christmas Eve came, they joined the carolers strolling down Lake Shore Road, aglow with candles in paper bags. A soft snow was falling and peace seemed to fill the earth as they sang the traditional songs about a silent night and the little town of Bethlehem. By the time they'd made their way back to the condo, their cheeks were red and they needed hot chocolate to warm up.

"Do we get to open presents tonight?" Aunt Ethel asked.

"Presents?" Maisy looked amazed.

"What do you think is in all these boxes?" Aunt Ethel chuckled.

Face beet red, Maisy made an admission that absolutely broke Diana's heart. "My mother always wrapped empty boxes. She said decorations were what the season was about. No one actually got presents in those boxes on TV...or so she said." Her voice faded.

The air was sucked from the room. The only sound was the spitting and crackling of the fire. "Okay, want to help me hand these out, Maisy?" Will broke the tension by grabbing a couple of gift bags. "I can assure you these actually contain something. If you don't like it, you can exchange it or regift it." That caused a laugh, and Will had to explain the whole regifting thing to his niece. The frantic rustle of paper was followed by exclamations of surprise. Clothing and kitchenware, candles and special teas. Will's father gave him a drill. "You can't own a home without a good drill. Just too much to do."

A home? Was Will buying a new house? Pouring another glass of eggnog, he wore a secret smile. The women had baked Christmas cookies that day with Maisy. Diana was glad to see the girl's appetite had changed since she'd been eating regular meals. By the time midnight came, Will's parents had gone off to bed and so did Maisy, probably eager to play with her new iPod. Will and Diana drove her grandmother and aunt back to the yellow bungalow. Red Arrow Highway felt so peaceful under a light coating of snow.

Before Grandma Kit retired for the night, she pulled Diana aside. "Just want you to know, I think you're wonderful with Will's niece." While Diana's eyes brimmed, her grandmother kissed her cheek the way she always had, smelling of White Shoulders. "Maisy appreciates your kindness. You know how hard it can be sometimes."

"Yes, I know." Her grandmother shrugged because in their family, they never made a big deal of things. "Sleep tight," she said as Grandma Kit closed the door.

While the older women settled down, Diana cherished the gift her grandmother had just given her.

"You okay?' Will asked, coming up behind her.

"Perfect." She turned and buried her face in his shoulder, so warm and wonderful. "They really like you."

"Then it's mutual. You have a great family."

"Certainly not perfect." Turning, she began to pick off the refrigerator magnets and tossed them in the trash. What good were painful memories?

"No family ever is. Here, let me help." Will joined her.

When the refrigerator was a clean slate, Diana made decaf and the two of them settled onto the sofa. "Such a busy week," she said, grateful that Rachel had helped her with Hippy Chick.

"Sure has been." Wearing one of his secretive smiles, Will took a sip of coffee.

"My grandmother is so happy to be here, Will. And so is Aunt Ethel. And it's perfect having your folks visit at the same time. They all get along so well."

"Just like one happy family." He rested his mug on the coffee table.

She liked the sound of that. "Yep. I guess so."

Taking a small box from his pocket, Will said, "Just one thing more. Maybe we should make this family thing official. I love you, Diana, and I know you feel the same. Will you be my wife?"

"Oh, Will." Diana's hands shook as she untied the silver bow and unwrapped the box. "Are you sure?" When she flipped open the lid, a beautiful solitaire winked up at her.

"Will you make me the happiest man in the world?"

She couldn't get the words out fast enough. "Yes. Yes!"

"Shhh. You'll wake up the whole place. I want you to myself for a little while." After slipping the ring on her finger, he quieted her with a kiss warm enough to heat her heart and soul forever.

# Epilogue

## Five Months Later

"You doing okay, Harold?" Diana fidgeted with her hyacinth Juliet cap.

"Yes, ma'am. I sure am, Diana." Wearing a light blue sport coat Will had bought for him, Harold stood tall. His standby winter hat had been put aside today to walk Diana down the path to the gazebo.

Outside the glass exit door, a June breeze carried the promise of summer. But the only promise Diana needed was in Will's eyes. She didn't need any vows. His steady gaze told her everything she needed to know. From this day forward, their lives would be linked. They'd meet happiness and tears together, stronger because of each other. Waiting for her at the gazebo, he looked so handsome in a new sand-colored linen suit. No tux for him, he'd said. He wanted a suit he could wear again, and she figured he was thinking of how the ladies would like it at the Sunday dances. So practical. Underneath his polished exterior, Will still was a boy from Beanblossom, Indiana. She wouldn't have it any other way.

A trip to Second Hand Rose with Phoebe, Carolyn and Mercedes had turned up a wedding gown with scalloped cap sleeves, a pattern repeated in the floor length skirt that rustled when she walked. The demure neckline was a contrast to the revealing dip in the back. Thank God for Chicago people who brought their designer clothes to the consignment shop on Red Arrow. The dress was worthy of a runway, at least in her eyes. Her Juliet cap of blue hyacinths anchored a tea length veil.

Fidgeting next to them, Maisy swished the long glass-green dress that made her feel like a mermaid...or so she said.

Chairs arced in rows bordering the path. Residents had been gathering for the past hour, carefully choosing their seats for the best view. "Good grief, they'll all have sunstroke," Jan had fretted. "Why don't they wait?"

"What? And miss that end chair?" Diana had teased. But their interest pleased her. The whole group felt like family.

The sunny June day didn't have the intensity of July. Will and Diana had purposely chosen a date before the arrival of seasonal tourists. Today the ladies were all dressed in their Sunday best, some with hats. A cloud of competing perfumes hung in the air. Even the older gentlemen had spiffed up, with Tim sporting a new bow tie.

In the front row sat their families. Paul and Marianne beamed at their son, while next to them Grandma Kit and Aunt Ethel whispered, no doubt with a hankie in their hands. How Diana wished her grandfather could have been here. But she knew that somewhere Grandpa Stanley was watching.

She glanced up at the clock on the wall. "Ready, Harold?"

One final swipe at his thin hair, Harold nodded. "Yes, ma'am."

He held the door open and she stepped into the sunlight. When the musician at the keyboard saw Diana emerge on Harold's arm, he struck up the traditional wedding march. Will and Diana both wanted everything to be a bit old-fashioned.

Hearing that first chord, Maisy asked, "Is it time, Diana?" Due to Phoebe's talent, Maisy's honey brown hair had been restored, sporting a gleaming green streak. She looked so sweet, a far cry from the angry girl who'd been dropped off in a snowstorm months ago.

"Yep, this is it." They shared a nervous smile. "Pass Uncle Will and then just stand on the left. Cole is on the right." Maisy was spending a trial summer in Gull Harbor. Will's parents had rented a house near the beach. "About time we take a vacation," Paul told them. But they all knew Paul and Marianne wanted to be near their granddaughter. The teenager would be staying with Diana and Will this summer after they returned from their honeymoon, camping in the Upper Peninsula. They'd take it from there. Delinda's new life in Florida had no room for a teenager, so some things had to be worked out. But Diana and Will both felt optimistic.

Her eyes swept the crowd. Everyone she cared about was here. A sense of completion filled her.

"Ready, Harold?" she whispered. Maisy was about six feet out and everyone was waiting for the bride.

"Yes, ma'am. Sure am." With a cheek-splitting smile, he stepped forward, Diana on his arm. Heads swung their way. Diana had dressed in Will's office so no one had seen her gown yet. As they passed, approval hummed through the guests, all craning their necks for a better view. A couple of the women even popped up like jumping jacks. The photographer began to snap photos. Maintaining a smile was no problem for Diana. This was the happiest day of her life.

Not wanting to hurt anyone's feelings, she didn't have bridesmaids except for Maisy. But as she slowly passed Phoebe and Carolyn, they gave her a thumbs-up and Mercedes beamed. In the row behind them, Kate and Cole sat on one side of Sarah, her hands folded complacently on a bulging tummy. Her baby was expected in August. Chili and Ignacio were on the other side, with Chili giving her usual running commentary.

When they reached Will, Harold stepped back. "Gotcha here, safe and sound. Right, Diana? Safe and sound."

"Yes, you sure did," Will assured him, winding Diana's arm through his.

With a pleased smile, Harold took the seat next to Will's father.

"You look beautiful, sweetheart," Will whispered.

Her heart so full of love and joy, Diana didn't trust herself to say a word. So she squeezed his arm and turned to the minister.

Later their guests passed through the reception line at the Whittaker Woods Country Club. Will had insisted that their party be here, where it all started. "You're such a romantic," she'd teased.

"Oh, and you're not?" he shot back with a grin.

Okay, Will had a point. They were alike that way. She'd never forget that first pizza he'd brought her or the bag of weeds at the road. A relationship was created from small gestures and big moments. And it took time. Diana knew that now.

Dinner passed in a blur. She could hardly eat a thing. Around them, guests chattered and laughed. Everyone was so happy for them. But when the quartet began to play, she turned to Will. She didn't need a vocalist to recognize this song. "Did you request this?"

"Of course." Leaning over, he kissed her cheek.

Strains of "I Only Have Eyes for You" filled the room. She could hear their guests sigh and saw Chili and Sarah exchange a glance. Did they remember that Firemen's Ball as vividly as she did?

Diana turned to her husband. "Dance, Mr. Applegate?"

"With pleasure, Mrs. Applegate." He swept her away in his arms.

As they whirled around the dance floor, she was filled with gratitude. Her feet hardly touched the floor. How lucky that she'd found Gull Harbor. Oh, she'd come to the town for all the wrong reasons. But as Carolyn reminded her the other day, she'd put her stamp on it. Paid her dues and owned it. Sure, she'd met challenges, like the burns she thought marred her forever. But those stumbles along the way gave her a chance to see the true depth of Will's love. And Maisy was right. The half-moon indentation on her cheek had paled to sexy.

Humming, Will guided her around the floor.

"What, no twists and twirls?" she chided after steps that were more a waltz than California swing.

"Later," he promised, one hand edging onto her bare back.

She released a shiver. "Later." For them there would be a later.

Always.

Will anchored her. She knew that now. "All packed to go camping?" he whispered against her ear.

"Yep. All set." Had she packed enough bug spray? Diana had no idea what awaited her.

The music changed tempo. "Ready?" Will was gathering himself. She'd felt that energy before.

"You bet." She'd been practicing. And boy, she'd show him.

That would probably never change either.

# THE END

Want to read more about the women of Gull Harbor and the men who resurface from their past to test and tantalize them? Here's an excerpt from *Coming Home to You*, the first book in the series Man from Yesterday. Kate Kennedy returns to Gull Harbor after her mother becomes ill. She doesn't even get to the house when she runs into a guy she knew in high school. She's never forgotten Cole Campbell. What woman could?

The thumping started when Kate Kennedy reached Greta's Gifts on Red Arrow Highway. Cheese curls churned in her stomach as she tapped the brakes. Almost home but something was wrong with the kayak strapped to her roof. Gravel crunching beneath the tires, she pulled into Greta's and parked. The sun bounced off the hood of her SUV, but a cool May breeze bathed her face when she cracked open the door.

Welcome to Michigan. Her eyes felt grainy from fourteen hours on the road, but she was home.

Stretching, Kate breathed in the lake, damp and beachy. The tightness in her shoulders eased. Pine trees caught a high spring gust and the familiar rustle made her smile. Her stomach gurgled. Not much to eat the whole ride from Boston except peanut butter and jelly, plus bags of cheese curls washed down with coffee.

Looking up, she exhaled. At least she hadn't lost Gator, her green kayak. A red security tie flapped in the breeze. Must have lost the other strap along the way. Kate scrubbed her face with hands shaking from all the caffeine. A semi roared past, kicking up dust. She tugged up the zipper on her hoodie.

"Doggone it, Gator. I want to be stretched out on the beach, not wrestling with you."

The kayak slid a bit more. Too bad she'd left her small kitchen stepladder in the Boston condo, along with a lot of other stuff. When she yanked the remaining red band, it fell away in her hand. One frustrated shove and Gator retaliated, smacking her square in the chest before clattering to the ground. The pain bent Kate over like a paper clip. She almost didn't hear the door slam behind her.

Blinking furiously, she pulled herself up, grateful for the sunglasses. No way would anyone see Kate Kennedy cry. A man ambled toward her in work boots, worn jeans, and shoulders that tested the seams of a beat-up jean jacket. That walk looked familiar and her heart kicked up a beat. He wore aviator sunglasses, so no telling for sure. A black and white dog hung out of the pickup, Great Dane ears pricking forward. Big muzzle, big dog.

"Need some help?"

Yep, it was him. Kate's legs weakened but she straightened. "No, I'm fine."

His eyes shifted to the kayak. "Doesn't look fine to me."

She fisted her hands on her hips. "I'm fine. And so is Gator." Her chest throbbed.

Blue eyes swept like a July wave over the tops of his sunglasses. "Gator?"

She swallowed. "My kayak. Seemed appropriate."

"I see."

But Cole Campbell had never understood why Kate wanted all her belongings named and in their proper place. Shoot. They'd been on the high school debate team together, and he didn't recognize her? Maybe it was her recent drugstore dye job. She'd had brown hair in high school. Now she ran a hand over blonde hair, crisp from two days of neglect.

He swayed back on his heels, a Good Samaritan with second thoughts. The two empty seats of the kayak stared up at them. "Lucky you didn't lose it on the road. Could have smashed into another driver. You need to batten it down."

How she used to hate being lectured by him. "Thought I did. It was dark when I loaded it."

"Try doing it in the daytime. You could kill somebody."

"I left at midnight."

"Midnight?" He lowered the glasses and his eyes darkened.

Her chin came up. "Highway's quiet at night. Just the truckers."

"Exactly. Truckers. You think that's safe?" He obviously didn't. But that was none of his business. "I've, ah, probably got some rope in the back." She seriously doubted it.

"I'll be glad to help." Cole's attention shifted to her jeans. The corners of his lips lifted. "You saving that for something?"

Kate looked down. A cheese curl was caught in a warm spot and she batted it away. No time for games. Especially not with him.

His eyes flitted from her to Gator and back. A stern mask slipped into place. Cole's teenage acne had left faint pockmarks that definitely didn't detract from his macho appeal.

Was he going to help her or not? Her chest throbbed. Could

this day get any worse? The boy she'd lusted for in high school didn't even recognize her. Kate's throat closed. Nothing like feeling forgettable.

In two thrusts of his muscular arms, Cole had Gator back in the rack on top of her SUV. Disgusting how easy he made it look, but it gave her time to enjoy the view. Cole Campbell had definitely left "gawky" behind.

"Thank you."

Wheeling around, he caught her staring and grinned. "Got that rope?"

Her face burned. "Sure. I'll get it. Let me just check Bonita."

"Bonita?" He tilted his head.

"My car." One glimpse of the pretty blue SUV on the lot and she knew it was Bonita.

"Sure. Right."

Popping open the back gate, Kate launched herself into the tightly packed boxes and bulging trash bags. Her rear end felt big as a helium balloon.

"Finding anything? I might have something in the truck."

Feeling him hovering, she tried to squeeze her butt tighter.

When she heard the scratch of his boots, Kate thought maybe he was leaving. Her disappointment surprised her. After all, she wasn't at her best. If you're going to run into an old flame… well, a man you wanted to be your old flame… a girl should look hot, not sweaty.

Kate was sweaty. And not in a good way.

Finally, she climbed out empty-handed. Cole was ambling

toward her with a roll of heavy gauge rope.

"That looks serious." Her mother wouldn't even be able to get a clothespin around this sturdy stuff, although she'd probably try.

"Want to stand on the other side and catch this?"

"Sure." *I'd hold anything for you. Like my breath.*

While Cole tossed a length of rope over the kayak, his dog watched from the pickup with mild interest. Grabbing the rope, Kate threaded it back and he knotted it securely. "First, I like to tighten the bow and then the stern."

"You kayak?"

Whipping out a Swiss army knife, he cut the rope. "Way too much work. I sail."

Of course. She pictured an elegant yacht skimming Lake Michigan. Samantha McGraw would be rubbing her tan body against his. Kate didn't need the instant replay. Had enough of that in high school.

Cole worked with calm efficiency, the way he'd handled Student Council or Debate Club.

Oh, yeah. He'd handled their debate group just fine.

When he turned back, his eyes went to her hair. Smiling, Cole whisked something from the mess. Her breath left her body.

Maybe she was just tired.

Or maybe she was desperate for a man's touch.

He handed her a cheese curl. "You missed this."

"Great. Thanks." She jammed it in her jean pocket and then felt stupid. Was she going to press it in her high school scrapbook? Kate slammed her back gate shut.

Cole's eyes rested on the Massachusetts license plate. "Passing through or coming for the summer?"

"That depends." He still didn't know her? She edged toward the driver's door. "Thanks for your help."

Cole cocked his head to one side, like he was listening to her voice. "Sure. No problem."

"Got to get to an appointment." Maybe a shrink. She opened the driver's door so fast she almost cracked herself in the mouth.

"Ah, huh. Well, good luck."

"Right. Thanks." Kate needed more than luck this trip. Without looking back, she peeled out and did a U-turn on Red Arrow. In bad need of a friendly face, she headed into town. To read more, visit any online bookstore: Amazon, Barnes and Noble, Kobo or iBooks.

# Other Books by Barbara Lohr

## Windy City Romance series

Finding Southern Comfort
The Southern Comfort Christmas
Her Favorite Mistake
Her Favorite Honeymoon
Her Favorite Hot Doc
The Christmas Baby Bundle
Rescuing the Reluctant Groom


## Man from Yesterday series

Coming Home to You
Always on His Mind
In His Eyes
*Note: the books in these series all stand alone
or can be read in a series.*

# About the Author

Barbara Lohr writes heartwarming romance with a flair for fun and subtly sexy love scenes. In her *Windy City Romance series*, feisty women take on hunky heroes and life's issues. Her *Man from Yesterday* series provides a provocative glance back at "what if." When she's not writing, she loves to bike, kayak, golf or cook. She makes a mean popover. Barbara lives in the South of the USA with her husband and a cat that claims he was Heathcliff in a former life.

For more information on the author and her work, or to sign up for her newsletter, please see:

www.BarbaraLohrAuthor.com

www.facebook.com/Barbaralohrauthor

www.twitter.com/BarbaraJLohr

# Acknowledgements

Many thanks to Romance Writers of America and Central Ohio Fiction Writers. The loops and forums of writers who address writing and publishing issues are also invaluable to me. An extra loud shout out to my Street Team, the readers who support me in so many way!

For my daughters, Kelly and Shannon, when we shared Judy Blume and Madeleine L'Engle together, we never saw what lay ahead. Keep those reading lamps on over your beds. My grandchildren, Bo and Gianna, bring me such joy and will probably appear in quite a few of Mama B's novels. To my husband Ted, words aren't adequate to thank you for your love and support, especially when my computer crashes and you have to provide tech support. May we have many more wonderful years together that include trips to Leopold's for ice cream.